MISSPELLED

Magic Gone Awry

Edited by
KELLY LYNN COLBY

Cursed Dragon Ship
PUBLISHING

ISBN 978-1-951445-23-2

ISBN 978-1-951445-24-9 (ebook)

For all those who made a mistake and things didn't quite turn out the way you expected. There's still a happy ending. You might just need a little magic.

Contents

A Measure of Magic

MIRIAM THOR

In retrospect, Elliana should have seen this coming. Or at the very least, as one of the most powerful mages in the kingdom, she should have considered that it was a possibility. In her defense, though, her magic had been part of her since the day she was born, its presence as natural as the blood in her veins. It had never occurred to her that anything could separate her from it. But apparently, her magic was attached to her body, not her soul. It would have been nice to know that *before* she tried a body-switching spell.

"Paige, is everything alright?"

Elliana snapped her attention back to the woman with the broken arm. Mary? Molly? Definitely something with an M.

"Everything's fine," Elliana lied, not wanting to add to her patient's distress.

She tried one more time to reach for her magic as she usually did. In response, Paige's magic trickled through her, a brook compared to her usual waterfall. There was no way she could fix this woman's arm with so little magic. How did her friend possibly work as a healer with such limited power at her disposal?

Elliana could practically see Paige rolling her eyes at that question. Which was weird considering those eyes were part of the body Elliana currently inhabited.

1

Tucking her brown hair behind her ear, Elliana thought back to the few times she'd seen her friend use magic. Paige had drawn some glowing symbols in the air. When Elliana had asked about them, Paige had shaken her head in exasperation.

"They're runes, Ellie," she'd said. "They help people with normal amounts of magic amplify and focus their power."

At the time, Elliana hadn't thought that information of any use to her, but now ...

She glanced at Paige's bookshelves. Now, they were her only hope to heal this woman and maintain her friend's reputation.

Trying to look confident, Elliana walked to the shelves and skimmed the titles, pausing at one called *Healing Common Injuries and Maladies*. Since broken arms seemed fairly common, she grabbed it and flipped through the pages. Thankfully, it didn't take her long to find the right spell. She traced the runes with her finger a few times, then practiced drawing them in the air.

Her magic—well, technically Paige's magic—tingled, eager to combine with the runes. Elliana smiled. She could do this.

After practicing one more time, she hurried back to her patient's side.

"Just hold still," she said and reached for Paige's magic again.

This time, when she felt the trickle of power, she focused it on her finger and carefully drew the runes, marveling at how they appeared in front of her, as if she was painting the air. For a moment, the runes hovered, glowing the deep green of Paige's magic. Then they faded, and the woman sighed with relief, her arm back to normal.

"Thank you, Paige," she said, standing up. "I'll bring your payment as soon as we bring in the harvest."

"Okay," Elliana replied, forcing a smile as a wave of fatigue swept through her.

"See you soon," the woman said and left.

Elliana took a couple of deep breaths to steady herself. Had she done something wrong, or did Paige always find healing this draining? Given how tired her friend seemed these days, Elliana suspected the latter. She'd have to discuss that with her as soon as they got this mess sorted out.

She ran a hand down her face. Switching bodies with Paige had seemed like the perfect way to understand her people better. Because no matter how approachable she tried to be, Elliana knew they would never see her as anything but the baroness of Laveny, which meant they'd never be honest with or around her.

That was why she'd talked Paige into this plan. It was a shame it had to come to an end so soon. She'd hoped to spend at least one full day in her friend's shoes, but it couldn't be helped. If Elliana had Paige's magic, that meant Paige had *her* magic, which could be problematic. It had taken Elliana years to control the raw power that roared in her veins, and that was with her magic growing as she did. For Paige to have it dumped on her all at once ...

Well, the two of them just needed to switch back as soon as possible.

With that in mind, Elliana headed for the manor house, planning to use the servants' entrance, the way Paige did when she came to visit her mom. She hoped Paige had managed to keep her magic under control so far, and that she'd continue to do so until they switched back. It shouldn't be too difficult for her. Elliana had intentionally chosen a quiet day for the switch, one where nothing strenuous would be required of Paige while she was in Baroness Elliana's body. Her friend was pretty even-keeled, so the magic inside her should behave. Unless something out of the ordinary happened.

A trumpet interrupted her thoughts. When she glanced back, her mouth dropped open in shock. A carriage bearing the royal crest was on the road, approaching the manor house.

"Make way," the driver cried. "Make way for the Crown Prince!"

Elliana forced her mouth shut. The crown prince? Why in Bryolan had Ren decided to drop by unannounced?

She pursed her lips. Paige would undoubtedly be nervous about meeting royalty. This could be bad. Really bad.

Picking up her pace, Elliana promised herself when this was over, she'd give Ren an earful about the importance of scheduling royal visits. And possibly turn him into a squirrel while she was at it.

In retrospect, Paige should have shot down the body-switching plan the moment Ellie mentioned it. She knew better than to go along with her friend's crazy schemes, so she had only herself to blame for her current predicament.

Sure, Ellie was the baroness of Laveny, but Paige's mother had been her maid since she was a little girl. The two of them had grown up together. Despite the difference in their stations, they were true friends. If Paige had said no to the harebrained idea, Ellie would have listened.

Instead, Paige had gone along with it, and now look where they were. The crown prince of the entire kingdom had just arrived, and Paige wasn't sure it was safe for her to greet him. This morning, she'd made a hairbrush float to her with barely a thought. It had been more than a little unnerving. Since then, she'd managed to keep a cork on Ellie's magic, but she'd found that the stronger her emotions, the more difficult that became.

Now she was supposed to greet the crown prince—probably have brunch with him, too. It was a recipe for disaster, but what else could she do? It would be unbelievably rude for the baroness *not* to greet the prince. At worst, it could call Ellie's loyalty to the crown into question, and Paige couldn't allow that. So, she'd asked her mom to put her in a fancy dress and pin her blonde curls so they looked elegant. Now, she walked to the entrance hall, doing her best to keep her unruly emotions—and Ellie's magic—under control.

When she reached the grand staircase, Paige saw not one, but two, royal-looking men waiting at the bottom with their entourages. One of them, she recognized as Ellie's cousin, Renaldor, the Crown Prince of Bryolan, but she'd never seen the other man before. Her stomach quivered, and a nearby vase shook in response. Alarmed, she tightened her hold on the magic inside her. Or at least she tried to. It wasn't like she had much practice with that sort of thing.

When she was sure nothing was about to shatter, Paige squared her shoulders and walked down the stairs, careful not to trip on Ellie's elaborate dress. As soon as she reached the bottom, she dropped into a curtsy.

"Welcome to Laveny, Your Highness," she said, keeping her eyes downcast.

"Thank you, Baroness," the Crown Prince said, stepping forward. He was a few years her senior with curly black hair and tan skin. "I apologize for any inconvenience."

"Not at all," Paige replied, hoping she sounded polite enough. "How can Laveny be of service to you?"

The prince blinked like he was surprised, then said, "Allow me to introduce Duke Harvorth of Luthania." He gestured to the man behind him, who inclined his head.

Paige inclined hers in return, forcing herself not to curtsy. It wouldn't do for a Baroness of Bryolan to show subservience to a noble from another kingdom.

"The duke accompanied King Provenius to Bryolan to discuss a treaty with my father," the prince explained. "Since the negotiations have been lengthy, I offered to give His Grace a tour of our kingdom. We weren't planning to come to Laveny, but when he heard its baroness is a powerful mage, he insisted his tour wouldn't be complete without a demonstration."

Paige's heart skipped a beat. A demonstration? A duke from a neighboring kingdom was here to see Ellie demonstrate her magic? The candle sconces near the door trembled ominously. Paige clamped down the magic swirling within her and took a fortifying breath.

What was she supposed to do? She couldn't possibly give the man a demonstration, but she also couldn't refuse a request from the crown prince. That left one option. She needed to stall long enough for Ellie to switch them back.

"Of course, Your Highness," she said. "But you all must be tired from your journey. Surely, you'd like to rest and have some refreshments first."

The prince gave her an odd look but nodded. "That sounds nice."

Paige glanced around. Spotting a servant she knew, she called, "Bartholomew."

The servant looked surprised to be called by name, but he walked over obligingly.

"Yes, My Lady?"

"Please instruct the cook to have brunch sent to the dining room and have a few servants report there as well."

He bowed slightly. "Yes, My Lady," he said and hurried away.

Suppressing the discomfort she felt at ordering someone around, Paige looked back at the prince.

"If you'll follow me," she said and led the way to the dining room.

When they arrived, the servants she'd requested pulled out chairs for them.

"Please have a seat," Paige told the guests. "The food will be here shortly."

Prince Renaldor raised his eyebrows. "You won't be joining us, Baroness?"

The centerpiece quivered.

"Not yet, Your Highness," Paige replied, her hands trembling. "I need a few minutes to freshen up. I'll be back shortly."

The prince narrowed his eyes, but he nodded.

"See you soon then," he said and took his seat.

Paige curtsied quickly and fled the room. As she made her way to Ellie's chambers, she vowed she absolutely would not go along with her friend's next crazy scheme.

⁂

In retrospect, Renaldor should have sent a messenger to warn Ellie they were coming. If his wife were here, she would certainly scold him for not doing so. In all honesty, the idea hadn't even occurred to him. He'd just expected Ellie to take this unexpected visit in stride, the way she did everything else. Renaldor had known his cousin since infancy, and though she often got peeved with him, he'd never seen her flustered in his life.

Until now. Apparently, an unannounced visit from the Crown Prince and a hostile duke was enough to rattle Ellie's seemingly unshakeable composure. What Renaldor couldn't figure out was why. Ellie showed him the respect he was due, but she had never been nervous around him, or even his father. She'd also always been more than willing to put someone in their place with her magic. Why in Bryolan had that changed? It was like she was a whole different person.

Renaldor suppressed a sigh. Something was wrong with his cousin, and he was determined to find out what. As soon as the food arrived, he rose to his feet.

"I find myself in need of the lavatory," he said to both the duke and the servants.

"Of course, Your Highness," a serving boy replied. "I'd be happy to escort you."

"No need," he replied. "I know the way." He looked at the man across from him. "Excuse me, Your Grace."

The duke inclined his head, and Renaldor left the room. Instead of heading toward the lavatory, he strode straight to Ellie's chambers. The guard outside her door jumped to attention as he approached.

"Is the Baroness in there?" he asked.

"Yes, Your Highness."

"Please inform her I'd like a word."

"Yes, Your Highness."

The guard turned and knocked on the door. "My Lady, Prince Renaldor would like to speak with you."

After a moment, Ellie's voice replied, "Please let him in."

Obediently, the guard opened the door and held it for him. Renaldor walked in and found Ellie seated on the couch with another young woman who appeared to be a commoner. Seeing him, they both got to their feet. Ellie curtsied, and the commoner dipped her head, a familiar spark in her eyes. Renaldor stifled a groan. Suddenly, it all made sense.

"Ellie, what have you done?" he asked, glaring at the commoner.

"What have *I* done?" she snapped. "You're the one who decided to drop by for a magic show."

Whoever was currently in Ellie's body stared at her with wide eyes. Renaldor just shook his head.

"Duke Harvorth has been insinuating that our mages aren't up to par for a fortnight," he said. "When he asked to come here, I thought it would be the perfect opportunity to shut him up."

"Well, that's all well and good," Ellie said. "But would it have killed you to send a messenger ahead? If you had, we wouldn't be in this mess."

Renaldor looked between the two women. "And exactly what kind of mess are we in?"

Ellie sighed. "I wanted to know what my people's lives are really like, so I convinced Paige to let me switch bodies with her for a day or so."

"Paige?" Renaldor asked, trying to keep up.

"My friend," Ellie explained, waving at the body that was usually hers. "She's my maid's daughter."

Paige curtsied again, looking sheepish. Ellie glared at her.

"You really need to stop doing that in my body."

Paige stared at her in disbelief. "He's the Crown Prince!"

"And I'm a baroness," Ellie said. "You never curtsy to me."

"That's because when we were four years old, you threatened to turn me into a chipmunk if I ever did it again."

Ellie tilted her head. "Yes, I suppose I did." She turned back to Renaldor. "Anyway, this morning, I cast a spell to move my soul into Paige's body and hers into mine. I thought it would be easy for me to switch us back, but there's been a slight complication."

Renaldor braced himself. "And that is?"

"Apparently," Ellie said, "magic is attached to the body, not the soul. So now, I have Paige's magic, and she's got mine. And since Paige's magic isn't strong enough for me to undo my spell—"

"I have to do it," Paige chimed in. "But I'm telling you, Ellie, I can't."

Ellie put a hand on her hip. "Of course, you can. You have my magic."

"Yes, but not your *control*," Paige said. "And you already told me you didn't use runes to cast the spell, so I can't undo it."

"But you don't need runes," Ellie said. "You just have to...to feel it and make it happen."

She made it sound like the easiest thing in the world. Renaldor resisted the urge to roll his eyes.

"But I don't know how to do that," Paige said, wringing her hands. "And if I make a mistake, it could be disastrous."

Ellie shook her head. "That's not—"

"She's right, Ellie," Renaldor cut in. "A spell like that is complicated. And for someone not used to instinctual magic, it could be dangerous."

Ellie turned her piercing gaze to him. "So, what do you suggest? That we stay like this until Paige feels comfortable switching us back? That might have been an option if you hadn't brought a duke here for a magic *demonstration*, which we both know is code for a fight with his pet mage!"

Paige gasped. "It is?" she asked, her face going white. A vase on the end table shattered.

Renaldor jumped, then looked at Paige in alarm.

She covered her mouth with her hand. "I'm sorry," she mumbled, tears filling her eyes.

The couch started to shake.

Ellie grabbed her by the shoulders. "Breathe, Paige. It's okay. We'll figure it out. Just breathe."

Paige stared into her eyes and took a couple of deep breaths. The couch stopped shaking, and Ellie took a step back, looking relieved.

"I'm sorry, Your Highness," Paige said, her eyes downcast.

Renaldor shook his head. "There's no—"

"Don't apologize to him," Ellie interrupted. "This isn't your fault. Mine, yes. His, somewhat. But not yours. You've got nothing to be sorry for."

Paige nodded, biting her lip, and Renaldor couldn't help but feel sorry for her. It wasn't fair to put her in this position, and as much as he hated it, he knew what he had to do.

"I'll tell the duke you're indisposed and won't be able to do the demonstration," he said.

Ellie stared at him, shocked speechless for once. She understood the repercussions of that decision as much as he did, but there really wasn't another option.

To his surprise, it was Paige who said, "No, we can't do that. It'll make Bryolan look weak." She glanced at Ellie. "Right?"

Ellie nodded reluctantly.

Paige took a deep breath. "Well, we can't let that happen, so if I can't switch us back, I'll have to fight the duke's mage myself."

Renaldor's lips parted in shock. It wasn't often that someone truly stunned him.

"No," Ellie told her. "You're a healer. You don't know the first thing about battle magic."

"I...I'm sure I can figure it out," Paige muttered. "You said I just have to feel it and make it happen, right?"

Ellie crossed her arms. "If you can figure out battle magic, then you can figure out how to switch us back."

"That's different," Paige insisted. "Transferring souls is a lot more complicated than knocking someone over, and if I fail, the consequences could be much more dire." She sighed. "Admit it, Ellie. Me fighting the other mage is our best option."

"No, it's not. It's too dangerous," Ellie said and turned her gaze to him. "Ren, you can't let her do this!"

Renaldor looked back and forth between the two of them—Ellie, worried and desperate and Paige, scared but determined.

He clenched his jaw. It wasn't right to send an inexperienced mage into a fight like this. Even in an exhibition match, she could get hurt. Not killed—the duke's mage wouldn't dare go that far—but still hurt. He didn't want to put her in that situation.

But if he didn't, it would make Bryolan look weak. That wasn't something they could afford right now, not without jeopardizing the treaty. And as Crown Prince, it was his duty to do what was best for his kingdom.

Renaldor sighed. Sometimes, he hated being Crown Prince.

"If you're sure," he said, looking at Paige.

Ellie shot him an outraged look that promised retribution once she had her magic back, but Paige just squared her shoulders and gave him a firm nod.

Renaldor thought it was one of the bravest things he'd ever seen.

It was probably a good thing Elliana didn't have her magic right now. If she did, she might have lost control and blasted Ren across the courtyard. Of course, if she had her magic, they wouldn't be in this mess in the first place, but that was beside the point.

Curse Ren and his duty to Bryolan. If he got Paige hurt, she would never forgive him. She'd never forgive herself either.

Forcing those useless thoughts aside, Elliana peered around the bush she'd hidden behind and watched Paige walk to one end of the courtyard. Her opponent, a middle-aged man with an ego as large as his gut, strode to the other side, looking smug. If Elliana was in her own body, she would've had fun taking him down a peg or five.

She gnawed on her lower lip. She'd only had time to give Paige a few pointers about battle magic. Elliana just hoped it was enough.

As Ren stood to announce the start of the match, she shot him one last glare. When all this was over, she was definitely turning him into a squirrel.

When the prince called for the match to begin, Paige tried to do exactly as Ellie had instructed. She reached for the magic within her and pictured her opponent being knocked off his feet. Nothing happened.

She tried again, striving to put more feeling behind it. This time, a gust of wind hit her opponent, but it wasn't enough to knock him down or even make him stagger. What was she doing wrong?

Smirking, her opponent raised his hand and drew runes in the air. Instantly, Paige found herself unable to move. Panic filled her, and Ellie's magic lashed out in response, breaking the spell but causing no harm to the other mage. The man raised his hand and drew more runes.

Desperate to do something, Paige reached for the magic inside her again. Ellie had said her attacks were only limited by her imagination, so Paige tried to think of an attack that would subdue her opponent without hurting him too badly. After a moment, she imagined ropes appearing and wrapping around him. Nothing happened.

Before she could try again, an invisible force slammed into her, knocking her backward. She hit the cobblestones hard, then rolled onto her stomach. When she tried to stand up, what felt like an enormous weight settled on her back, smashing her into the cobblestones. Paige tried to reach for Ellie's magic to force it off, but the pain made focusing difficult. A large rock on the far side of the courtyard exploded. Unfortunately, it wasn't close enough to the other mage to affect him.

Paige clenched her fists. The prince had told her to concede if she felt like it was hopeless, but she couldn't do that. Not with her kingdom depending on her. She had to get out of this. But how?

"Is that all you've got, *Baroness?*" her opponent yelled, making the title sound like an insult. "I never expected you to be so weak. Admit defeat, and I won't break your ribs."

Gritting her teeth, Paige did her best to ignore the pain. Tears of frustration filled her eyes. This wasn't right. Luthania was going to think that Bryolan was weak. The treaty could be ruined because of her. She couldn't let that happen, but it was painfully clear she couldn't defeat this mage herself. That left only one option.

Praying she wasn't making a huge mistake, Paige closed her eyes. This time, she didn't try to summon the magic within her. She just wished with her entire being to be back in her own body and for Ellie to be in this one.

Elliana's world spun uncontrollably, and she lost all sense of her surroundings. When she got her bearings, she found herself lying on her stomach with an immense force pressing her into the cobblestones. Instinctively, she sent out a wave of magic, shattering the spell that held her in place. With the pressure gone, she was able to think and realized what must have happened.

Paige had managed to switch them back.

Elliana's eyes snapped up. She studied her opponent as she rose to her feet. The man looked surprised to see her moving, but still haughty and sure of his victory. That wouldn't last long.

A stab of pain turned Elliana's attention to her ribs. She ran a hand over them while exploring them with her magic. Two of them were cracked. A wave of rage washed over her as she healed them. That arrogant prick had hurt Paige. She met his gaze, hoping he could see the message in her eyes.

You hurt my friend, and now you're going to pay for it.

Without moving a muscle, Elliana sent her opponent flying backward at least three times as far as he'd thrown Paige. Before he could even think about moving, she made thick vines burst through the cobblestones and wrap around the man's legs, ribs, and shoulders. He winced as they squeezed tightly.

Elliana strode toward him, a predatory smile on her face.

"No," she said. "That wasn't all I've got. And neither is this. Yield, or I'll show you more."

The mage tried to move his hand to draw a rune. Immediately, Elliana caused the cobblestones to envelop them. The man's eyes widened, and then he grimaced as the vines tightened again.

"I yield," he hissed through clenched teeth.

"Wise choice," Elliana said and allowed the vines and cobblestones to release him.

She gave the man one last smile, then walked over to where Ren and the duke were waiting.

Renaldor felt a wave of pride as Ellie came to stand in front of the duke.

"Was that enough of a demonstration, Your Grace?" she asked. And though her tone was polite, her eyes held a challenge. "If not, I'd be happy to provide another."

Behind her, the vines disappeared, and the cobblestones fixed themselves, seemingly of their own accord.

Only twenty-five years of rigorous court discipline kept the amusement off Renaldor's face. This was why he'd agreed to come to Laveny. It was also why he planned to invite Ellie to be one of the crown's mages as soon as her brother came of age and could take over the barony. Ellie truly was remarkable.

"That demonstration was more than adequate," Duke Harvorth replied, barely civil. "Thank you for indulging me, but I think it's time we were on our way." He turned to Renaldor. "I'll go help my mage to the carriage."

"Very well," he replied. "I'll be there shortly."

When the duke was out of earshot, Renaldor smiled at his cousin. "That was brilliant, Ellie."

She narrowed her eyes. "I'm not the one you should be thanking."

Looking toward a bush, she gestured for it to come over. Renaldor was confused until Paige stood up from behind it and made her way toward them. Ellie turned back to him, her gaze fierce and calculating.

Remembering where that look had gotten him in the past, Renaldor said, "Need I remind you that turning Bryolan's Crown Prince into a rodent would undermine everything you two just accomplished."

She crossed her arms. "I suppose that's true. I'll let you off the hook ... for now."

Before Renaldor could respond, Paige reached them and dropped into a curtsy.

Ellie scowled at her. "I told you not to—"

"That was when I was in your body," Paige interrupted. "Now that I'm in my own, I'll curtsy to the prince if I like."

"Fine," Ellie said, rolling her eyes. Then her gaze softened. "Are you alright?"

Paige nodded. "What about you? I'm pretty sure I felt one of your ribs crack."

"Two, actually," Ellie said, "but I healed them with no trouble."

Paige frowned. "I'm so—"

"Don't you dare apologize," Ellie snapped. "You were brilliant. Wasn't she, Ren?"

Her eyes dared him to contradict her.

"Yes, you were," Renaldor said, looking at Paige. "You did Bryolan a great service, and you have my gratitude."

Blushing, Paige said, "It was my honor, Your Highness."

Renaldor smiled at her, then looked back at his cousin.

"I am truly sorry for the unannounced visit. Next time, I'll be sure to send a messenger, even if he's only a few hours ahead of me."

Ellie nodded, looking slightly mollified.

"But," he continued, "this situation was not entirely my fault. I trust you've learned something, too?"

"Yes," Ellie said, "I've learned that having so little magic is more difficult than I imagined." She looked at Paige. "Just fixing a broken arm was really taxing. Is healing always that difficult for you?"

"You get used to it," Paige replied with a shrug.

Ellie frowned. "If you say so. But I want you to promise you'll ask me if you need help."

Paige's eyes widened. "But Ellie—"

"But nothing," Ellie said. "I won't have my people dying or you half-killing yourself to heal them. Not when I could fix it so easily. And I don't understand why—"

Renaldor cleared his throat, giving his cousin a pointed look.

Ellie met his gaze without flinching. "Yes, obviously, I learned my lesson about experimenting with spells. Happy?"

He sighed. One day, when he was king and she was his chief mage, they were going to have an interesting time indeed.

"And I learned that I should look for all possible pitfalls in Ellie's crazy schemes before agreeing to them," Paige said with a cheeky grin.

Ellie blinked, then burst out laughing.

"Yes," she said between giggles, "I suppose you should."

Renaldor looked at Paige thoughtfully. In the last couple of hours, she'd proven herself to be both loyal and courageous, and she seemed to have a good head on her shoulders. If she could also rein in some of Ellie's wilder plans, it might be a good idea to have her at court. With luck, one of his younger brothers might even fall for her, and she could officially be on his council when he became king. It was an idea worth considering further.

Ellie studied him. "You've got that crafty look on your face. What are you thinking?"

Renaldor shook his head, knowing he couldn't keep the duke waiting any longer.

"Nothing that can't wait." He smiled at them both. "Thank you for everything you did today. I won't forget it."

"You're most welcome, Your Highness," Paige replied.

"Neither will I," Ellie said at the same time.

Renaldor's lips quirked. It was good to see their expressions on the right faces this time. He hoped to see them both more often in the future.

"Good day," he told them and turned to walk away.

As he made his way to the carriage, Renaldor decided he really should thank the duke for requesting this detour to Laveny.

Meet Miriam Thor

Miriam Thor grew up in Louisiana. After graduating from high school, she moved to North Carolina where she attended Gardner-Webb University and earned her bachelor's degree in American Sign Language and elementary education. After graduation, Miriam remained in North Carolina for several years. While there, she met and married her husband. Recently, the two of them moved to Alabama. Miriam is currently employed as a sign language interpreter at a middle school.

In second grade, Miriam's teacher encouraged her to write to her heart's content, so she started doing that and never stopped. Her first short story was published in 2016. She likes to write a variety of genres, but fantasy is her favorite. Occasionally, Miriam also dabbles in poetry, but only when inspiration strikes. Her published works include a young adult fantasy novella entitled *Wish Granted*, a contemporary Christian fiction novella entitled *Her First Noel*, several short stories, and a handful of poems.

When Miriam is not writing, she enjoys reading, doing martial arts, spending time with her husband, and cuddling with her cats. She also loves to eat sweets, especially cookie dough, cheesecake, and anything chocolate.

To learn more about Miriam or to find her published works, you can visit her website: https://miriamthor17.wixsite.com/author. You can also follow her on Twitter (@Miriam_Thor17) or subscribe to her blog: threecs.org.

Sophronae Snafua

MADDI DAVIDSON

I don't believe it," Cassidy said.

Sophrona took another sip of her butterfly pea flower tea, the bright magenta concoction leaving a slight stain on her upper lip, which matched the color of her tinted hair. She hadn't seen her goddaughter since the funeral for Cassidy's parents, six years earlier. The tall, angular teenager had grown into a shapely twenty-three-year-old woman strongly resembling her late mother.

"Why are you here, my dear, if you think what you mother wrote was a lie?"

"I want you to admit you're an old fraud, or prove to me you're not," she said.

"But I *am* an old broad," Sophrona replied, somewhat puzzled.

"Fraud, old *fraud*. Prove you are not an old fraud."

"Oh! Well then, what would you like me to do? Display my magic license from the seventeenth century?"

A movement outside caught Cassidy's attention. Through the sitting room's bow window she saw a young boy of about four pulling a red wagon carrying a slightly younger girl, his sister judging by the matching coal black hair and widow's peak.

"A red wagon. Mother said you could conjure things up, so cast a spell to make a red wagon appear. A small one, about so big." Cassidy held her hands about a foot apart.

Sophrona's countenance brightened. "What a wonderful idea. I haven't done that spell in over a century. There is so little demand for my services anymore since few people believe in magic. Come with me."

Sophrona led her goddaughter into a sleek modern kitchen spanning the rear of the small home. Blazing white cabinets were complemented by a huge center island with teal blue cabinetry, large stainless-steel appliances, and acres of quartz countertops.

"*This* is where you work?" Cassidy said.

"You were expecting a black cauldron hanging in a brick fireplace?"

"Mother wrote you were ancient, so ..."

"You have to be patient in my line of work, but black cauldrons take too long to heat up and they're hard to keep clean. Plus, without ventilation a lot of spells smell like three-month-old decomposing warthog."

"Ancient, not patient. *Ancient!*"

"I am old, dearie, but I keep up with the times, except for that Internet stuff. Can't seem to get the hang of it."

Sophrona removed a thick leather-bound book with a gold-tooled spine from one of the cabinets and paged through until she found the appropriate spell. Tottering around the kitchen and talking to herself, she gathered ingredients while periodically consulting her book.

As Cassidy watched her work, she thought about her mother's letter. "To be opened by my daughter if she is still unmarried at twenty-three," had been scrawled across the front in her mother's haphazard script. For years Cassidy had speculated on its contents. Never had she imagined that it would contain a tale of magic.

Standing a smidge over five feet tall, Sophrona used a step stool to reach a small, brass pan hanging over the center island. She filled it with water, placed the pan on the gas stove, and added over a dozen items including fresh red dragon fruit, green coffee powder, chile pepper, star anise, and two handfuls of low-calorie sweetener. She

brought the concoction to a boil, then let it simmer, stirring occasionally. At the last moment, she tossed in a handful of cinnamon candy.

"Time for the incantation," she said. "Stand back." Checking the
book one last time, she raised her hands. "*Appareat rubrum draco*!
Dragon appear!"

Little orange flames blazed at the tip of Sophrona's fingers. The
smell of sulphur filled the air. Smoke poured out of the pan onto the
floor followed by flashing glitter. When the haze cleared, a six-inch
red dragon lay on the tile floor. As the last glitter fell, the dragon
sneezed, a tiny blue flame flaring from its snout.

"It's a red dragon. I asked for a red wagon," Cassidy said.

Sophrona's face fell. "I thought you said wagon, but I didn't think
that could be right. What would you do with such a thing?"

"Well, I certainly can't use a baby dragon. How would I explain it,
particularly when it reaches full size?"

Sophrona picked up the dragon, placed it on the island, and
began to caress the creature's back. "This is as big as it gets. Anyone
can make a dragon, but it requires a deft touch to miniaturize it." The
dragon expressed its pleasure at the stroking with deep sighs and
puffs of purple smoke, then rolled over for a belly rub.

"Dragons are loyal and loving and make great pets," Sophrona
said. "You only need to let it out once a day to stretch its wings,
preferably after dark."

Observing the little creature coo in pleasure, Cassidy was struck
by the fact that she was looking at something that didn't exist, but
had been conjured out of thin air—and a handful of ingredients—by
a doddering old woman. Her mother had been telling the truth about
Sophrona. "You *are* a fairy godmother," she said.

Sophrona's eyes brightened. "Then you'll let me find you a
husband like your mother suggested. Here," she said, grabbing a pen
and a pad of paper. "Write down what you want. My hearing is a bit
off, but my eyesight is good when I wear my reading glasses,
assuming I can remember where I left them."

Cassidy paused. According to her mother's letter, Sophrona had
brought her parents together. Her father had set sail on a calm day in
St. Petersburg, Florida, only to be blown off course by a freak wind-

storm, which carried his boat south, around the tip of the state, and up the East Coast to deposit him on the sand at Myrtle Beach, South Carolina in front of her sunbathing mother. However, that all happened thirty years ago. Sophrona had admitted she'd not done much magic lately.

"Are you sure you can handle it?"

"I'll admit it's one of the hardest spells to do. One has to summon a man who will not just meet a woman's expectations, but fit with her essence. Imbuing the spell with the necessary force to bring the couple together is challenging, but just last century I brought a woman all the way from America to meet the future king of England. She had to divorce her second husband, and her beau had to abdicate the throne. However, he was a prince at the time they met so my record is unblemished in that regard."

"What if I don't like him? The man who appears. Maybe I just don't find him sexy. What then?"

"My dear, once a woman reaches twenty-three, she's virtually out of marriage prospects. All my goddaughters have been grateful to have any man agree to marry them rather than remain an old maid."

"Times have changed. Women are having careers and getting married much later, if at all. I have years ahead of me to find someone."

Sophrona slumped in her chair. In her younger years, she had scores of godchildren. Now she had only three left, two of whom were married and childless. Cassidy could represent her last chance for more godchildren.

Recognizing Sophrona's disappointment, Cassidy attempted to soften the blow. "I know you can cast a spell but ... just not now. I'd like to try traditional means first. As a school teacher, I don't meet many unmarried men, so I've joined a singles group at church and a big health club."

"Humph. The traditional method is to call on your fairy godmother."

"I don't know anybody else who has one, unless you count fairy-godmother.com."

"What on Earth is that?"

"An online dating site guaranteed to find you a prince charming."

After Cassidy departed, Sophrona gave herself a pity party, wallowing in feelings of low value and regretful she hadn't embraced the Internet where, apparently, her services were wanted. After an hour of sorrow and a shot of eighteen-year-old single malt scotch—over the centuries Sophrona had learned to appreciate the good stuff—she started steaming: rice for dinner and anger at not being appreciated.

"Just because I haven't done a lot of magic lately doesn't mean I can't. I've been busy with my literacy volunteer work and my golf leagues. And since I broke my last working wand, I've had to channel power through my fingertips, which is a *lot* harder than it looks. People look at me and think I'm old and useless. I can't deny the old, but I am *not* useless." The pep talk raised her spirits immensely, and the rice was good, too, after she threw in pinto beans, pineapple salsa, and fresh avocado.

"If my goddaughter doesn't want magic, I won't use magic, but I can still help," she said to the little dragon nibbling away on the remains of her avocado. "I can compose a personal ad for her: young lady of twenty—okay, I'm fudging her age—who is educated, pretty, and fun-loving, wants a husband who is wealthy, stylish, handsome, fascinating, and doesn't throw used towels on the bathroom floor. What do you think?"

The dragon had dozed off, emitting avocado-green smoke puffs as it snored.

Sophrona perused the personal ads in the local paper and was dismayed to discover they used a language that was as unfamiliar to her as spells were to mere mortals. After another tip of the bottle to buck up her spirits, the acronyms began to make sense and she was able to compose an ad for her goddaughter. "SWF ISO M for swinging time. Call Cassidy at 335-444-2730."

A week after the ad first appeared, Sophrona answered the door to her furious goddaughter waving a folded newspaper.

"What in the world were you thinking?"

Sophrona strolled over to a side table and picked up her reading glasses. Taking the paper from Cassidy, she perused the item circled in red ink.

"Well, I had a tad of single malt whisky. Helps with the creativity. Have you met anyone nice yet?"

"Thinking. What were you *thinking*? Not drinking, although that explains the fiasco."

Cassidy ranted for several minutes, speaking so quickly that Sophrona didn't catch most of what she said, except she'd been badgered by a "creamy dessert" or "sleepy pervert" or maybe "creepy servant." Tiring of Cassidy's histrionics, Sophrona took a seat in her easy chair.

Realizing the awkwardness of towering over her godmother while yelling at her, Cassidy stopped speaking and slumped onto the couch.

"So you didn't meet anyone nice?" Sophrona had surmised this might be one of those times she should act the fool. Not that it was a stretch.

"How could I with that ad?" Cassidy explained to Sophrona that M meant married, not male, and swinging was a term for married individuals who enjoyed sexual experiences with other married or coupled individuals.

At the latter revelation, Sophrona blushed excessively. She excused herself and disappeared into the kitchen. Happily she still had some Scotch left. When she returned, Sophrona carried a tray with a pot of tea and two tea cups.

"If it's the butterfly pea tea, I'll pass," Cassidy said.

"It's orange pekoe with more than a little whisky."

"In that case, I'm in."

"I'm terribly sorry," Sophrona said after taking a few sips of tea.

Godmother and goddaughter reconciled over several cups of whisky tea with Sophrona promising not to interfere while Cassidy followed her own methods of meeting men.

However, when several months had passed with Cassidy still not married or engaged, Sophrona resolved to take action. Mindful of her previous debacle, Sophrona abstained from alcohol for a full day before starting the complex and taxing spell to bring Cassidy true love.

"Arms of an oak for a strong man," she said dropping oak branches into a large non-stick pot filled with water.

"Essence of woman." Sophrona added a few strands of Cassidy's long-dark hair to the pot. Not being a cleaning fanatic, she'd been able to pluck the hairs from the couch where Cassidy had sat on her last visit three weeks earlier.

When the concoction began boiling, she stirred in a bird's nest for love of home, lemon zest for enthusiasm, basil and garlic for seasoning, a touch of chamomile for good health, and finally salt and pepper to add excitement to the relationship.

Holding her hands high, Sophrona intoned, "Power of all, I command you to send my goddaughter a true prince to love. *Omni virtute praecipio tibi filiam meam Deus caritas est princeps.*"

That's what she meant to say, but due to a heavy hand with the pepper, Sophrona involuntarily sneezed as she reached the end of the incantation and "*princeps*" was mangled. A low menacing growl emerged from the pot and whisps of black fog rose to the ceiling.

"Oh dear! What have I done?"

She discovered the answer a week later.

"I'm in love," Cassidy said. She was nearly breathless on the phone. "His name is Max, and he's a real sweetie. We just got back from a run. We're having such fun together, and he sleeps in my bed. I've never felt such delicious kisses! He even licks my ankles! I've been doing some reading about him. Did you know the breed is known for being fearless, intelligent, and loyal?"

"Breed?"

"Yes, didn't I mention he's a German pinscher? He just appeared on my doorstep one morning. I notified local vet offices and the animal shelter, but no one claimed him. The vet says he's about four years old and in great shape. I think the name Max suits him."

After she hung up, Sophrona skipped the tea and went straight to the whisky.

Perhaps she was the tiniest bit rusty, Sophrona thought. A few small spells would help shake out the cobwebs. A wand would help, too. Hawthorn, of course. It was hard to go wrong with one of the Faerie Triad woods.

During the next new moon, Sophrona cut off a small branch of a neighbor's hawthorn tree. She sanded off most of the bark and brushed it with tungsten oil. After a few passes over an open flame, she was ready to test the new wand.

Sophrona thought of her golfing friend, Julia. "Poor woman has been playing the game for forty years and never experienced the thrill of a hole in one. *Sit amicus meus Iulia facere foramen unum iaculat.*" Sophrona gave her new wand a little wave, orange flames shooting from the tip. A small cloud of green smoke flew toward the window, and the smell of fresh grass permeated the kitchen.

Within a week the wished-for event occurred. On a par three hole at the municipal golf course while golfing with Sophrona, Julia's drive caromed off a maple tree and was picked up by a squirrel who carried it forty yards onto the green, dropping it in the hole.

"Ugly, but at least it worked," Sophrona muttered.

She continued to cast small spells, including transforming the little red dragon into a gorgeous ruby-throated hummingbird. She missed the cooing, but enjoyed seeing the tiny bird when it visited the feeder, and not having to worry about the creature accidentally starting a fire.

Brimming with confidence from her successes, Sophrona once again tried the prince spell, this time with a small addendum. "*Debit amor Pinscher.* He must love Pinschers."

As the odor of new leather and navy blue smoke emanated from the pot, Sophrona let out a huge sigh of relief. The signs looked good.

"I've changed health clubs," Cassidy announced on her next visit.

"You've met someone?"

"Yes, and not in a good way. At my old club there was a dirty old man who kept following me around from machine to machine, trying to chat me up and pinching my rear end."

"Pitching? Like Don Drysdale?"

"Pinching. *Pinching!* He's a bigwig politician, and I knew the club wouldn't take any action. So, I quit."

Sophrona knew she'd blown the spell somehow. *You've lost it, old girl. You can't do the big stuff anymore.*

The only saving grace was that Cassidy seemed genuinely happy with her new health club. "I've even made a few new friends," she said, which Sophrona heard as "a few blue pens."

On a beautiful, bright July day, Cassidy appeared at Sophrona's door with a dozen roses. "You did it!" she said as she threw her arms around Sophrona. "Thank you, thank you! I'm sorry I ever doubted you. He's perfect!"

"Who?"

"Brendan, of course. I met him at my new health club. It was love at first sight. We've been dating for a month, and he proposed last night. Oh Sophrona, he's the prince I've always dreamed of. When he told me that his name is derived from the Old Welsh, meaning Prince, I knew you had brought us together."

Over the next thirty seconds while Cassidy held her godmother in a bear hug, Sophrona felt stunned, then contemplative, then elated. "I'm so glad it has worked out, dear. Not one of the easier spells, as I said. Had to go through a little intermediate step to get you to the right health club."

Over cups of tea, sans alcohol, Cassidy shared her joy and informed her godmother that the wedding would be in September. Of course, Sophrona must come. She and Brendan were looking for a house, but she would continue to teach.

"What about children?" Sophrona asked.

Cassidy laughed. "There's no rush. We're not even sure we want any. Besides, we have a child: Max."

That evening Sophrona prepared another spell. "This is for their own good. *Benedicat cum multis felis.* Bless them with many children."

Black, tan, and white tendrils of mist rose into the air as Sophrona heard faint mewing sounds from the pot.

"That's not right." She peered at her spell book. "Oh no! It should have been *fillis*, not *felis*! I want children, not cats!"

Meet Maddi Davidson

Maddi Davidson is the pen name for two sisters—Mary Ann and Diane Davidson—who, by mutual agreement, live on opposite coasts of the USA. Together they have published several novels, a non-fiction book, and numerous short stories. Their tales range from the murder of a deranged scientist attempting to resurrect the dodo to a spurned wife hacking the pacemaker of an ex-husband who richly deserved it.

Call Mountain Blood

CHRISTOPHER COLLINS

G raki looked at the sand spilled on the reed mat and blinked.
Call, Mountain, Blood.

What am I supposed to do with these? he thought to himself, as a flush of panic began to creep up the back of his neck.

"Uh, Firmizkt remains mysterious this evening, Chieftain," he mumbled quietly to the dark form across from him.

This and every other evening. His heart beat faster. The flush spread across his neck and into his cheeks. Graki was sure it could be seen glowing from behind the carved wooden mask he wore over his face. He leaned forward self-consciously, just in case, and the mask slipped, blinding him. He readjusted it with one skinny, green hand. It rubbed uncomfortably, heavy, on the bridge of his nose. He read the spilled sand again, trying to find some meaning in what he saw there:

Call, Mountain, Blood.

He read the sand, but it made no sense.

"What does it mean, Shaman?" asked Chief Uluk. Large for a goblin, his size—more importantly his general cruelty—more than qualified him for the job of clan chieftain. He sat staring at Graki in a way that could bode only ill fortune.

Graki poked at the sand runes. The smoke from the fire irritated his eyes.

"I, uh," Graki said. "This is a puzzle, Chieftain. Firmizkt speaks tonight in tongues." He blinked again, willing the sand piles to change before him or to spark his imagination. He'd never been quick with his thoughts.

"And you are the voice of Firmizkt, Shaman. It is your place to speak his thoughts." The chieftain's voice filled the hide hut in which they sat, though it sounded far away to Graki.

"Tell me *now* what Firmizkt wills for the raid tomorrow." Uluk thumbed the wood handle of a cruel-looking, curved dagger he held backward in his right hand.

Graki's breath came faster as the panic in him rose. His lungs burned from the smoke. A ringing sound filled his ears.

Uluk's voice seemed to come from a distance as the chieftain continued to speak, "You *must* give me Firmizkt's blessing, Shaman. I need all of my boys' strength tomorrow. I need them to have the blessing of their god. You will give me this," the chieftain continued.

Graki stared at the piles of sand, willing Firmizkt to talk to him, but expecting the god's customary indifference.

"Call, Mountain, Blood. Firmizkt is..." The shaman trailed off. His stomach churned, and sweat dripped from his brow.

The terrible, gleaming dagger filled Graki's vision as the shaman's sight narrowed into a dark tunnel. Uluk's thumb rubbed back and forth over the polished wood. Over and over. Over and over. Sharp, black nails somehow as intimidating as the pitted dagger. The chieftain's insults were fully muffled now, incomprehensible. Graki could hear only the sound of his rapid breath, could see only the vicious nails.

"No, I...I..." He tasted the rusted iron of the dagger in his mouth. The weight of the wooden mask was an anchor, dragging his face toward that hand with those dark, sharp, dangerous claws.

Graki vomited into his mask. With nowhere to go, the bile and acid splattered up into his eyes and nostrils and down his bare chest. Uluk leaped up, swearing and shouting, the dagger flung to the side.

"Worthless shaman!" he roared, and clubbed Graki across the ear with the inside of his fist. "You worthless—"

"It's not..." Graki's eyes and nose burned, his stomach heaved. His clubbed ear felt as though it were torn off. "I...I..." The shaman stammered between retches.

He huddled against the tent wall, Uluk towering above him. The fire made the chieftain's shadow that much larger, huge, black. A commotion stirred outside with shouts from far away. The chieftain leaned over Graki, bashed the shaman across the side of the head again. Long black claws stretched from the hands of the shadow toward the smoky ceiling as Uluk raised his own. Graki cowered, unable to breathe, unable to think.

"It..." he began again. The room shrank, the fire flared. He could hear only his words now. "It's not for you! Not for you! The mountain moves! For you! For you! The mountain moves!"

"That is not a telling!" roared Uluk, striking the shaman again.

Darkness closed over Graki.

———

He woke later that night to pain but blissfully alone. His head ached, and his throat burned. Dried blood crusted his split ear. Graki tried to push himself up from the floor, and bright white light flared across his vision. A stabbing in his head threatened to cast him back into unconsciousness with each movement. The scattered fire had burned down to embers on the packed dirt floor of his hut and provided little light or warmth. Chieftain Uluk was nowhere to be seen.

Panic took hold of Graki as the events of the evening came flooding back. The chieftain knew he was a fraud. Firmizkt had not spoken to him, there was no telling, and Uluk had attacked him for it.

This was it. The charade was over, and now the entire village would know. They'd all know he'd faked each of their tellings. That there was no guidance from Firmizkt. He had to get away before they came for him. What was the punishment for being a false shaman? It had never happened for as long as Graki could remember. It hardly mattered. Uluk was fierce and cruel, especially when he was angry.

Graki shuddered at the thought of the torture he would endure if he could not escape.

He dragged his aching body to the corner of his hut containing two earthenware pots, pain still stabbing his brain with each movement. He raised the smaller of the pots to his lips and drank deeply of the cool water inside, then spit a mouthful to clear the acidic taste from his mouth. One of his teeth was loose.

Graki dumped the contents of the larger pot onto the floor and went about gathering supplies. Salt hare meat, several hard-dried biscuits, a small bag of nuts and seeds were thrown into the large pot. The smaller pot of water, wrapped with twine, nestled into the bottom. He hesitated, then grabbed a skin of strong karak. If he lived, he would need a strong drink.

The shaman grabbed a ragged wrap from a pile of cloth he used for a bed, and, looping it a few times, lay it on the floor and set the pot inside it, before bringing up the sides into a sling. He tied it across his shoulders and onto his back, grabbed his robe from the floor and reached for his mask. He paused. What good would the mask do now? Who would he wear it for? He wasn't a shaman, and anyone who knew him as one would now know he was a fraud.

The mask lay on the floor of the hut, its wood face carved into a fierce grimace, and outlined with ash paint, serious and intimidating. Red-painted reed hair stood straight up from the wooden brow, and carved wooden rings pierced its ears. Dried vomit crusted its inside. Graki wavered, tears threatening to spill from his eyes. In one swift movement, he grabbed the mask and tossed it into the sling on his back. He took one more look at his hut, squalid and plain but his, and slipped quietly through the curtain blocking the doorway and out into the dark.

⁂

He entered a small clearing in the forest at the bottom of the valley as the moon rose from behind the ridge. A huge, white block of stone occupied the center of the clearing, almost as tall as Graki and as wide on two sides, twice that length on the long sides. The massive rectangle of limestone had the feel of even more mass than it actually possessed, as though it were pressing forcefully into the earth. A rust-colored stain marred the pristine white surface, spilling down the middle of the two long sides like a red waterfall down cliffs of bone.

The stone table was a human place, Graki knew, where the tribes of man celebrated their autumn harvest feasts and performed sacrifices to their gods. It was not frequented this time of year though and was secluded and safe enough for the night.

His strength seemed to give out at the sight of the table, the last reserves of energy fleeing as he finally recognized a landmark from the map in his head. With the last of his will, he forced himself to build a small camp on the dark side of the stone, gathering some dry tinder for a fire, and unpacking a little of his food. Exhausted, he leaned his back against the cold stone and tossed bits of the salt hare meat into boiling water to soften it. He took a large sip of the goat-milk karak from a leather flask, grimacing at the flavor and the burn of the alcohol. The gravity of his situation hit him all at once.

What had he done? How long could a single goblin make it on his own in the world, especially one like Graki who was small, weak, good for nothing. He wasn't even good at pretending to be a shaman.

Not for lack of trying. Tamoct, the shaman that preceded him, had apprenticed Graki as a child. He'd taught Graki how to mix the herbs and where the mushrooms grew. He had shown Graki how to make the ceremonial fires, how to read the sand spills. He'd taught Graki all the old rites and all the lore. He taught Graki how to speak to their god, Firmizkt.

Firmizkt never spoke back though. Graki took another mouthful of karak.

Why? Why did Firmizkt not speak to him? Why was he not worthy? Graki had been the most attentive apprentice. He learned the ways voraciously, gorging on the information given to him by Tamoct. He did everything exactly as Tamoct did, but when he spoke to his god, there was never an answer.

The sand spills were supposed to be the direct word of Firmizkt. Graki could read the telling of the sand as it flowed from his palm and between his fingers into mounds on the reed mat, but they made no sense. Random and disorderly. His god had nothing to say to him, or else his god gibbered and babbled. Graki flushed, embarrassed at blasphemy committed against an absent god.

He took another sip. The rabbit meat boiled quietly in the cook pot. Long shadows cast by the fire lengthened further and darkened, together with his mood.

At first Tamoct waved away Graki's failure as the learnings of a young shaman, but as the years went on and Graki was unable to perform a coherent tell, the elder shaman had grown suspicious. As his patience dried up, Graki's mentor became more cruel and abusive. Eventually, Graki decided if Firmizkt would not speak to him, he'd just have to pretend he did. He read the sands and made up fitting tells. He performed the rites each day, mixed the herbs and gathered the mushrooms. He spoke for a god that would not speak.

Now here he was, alone in the wilds on the run from Uluk, who would no doubt kill him if he was caught.

Graki stood abruptly, feeling himself sway drunkenly as though he were an observer not within his own body. He picked up the pot of boiled rabbit meat and the flask of karak, set them upon the table, and climbed up on the rock. He stood in the center of the stained stone and stared at the moon for a moment. His ear still ached. Tears flowed quietly from his eyes.

He knelt, and cupping his hands, took some of the warm water from the pot. He gingerly washed the dried blood from his ear and nose. Blood and water ran down his forearms and dripped off the points of his elbows. He took another sip of karak, spit it out onto the table, and prodded his loose tooth with his tongue. Then he took another large mouthful of karak.

Graki washed the blood from his face and the ceremonial ash tattoos from his arms and chest, the red and white mingling into a gray-brown pool on the stone table, running down the sides along the rust-colored stains. When he finished, he stood in the center of the stone, green skin dark in the moonlight. Cold wind blew over him. Graki looked again to the moon, silver white and cold. A sneer curled his lip. Drink, anger, and fear clouded his mind.

Graki screamed. In the silence that followed, he saw himself standing in a pool of blood and ash and tears and moonlight on the stone table. He felt somehow both small and fierce at the same time. He screamed again, raising both hands into fists above his head. Once more he screamed, digging his nails into his palms, until his throat was raw and his head ached.

He took a deep breath. Then he sobbed, tears spilling down his cheeks like rivers. Finally, he sat at the edge of the table, legs hanging from the side, shoulders slumping. He gazed around at the dark clearing. He wiped his eyes and slid off the rough limestone block, curled up in a ball by the fire and fell asleep, spent.

⁘

He woke sometime later to a clinking, tapping sound from the other side of the table, followed by what sounded like heavy scrabbling and more clinking. His breath caught in his throat. Uluk had found him.

Graki rose quietly and crept slowly around the huge stone slab, heart beating as though it might break out of his chest. His back pressed firmly to the side of the block, he took a deep breath and steeled himself. With a quiet whimper, he slowly peered around the corner toward the source of the noises.

In the light of the moon, he could just make out a huge, dark shape. It was easily the largest living thing Graki had ever seen, though he wasn't yet sure just what it was. It sat huddled over, its back leaning against the same stone table on the other side of which Graki had so recently been sleeping. The thing's attention was focused on something in front of it. It sat hunched over, poking at whatever it was that sat on the ground in front of it. It took a few moments for the shaman to realize the thing was covered in fur. An instant later, Graki recognized just what he was looking at: the largest bear he had ever seen.

Graki gasped and retreated back around the corner of the great stone table. A bear! He had no way to defend himself against a bear. He racked his memory for some helpful tidbit of information. Goblin folk wisdom instructed warriors to stand their ground against bears black of fur and small of stature, yelling, throwing

34

rocks and poking at it with their spears to make themselves too much trouble to eat.

Graki wasn't sure how big the black-clad ones were, but the monster on the other side of the great block certainly wasn't "small of stature," and it was too dark to tell just what color fur it possessed. In any case, he had no weapons with which to make himself pointy and unappetizing. What else?

The other bear, "the brown one," was large and dangerous. Wisdom told the goblin warrior to pretend to lie as though slain when in the gaze of the brown one and to silently pray to not find themselves actually so.

As a shaman, Graki should be able to speak with the animals of the wood, including this giant bear, to praise it as a lord of the forest and ask for safe passage. Goblin lore was filled with ancient stories of shaman seeking the council of the owl or news from the red fox. As a shaman, he should be able to commune with the bear. Unfortunately for Graki, he was a false shaman.

The goblin slumped to a sitting position and tried to catch his breath. What could he do? If he stayed, the bear would no doubt eat him. If he ran, it would catch him, and then eat him. He took a deep breath. Graki had run from one beast already today. That was enough. He would stand his ground, however it turned out. What else was there to lose now? The foolhardy—and certainly still somewhat inebriated—shaman squared his shoulders and stepped from behind the stone table.

"You there! Leave this place!" He shouted and jumped, waving his arms and trying to look threatening.

The bear looked up sharply from whatever it was that held its attention, its focus now fully on the goblin shaman. Graki wilted a little under the intense gaze.

"This is, uh, a human place, not a bear place." Inside, a voice well-known to Graki rolled its eyes.

"Not a bear place?" You aren't even well-spoken with animals. The goblin briefly fought back embarrassment, and then did so again when the same part of him continued, *Do you jest? Now is the time to be embarrassed? And in front of a bear?*

35

Graki punched the side of his head with the fleshy part of his fist in a fit of self-loathing. A sharp pain from his injured ear brought his focus back to the moment. Pushing aside his internal daemon, he took a deep breath and, with a backbone formed of adrenaline and fear, Graki stepped toward the bear and raised both arms above his head.

"Leave now!" he shouted. His mind frantically searched his shaman teachings for the true name of the brown ones. "Leave now, R'tk! This place is not for you."

A silent, dark mountain, the bear sat watching the goblin. It blinked once, slowly. With a grunt, it began to stand. Graki's pot, cracked and broken, fell from its grasp as it hauled itself onto all fours. The pot was almost empty; the bear had been eating Graki's food. He cursed himself silently. He should have strung the pot up a tree before he slept. This was a danger of his own making.

The bear continued to rise. With an illusion of slowness born of its massive size, the giant hauled itself up onto two legs and stood staring at the shaman.

Graki gulped but stood his ground with arms raised. He felt weak and small, an unarmed goblin against a mountain. Naked to the waist and wearing only his loincloth, he could not make an imposing figure. He wished he'd still worn his mask and ceremonial markings to seem more intimidating. But there was no escape now. He stepped forward once again.

"Begone, brown one! R'tk, lord of the wood, return to your home!" he shouted.

The bear watched him for a moment, then raised its arms in imitation of the shaman's stance, lowered its massive head and roared. It went on for what seemed like forever, the bear's huge dark mouth wide, spittle flying, and massive teeth gleaming in the moonlight. The roar washed over Graki like a wave—deafening, terrible, and glorious.

When the bear finally stopped, its roar echoed around the clearing and the forest beyond for some time before fading. The world was deathly silent, and for a second Graki thought he was deafened before he realized he could hear himself breathing, gasping. He whimpered, his bravery fled, as his knees gave out and he fell to the ground.

The bear lowered its arms, still standing. Towering at its full height, the brown one was now lit by the remnants of the fire on the other side of the stone table. Its fur, Graki saw, was not just brown, but multi-colored. Large swaths of its chest and arms and head were furred in red, or black or white. A ring of white fur wrapped its right arm above the elbow. Another fell over its shoulders and collarbones as though it were a livery collar. The overall effect was that of war paint. *Or ceremonial paint...*

Graki blinked in surprise. The pattern of the white fur was the same as the ceremonial ash paint Graki had worn every day of his adult life: the markings of a shaman. The same markings he'd washed off with his blood as he'd sat on the stone table earlier.

The bear grunted and fell onto its bottom, mimicking Graki again. It sat and stared at him, but did not move.

The sun rose slowly, gently, over the eastern hills. Birds sang in the trees around the wood. Small animals went about their morning activities, searching, as always, for food.

Graki still sat where he'd stumbled the night before. The great bear sat facing him. Neither had moved in the hours since their meeting, though the bear did look around the clearing or, occasionally, scratched itself, or yawned. Graki got the distinct impression that it was bored. The shaman, on the other hand, was not.

Fear replaced with curiosity and wonder, Graki's mind raced. This was no normal bear before him. That he was not at this very moment slowly digesting in the thing's stomach spoke most immediately to that fact, but even more, what bear had markings like that? The white fur was definitely in the same pattern as those worn by goblin shamans for, well, forever. The red fur "war-paint" across the bear's eyes and chest resembled the markings the human tribes sometimes gave themselves, smearing the blood of animals sacrificed at the stone table across their bodies. Feathers were twined here and there throughout the bear's fur, blowing gently in the wind.

What held Graki's attention, however, was the crown.

Floating slightly above the great bear's head was a translucent, faintly glowing circlet of ghostly vine and bone and wood. It moved in place as the bear took in its surroundings, turning and tipping in whatever direction the bear looked. When he'd noticed it finally, the crown had glowed ever so faintly blue, as though it were barely there. It grew brighter with the rising of the sun, but still, if Graki hadn't been paying close attention, he would have missed it.

Contrary to what he'd thought the night before, this thing was not one of the great bears, but without realizing, he'd already called it by its true name, R'tk. It was proper for a shaman to address the noble animals by their familial name, but what sat before him was the namesake of the bears. This was not just one of the great bears. What sat before Graki was *The* Great Bear: their celestial father, The Great Brown One, R'tk itself, God of the Bears.

Why is he here? Graki wondered. R'tk was in the clearing with *him*, the lowly shaman. Or rather, the false shaman. His own god wouldn't send him so much as a premonition, and now *right in front of him* sat *the God of all Bears!* What was he doing? Graki searched through his memories again, trying to recall the lore.

The gods of the noble animals wandered the celestial forests, the prime embodiment of their kind. They were said to offer their protection to their family or pack or herd when it was needed, and the animals were said to worship them. The wolves prayed to their goddess at the full moon, and the stag bowed their great antlers in respect to their god. R'tk was one of the Great Ones, a higher order of the gods of the noble animals with few peers, but the shaman couldn't remember what set them apart from the others.

The animal gods were sometimes worshipped, or at least revered, by others, too. The humans, Graki remembered now, painted themselves in the blood of a sacrificed boar or lamb before war, asking for favor from R'tk to make them fierce and strong. The very stone altar in this clearing was even stained red-brown with the blood of their sacrifices.

Graki recalled his actions the night before when, drunk and despondent, he'd stood on the human's stone table, crying. He'd cried and screamed at the stars themselves and then washed his ceremonial paint and blood and tears right there on the altar, leaving them pooling with spilled Karak and bits of rabbit meat.

It was him. He'd somehow summoned R'tk to him, in this place of power. Graki had called, and The Great Brown One had come.

But, why is he here? Why would The Great Brown One come to me? Graki's mind boggled, and then the realization of who truly sat only feet from him crashed like a wave over him. *The Great Brown One! Oh! Oh no...*

With a flash of utter, torturous, embarrassment, Graki recalled what he'd said the night before. He'd called out to The Great Brown One. Respectfully, but... The familiar flush crept again up the back of Graki's neck.

I...I gave him an order! I ordered Great R'tk to leave! Graki sat, mouth agape, in disbelief at his own actions. *What do I do now?*

As swiftly as he possibly could, Graki lifted himself from his seated position and fell to his knees, prostrating himself before The Great Brown One.

"O Great R'tk, please, please forgive me! I did not know to whom I spoke, O Great Brown One!" he cried out loudly into the earth, his face pressed to the ground. "Forgive me, I beg of you!"

The shaman lay face down in the dirt before R'tk, trembling with eyes closed tightly, awaiting his judgement. A moment passed, then two. Finally, he heard a snuffle and a grunt. Graki puzzled.

"O Great Brown One, I...I do not understand! Please, um, tell me what I may do to atone for my actions, Great R'tk!"

Silence.

Graki risked cracking an eye and looked up slowly. R'tk was gone. He shot up in surprise. Hastily, he looked around. There, at the edge of the clearing, The Great Brown One lumbered slowly on four paws toward the wood, his back to the shaman. As he reached the tree line, he stood, yawned, and scratched his back on a tree.

Unsure what to do, Graki inched slowly, painfully toward R'tk.

The Great Brown One continued to scratch on the tree as he approached.

"O Great Brown One," he began, and kneeled, "Great Brown One, please, forgive me. I did not know. Tell me your will." Graki knelt, hands raised above his head. He waited. R'tk responded with a grunt, stopped scratching, and wandered past the goblin back over to the stone table.

Graki trailed at a respectful distance behind R'tk. "O Great Brown One, if I may, why have you come? What must I do? Why have you come here to me?" He flushed again at his presumption. "Not, ah, not that you came here to *me*, ah, O Great R'tk."

As he neared the stone table, R'tk stopped at the remains of Graki's pot and poked at them. He picked up the largest piece with his two great paws and brought the crockery to his mouth, looking for any remaining food.

R'tk ate my food. The thought crossed into Graki's mind, unbidden. "Great R'tk, tell me what you would have me do. Why have you come?"

R'tk's ears twitched toward him as he spoke. He looked for a brief moment at the shaman, before tossing the remnants of the pot to the ground and picking up another to inspect.

"Great Brown One, will you not speak with me?" Graki asked. R'tk dropped the second piece of pottery and stood. The Great Brown One turned from Graki and walked toward the clearing edge again. Graki followed.

R'tk reached the edge of the wood and entered, shaman trailing behind. The Great Brown One walked without apparent purpose, moving from tree to tree, sniffing the earth, and picking at unseen things. Occasionally, he raked his giant claws across the trunk of a tree, tearing furrows in the wood. The shaman watched as R'tk, utterly indifferent to his presence, sat for a moment and sniffed, then stood once again, headed in a new direction.

Graki trailed R'tk through the woods, occasionally trying to gain the bear's attention with no success. He could feel an annoyance rising in him, curiously much the same as the flush of embarrassment he was so used to. His heart beat faster; his breath came quicker.

Eventually R'tk and Graki came to a break in the wood with a small river. White water crashed and gurgled across a small cascade of rock and spray. R'tk wandered slowly into the shallows and stood there, still. The shaman stood nearby, watching.

"Great Brown One, please tell me why you have come? Did you come here for me? What do you want of me?" Graki pleaded with R'tk. "Why do you ignore me, Great R'tk?"

The annoyance in Graki was slowly replaced with anger. "Great Brown One, speak to me. Have I done something wrong? Why am I shunned?" The feeling of emptiness and loss from the night before grew again in the pit of Graki's stomach. "What have I done? You must have come to me at the altar, but you will not speak with me? Am I not worthy enough?"

In one quick motion, R'tk struck a fish as it jumped across the cascade, catching the thing in his mouth. The bear sat, waist deep in water and ate.

Graki snapped. "Don't you see me? Why won't you speak to me? Firmizkt won't speak to me or share with me the telling from his place in the heavens, and you ignore me. You're right here in front of me, and you won't speak to me? You will not even *look at me*? R'tk, speak to me. I am *not* without worth! Speak to me!" he screamed at The Great Brown One.

R'tk paused and looked at the shaman, then resumed his meal.

Graki sagged. He *was* without worth. His own god Firmizkt would not acknowledge him. R'tk would not acknowledge him. This great bear was just that, a bear. The Bear of Bears cared little for a lowly goblin. Graki turned away from R'tk, tears welling, defeated.

He wandered slowly back in the direction of the stone table, his feelings of insignificance utterly confirmed. What would he do now? He was a weakling, a false shaman, a mere goblin in a huge world with nothing to offer and no way to protect himself. What was worse? A god so silent and indifferent to his prayers that it might as well not be there, or a god present right in front of him, utterly, totally indifferent?

The sun shone high above the clearing as Graki approached, the great, white stone altar dominating the center and appearing to glow in the bright light. He stumbled up to the remains of his campfire and sat, his back against the warming stone. Half the day and all of his food was gone. He might be able to use his shamanic knowledge to forage for some food, but he no longer had the strength or will to move. It would be a hungry night. He clenched his teeth and sighed.

"Get up," he said to himself. "Get *up!* You need to leave before he returns."

"*Return?*" said a voice behind him. "We just got here."

Graki jerked and threw himself away from the stone table with a strength born of absolute fear. Crouching above him on the table was Uluk. The shaman was blinded by the sun crashing over the shoulder of the chieftain. Even with features cast in shadow, Uluk was unmistakable. Dark and terrible, the chieftain loomed over the shaman. The long-bladed dagger was once again held backward in his hand. Uluk's free hand stretched slowly toward Graki, sharp fingernails pointed toward him in an accusatory gesture.

"You have been here for a while, though, haven't you? You left us, so rudely. Who gave you permission to leave? You're mine, Shaman." There was a cruel chuckle, and Graki saw through wide eyes four other goblins to Uluk's right, the chieftain's personal guard.

"You're coming back with us, Shaman, and we're going to make sure you don't leave again," Uluk sneered.

The shadowy shape dropped off the stone altar and walked slowly toward Graki. His guard drew their own daggers and followed.

"No!" Graki cried out, scrambling back away from Uluk. "Leave me alone, please! Leave me alone!"

"It's too late for that," Uluk replied, raising his dagger. "You need to be taught a lesson, Shaman. But that's not you, is it? You are no shaman. You've lied to me for so long. That makes me look weak to the clan. They think it was a bad sign. They need to see that you can't get away with that." Slowly, slowly, Uluk stalked closer.

"No, please," cried Graki. "No."

"Oh, yes, Shaman. What shall we do? Remove a finger for each lie? I don't think you have enough of them. No, I think we just remove a strip of your flesh. You'll probably live through hundreds of them!"

"No," whispered Graki. "Please, no."

Uluk loomed over him, close enough that Graki could smell the leather of the chieftain's armor, the stink of his sweat. The dagger gleamed, closer and closer to Graki. Closer and closer. Graki's eyes widened and rolled back in his head. His breathing came fast and ragged. There was nothing left in the world but the shaman and Uluk and his dagger and nails. Graki whimpered.

"Oh, Shaman, shhhhh. Quiet now. This is going to hurt."

"No!" Graki cried out. "No! *The mountain moves for you! The mountain moves for you!*"

Graki's desperate cry was echoed, drowned out by a roar from the edge of the wood, vibrating the very insides of the goblins, surrounding them, washing over them. A roar unlike any that had existed. A roar that threatened to crush their ribs with its very presence, stealing the air from their lungs, assaulting their senses.

Uluk jumped, and fell back away from the noise, seeming to shrink as he tripped and scrambled away, attention no longer on Graki. Behind him, the warriors steadied themselves, bracing for something. With great effort, Graki looked toward the sound of the noise, dazed.

R'tk charged toward the altar, massive bulk moving faster than seemed possible. The great claws tore into the ground as it ran, shredding the grass and soil. He roared again, huge mouth open, great teeth gleaming. His eyes were now all black, dark as iron. The Great Brown One tore through Uluk's guard, slashing and biting and rending limbs from bodies. They stood no chance against the mountain of fur and teeth and claws. Passing one, R'tk's claws ripped across the guard's stomach, spilling entrails to the ground. Reaching another, he clubbed the goblin with one great paw, breaking bone and sending the guard flying. Within seconds, the four goblin guards were relieved of their lives. R'tk paused for a moment, rose once again to his full height, and turned toward the chieftain as Uluk raised his wicked dagger and shouted in fear.

R'tk fell upon Uluk, and the chieftain disappeared under the bulk of The Great Brown One, screaming in fear and stabbing at R'tk with his dagger. R'tk landed with one giant fist crushing Uluk's chest. As the chieftain clawed and stabbed at R'tk's paw, The Great Brown One raised his other massive fist and raked his claws across Uluk's body, once, twice, again. The chieftain stopped moving and fell silent. The clearing fell silent with him.

R'tk sat back and rose on two feet, raised his front paws above his head and roared again, shaking the trees, filling the sky. Then, he dropped back to all four and turned toward the shaman.

R'tk lumbered toward Graki, jaws and claws and chest stained red with the blood of the chieftain and his warriors. Graki stood, for the first time in his life, unconcerned by the close presence of power. It was clear R'tk had come to protect him from Uluk. Somehow, in his heart, Graki knew The Great Brown One was no threat to him.

R'tk stopped before the shaman and lowered his head to Graki's face. Giant brown eyes looked into his, into his very being. Graki looked back. R'tk raised his massive paw, still bloody from battle, and placed it upon Graki's chest for a moment. When the bear withdrew it, a massive bloody paw print stained the shaman's chest from shoulder to shoulder, neck to navel. As Graki watched, the blood appeared to dry, drawn into his skin, and he was left with a huge red tattoo.

This bear, The Great Brown One, had come when Graki called and had protected him when he needed protecting. And he *had* called. Graki *was* a shaman, just speaking to the wrong god and listening for the wrong answer. Great R'tk was *his*, and he was a member of the Great Brown One's sleuth.

R'tk turned and walked away into the wood, pausing once to sniff the air. He faded as he retreated into the tree line and was gone.

Graki stood in the clearing, the weight of a lifetime lifted from his shoulders. He placed a hand on the stone table for a moment, gazing up into the sky, before gathering the remains of his things and setting off into the woods himself, leaving his mask lying in the dirt beside the altar.

Graki the goblin, Shaman of R'tk, headed away into the wood toward a new life.

Meet Christopher Collins

Chris Collins—known to the Legion of Dorks as Hammerdwarf —is a software engineer by trade, general-purpose geek by upbringing and Godzilla Hunter Extraordinaire by interest. While Chris is a correspondent and writer for OpenSource.com, contributing frequent articles about his latest technical obsessions, Hammerdwarf is decidedly less focused, enjoys writing fantasy and science fiction stories, brewing beer and streaming games of Dwarf Fortress. Both Chris and Hammerdwarf can be found on Twitter: @ChrisInDurham.

Be Like the Pigeon

MATT THOMPSON

Young Edwin is giving me that gimlet-eyed glare again. I don't think I can stand it if he speaks. I certainly can't stand it if I do, so why should I give him the satisfaction?

Logs crackle in the fireplace, barely warming our draft-ridden parlor. With a flourish of his most thaumaturgical cloak, Edwin sweeps a pile of papers from the rickety dining table and clears his throat. I fix him with my most baleful expression. It seems that his hubris, still intact after all that's happened, will not yet allow him to admit the obvious—that what he is about to utter, and the form in which it will be delivered, will be ludicrous beyond imagining.

And sure enough, when he opens his mouth this pile of doggerel comes out:

With words we haggle
Describing a thing/Yet not
Seeing its true form

He leans back in his chair and regards me with satisfaction—as if, in his mind, he's produced a masterpiece of the haiku form. Vanity! 'Twas ever thus with Edwin. Still, it would be rude to refuse the challenge. The wise elder brother I may be—albeit by less than an hour—but some sibling rivalries never cease.

The scattered, worthless reams of parchment still strewn between us are dotted with the evidence of our previous endeavors. Ignoring them, I focus on naught but the words I wish to say. Maybe, just maybe, this will be the time my asseverations vent in something approaching the form I intend, and the thread between brain and mouth shall once more be made whole:

There once were two sorcerous brothers
Who hated and feared one another
It wasn't surprising
The scorn had been rising
Since they were inside their poor mother.

A single snort of derision is all the reply I get. Well, then. No more poetry for now. To be cursed is bad enough. To be cursed because of your own flesh and blood—especially one so inept that he managed to hex himself into the bargain—is the cruelest joke of all.

Not that either of us are laughing. But someday I—and, more's the pity, he—shall speak freely again, devoid of these constricting meters that serve only to make us a laughing stock the length and breadth of the district. I fear, however, that today is not that day. I am coming to the inevitable conclusion that resources must be pooled if we are ever to escape this linguistic bondage. Edwin scrawls something on yet another piece of paper, then scrunches it up and hurls it into the fire with a disgusted exclamation. Ha! And ha! on myself. Ruminating on the often-overlooked limitations of knowledge, I turn my thoughts to lore, sorcery, and legerdemain.

With a sharp intake of breath Edwin prepares for yet another sally onto the lower slopes of verse. Thankfully, he only sighs; or, more likely, his own tongue has refused the command. He jams his hat crookedly onto his head and flounces from the room. Clogs clop on the stairs. Chuckling inwardly, I sink into a silent torpor, relieved only by the sputtering of the fire, and the cauldron's clank drifting down from our attic apothecary.

I must have slept. Dim embers glow in the grate. Dawn light seeps through the window. My bed calls. Later we can discuss the situation, as best we can within our Edwin-imposed strictures.

But...what's this? A faint odor of sulphur wafts through the house. He hasn't...? The smell is joined by that of charcoal, the resultant blend as rank and cloying as the grave. In my panic, I almost trip over the hem of my robe. Cursing the need to impress the simpletons who live around here with such superficial trappings of wizardry, I make haste to the stairs.

Yellow smoke billows from the landing. Waving the noxious brume away as best as I can, I clatter upstairs and rattle the door. Finding it locked, I make as if to utter a spell of unbinding before checking myself and barging the flimsy barrier open with my shoulder instead. Inside, the smoke is thicker than ever. Edwin is wreathed in gouts of the stuff, spilling from the lip of our cauldron in never-ending clouds.

In my haste, I call out to him, meaning to say something along the lines of, "What on EARTH do you think you're doing now, fool?" Instead, the following drivel spills from between my lips like stale effluvium from a standpipe:

An attic is not a good venue
For mixing up such a poor menu
The pot overfloweth
Calamity groweth
And this is why I can't defend you.

It's so poor I stamp my foot in despair. Edwin spares me barely a glance, shaking his head in contempt and continuing to stir. A sudden fury fills me. Why should I tolerate this endless malfeasance? I step forward and grab him by the shoulder, intending to make clear my level of disapproval in language that doesn't require words— sesquipedalian or otherwise. As he shakes me off, with more strength than I would have thought him capable, he hisses:

Be not so bitter
And yet/Be like the pigeon
Changing with the winds.

Is he trying to tell me something? The haiku, necessary research

48

has told me, is a poetic form containing more substance than some think. The syllabic construction is but one aspect of the whole. One must hint—subtly, mind you—at the ephemeral nature of the changing seasons. I believe they find that kind of thing significant in the Orient. Myself, I was barely aware of its existence until that night —was it only a week ago?—Edwin contrived to cast his bewitchment.

It happened, as these things do, on a moonless night. Clouds scudded across the moorland beyond the village. Edwin had retreated to the attic. We had been visited that day by a stream of local residents, both the wealthy and the pauperous. *Help us, please, Mr. Unwin*, they said to me, clasping their hands in pitiful prayer. *Our meadows are barren, Mr. Edwin*, they said to my brother. *Our houses list, our children starve, our cattle perish.*

But whatever torment had been cast over the land, whichever capricious deity was responsible for this imbalance of the cosmic order, was none of our business. And I know what you might be thinking—what kind of sorcerer behaves in such a cruel manner? One, the answer has to be, who understands the limits of their powers. The equilibrium of the world is not a thing to be trifled with. Only a fool would challenge fate in the casual manner Edwin thus attempted. Had I caught wind of his plans at an earlier stage, had I had even an inkling—well, would I have been able to stop him?

He was always one for the dramatic gesture, after all. At the age of four, to recall a prime example, he instructed our family abode—a most elegant and ensorcelled mansion that our Father, rest his bitter, necromantic soul, had spent the better part of a decade constructing —to grow feet, pick itself up, and march over hill and dale to eventually plonk itself into the ocean; having first cut a swathe through the countryside that you can still see today, albeit somewhat grown over. Poor Father never recovered from the shock. Madness followed, then death. As for Mother, suffice it to say that I imagine she sleeps uneasy in her own grave, her final days haunted by the grumble of ancestral spirits and intimations of eternal despair.

Edwin's life has been riven with a similar series of disasters. Watching him now, bent on his fetid task as if unaware a world exists outside his own head, a deep melancholy seeps through me. Our peripatetic existence since Mother's demise has barely afforded us a roof over our heads, the mundanity of our spell-weaving an affront to the higher realms themselves. And when the poor townsfolk, at the end of their tethers, came to us for aid—I had, of course, been most stringent in making sure Edwin's true abilities had remained hidden in the course of our incumbency here—he leaped at the chance to prove himself at last.

His spell, naturally, was artless, gauche, doomed to fail. Edwin works best when he allows his instincts to take over. When he tries to plan, to employ a level of cunning, disaster is sure to follow. It was only my desperate intervention on that blackest of nights that saved the village from obliteration. At the pinnacle of our house, chaos reigned. What devils had he conjured from the dark side? Vile wraiths, cackling demons, shapeless forms so eager to escape their confinement in Hell's dungeons they were battering—nay, mauling—at the flimsy thaumaturgic shield Edwin had hastily constructed.

I uttered words of command. The hellions retreated, a little. Wracking my brains, I spat out a holding spell, a filigree of subtle charm and fiendish guile.

Edwin stepped up beside me from where he had been cowering behind the herb cabinet. "Take these words," he cried, before I could clamp my hand over his mouth, "and keep them hidden! Demons, to your lairs be bidden!"

With that, he swirled his arms around in maniacal fervor. The cloud-spell hovering above our workbench turned colors I had never seen before and don't wish to see again. A screech sounded; a pop, a bang, and a roar, and the attic fell silent.

I staggered backward, my head aswirl. Motes danced before my eyes. Finally, I managed to clear my thoughts. A cough sounded. Edwin, his expression less sheepish than it should have been, wagged a finger. Before he could chastise me, I decided then and there I would take no more of his impertinence.

"Edwin, my brother," I tried to say, "the time has come to get some things straight."

Instead, I came out with this idiocy:

There once was a wizard who said,

"My brother is easily led
By his hubris and charm
So sound the alarm
For I think he might leave us all dead!"

Pitiful. And the subsequent days have been no better, both in speech and script. The limerick, my unforeseen yoke, is not a poetic form that lends itself to either subtlety or charm. Whatever I wish to communicate, whichever combination of words I direct my tongue or fingers to repeat, emerges as hogwash, twaddle, poppycock. Edwin, while seemingly imbued with a greater sense of gravitas, is faring no better. Possibly worse, in fact.

This week has been a purgatory I would almost sign my soul away to bring to an end. Which brings us back to the present moment, and the sulphuric miasma that threatens to overcome us. Edwin, lest it need saying, should not be let within a hundred miles of a spellbook. Or a poetry reading.

Be like the pigeon/Changing with the winds.

What kind of claptrap is that? Communicating entirely via metaphor is taking a toll on him, I fear. If he hadn't accidentally spouted his command that night in the form of a rhyme? If he had had the sense to leave the difficult work to those better qualified than he?

Then some other pandemonium would have revealed itself. I'm coming to the painful conclusion that if he got us into this, then only he can get us out. Edwin's talents are inscrutable, unfathomable, and undeniable. They also contain the seeds of greatness; albeit seeds that scatter to the four winds whenever he attempts to harness them to some great purpose.

He extracts a pouch from a pocket of his robe and shakes it into the broth. A puff of green-tinged smoke explodes upward and spreads out across the ceiling. He begins to mumble, his voice so low I have to thrust my face towards his to hear:

Thickets and brambles
Entrap us/Cast care skyward
And shake loose thy tongue.

It's a strange thing, but his meanings are getting clearer. I think

51

I'm getting the hang of this at last. "You mean...our tongues are held captive?" I attempt to reply. Of course, the words come out a little differently than I had intended:

A word is a dangerous thing
In the hands of a bird on the wing
If demons conceal
Then wizards reveal
And tongues shall once more freely sing!

Edwin nods, stroking his chin. I really am figuring this out. My rhyme, while unlikely to win any prizes, communicated even more than I thought I knew. If the demons Edwin summoned that night are truly in possession of our faculties, then the only thing to do is challenge them.

Hat askew, he wafts the tendrils of malodorous smoke away and declaims the following:

Leaves fall from the trees
As if our words/Once loosened
Renew, import clear.

By this I assume he means we must recast the spell we—he, I mean—so foolishly uttered. But how? Demons are unlikely to respond to poorly-conceived haiku, and even less to limericks, however cleverly worded. And broths and poisons are no good against the dwellers of the realms beyond, as my brother has finally realised.

Leaves fall from the trees.

Words trip from the tongue? But whose? Mine, I would imagine. The holding spell, at least, is seared into my memory. If I could just...

A peaceful calm steals over me. I let the words flow without thought:

Two brothers once sailed on the tide
'Cross turbulent seas far and wide
Their figurehead said
"Rough weather ahead
Let language itself be their guide."

A wind surges through the attic, clearing the smoke not a jot. Within its rush, vague, amorphous sounds form, syllable-like tones that shape themselves into a reasonable approximation of the spell. An alarming bubbling comes from the overflowing cauldron. Within the haze something else lurks, formed from the brume itself. A face, almost human. Almost, in fact, recognisable.

In a roil of mist another joins it, the two visages darting and swooping within the hellish stuff like evil butterflies. Edwin retches and coughs, his figure almost consumed. With an almighty roar the faces expand, filling the air above the pot.

Features sharpen. Eyes and noses and mouths coalesce into familiar—oh, so familiar!—forms. Their lips twist into leering grimaces, regarding the two of us with a contempt I'd almost forgotten.

Hello, Father.

Hello, Mother.

How lovely to meet you again. I would like my tongue back, if you please.

But no! I daren't speak. Not yet. Not while their enchantment holds. How long have they waited for this moment? Dear Father would assuredly take possession of more than my voice were I to make myself vulnerable.

A black tongue flicks out from between Mother's lips, sending a puff of smoke earthward. In a voice as loud as thunder, she cries:

There once was a woman who loved her two sons
But her kindness was repaid with tenderness none
So she took her revenge the best way she knew how
And their curse has a strength they shall not disavow.

The echoes die slowly away. That, I suppose, was poetry—of a sort. Well, well. It seems our beloved parents are caught in the same spell-web as Edwin and I. Maybe it was only Edwin's accidental stanza that had saved us from further iniquity? Although I'd like to think my holding incantation might have had something to do with it too.

Still, maybe not. Father's dingy sneer turns to a fearsome frown. He bares his teeth and spits out the following quatrain in the angry bark I recall so well:

With mortar and bricks I built my home with pride

Until one day my love was wrenched from me
By one whose power would be better nullified
Or better yet, cut down like a tree.

And I thought my own efforts were poor. It's almost embarrassing. Mother puffs out her cheeks and blows a cloud of soot at me. It tastes faintly of turnip, and it takes me a while to unclog my nostrils of the stench. Edwin emerges from the cloud, robe stained black, and assumes a splay-footed stance before them. If this is all they're capable of, the holding spell must still be working.

Which gives us an advantage. I suspect Mother and Father have surrendered the better part of their powers to the Lord of whichever domain they now inhabit. All Edwin and I need to do is break their hold on us and banish them for good.

Which, of course, is easier said than done—especially in our current state. Alack! How can we even think to exercise our influence while laboring under these restrictions? If only...

Edwin places his hand on his heart and puffs out his chest. Has he fallen into Father's trap? Indeed, that misty visage is licking its lips in greedy anticipation. Do they wish to possess us, to talk and walk through us? What terrible ambition drives him, even in death? Mother, too, has a smoggy look of avaricious longing on her face.

Too late, I leap for Edwin, in hope of wrestling him to the ground. But already the words trip from his tongue, and my efforts are for naught:

Home is a journey
Unending/Ever circling
Back where it begins.

Upon hearing this gibberish, Father's face stretches out in a most abominable manner. Cringing, I back away, scrabbling in desperation toward the door. But that will be no freedom at all, as our parents' mocking laughter roars over me in waves, and Edwin cowers before them.

My lungs fill with a vile stench, and a roiling figure towers over me, ready to pounce, ready to cast my mortal soul to the void.

And then a deafening *crack* sounds. Father hesitates, a frown creasing his billowing forehead. Another thunderclap. Grit showers down on me, powdery dust that tastes of lime and rot. The apparitions retreat, a little. The house begins to shake. What manner of devilment have we conjured up now? Or, I should say, what pandemonium has Edwin caused this time?

With a yaw and a sway the floor rises to meet us. Fissures appear in the walls. The structure holds—just. But...but...no, it can't be!

Edwin scrambles to his feet. The entire house jounces. With a lurch like that of a storm-stricken boat, we begin to move. Allowing myself the smallest of chuckles—small, because surely I am about to die—I rush to the window, Edwin beside me.

It would seem that this house's feet are chicken-like. It's as if they had lurked inside the walls for the entirety of our time here, just waiting to sprout. Knobbly legs extend upward into the foundations. Heaven knows what we must look like from the outside.

Father and Mother spin in frantic circles, dwindling second by second and engaged in a vicious battle to get back into the pot. Mother, I suppose, will be victorious. She always was. Father, for all his grandiose bellicosity, was not much more than a third-rate necromancer in life. Had I been less ethically engaged I might have ended up the same way. His pitiful jealousy of Edwin is what led him to lose his mind. And now, like the fool he always was, he's fallen for the same trick twice. A home is a castle, some might say. But if that castle is built on sand it doesn't take much to topple it. Edwin, more from instinct than reason, understands this implicitly.

The house increases its speed. Dust rains down. I wonder how we can stop it? I suppose we can't. Pumping like bellows, the scrawny legs thunder along, faster and faster. Fields and forests whip past. Edwin clutches my arm, shaking with a combination of terror and mirth.

A salt tang overpowers the vapor reek. Our parents have dwindled to wisps now, threading further apart with each jolt. At the exact moment they vanish with a smelly *pop*, the house skids to a halt.

Gulls screech. Waves crash. Edwin leans toward me, a conspiratorial look on his face. Sighing, I brace myself for his latest sortie onto the battlefield of poesy.

He leans in further. Reaching an arm out to brace himself, he opens his mouth and thrusts his face into mine, almost nose to nose.

"Run!"

The house tips backward at an alarming angle. It's only now that I remember what happened to our old family abode in its last moments. The cauldron skids past us and crashes into the herb cabinet, sending spices and tinctures flying. I risk poking my head out of the window. A hundred feet below us, sea-battered rocks loom. The giant chicken feet are digging into the soil—for all the good it will do; the coastal cliffs of this land have no more substance than cheese.

The pinnacle of the house is too far out to escape via the window. I scramble up the attic incline and batter at the brickwork, Edwin quaking at my heels and being of no use whatsoever.

But—

Didn't he just—?

So maybe I can...? I place a hand onto the unyielding wall, conjure up the deepest magic I can muster, and let the words flow:

Crack and split and rive and rip

Tear asunder, burst like thunder!

The bricks blast outward in a shower of mortar. I grab Edwin's hand and leap through. Just in time! As we tumble onto the grass the house begins to topple. Webbed feet cycle pitifully in the air. Edwin scrambles to his feet and sprints away. The house disappears with a mighty whoosh.

Seconds pass. The crash, when it comes, shakes the ground beneath my feet. A portion of the cliff crumbles away. In alarm I take Edwin's cue and retreat. I hardly wish to get this far and perish in the backdraft.

When I catch up with him, he's on his haunches, peering intently at a juniper bush. "Did you know, Unwin," he says, "that these berries can be used for—oh!" A silly grin blights his features. "It would seem we can converse as of old. How wonderful! Anyway—"

I leave him to it, and shield my eyes from the glare of the morning sun. Where to next? I suppose I'll have to take Edwin along with me. Leaving him to his own devices isn't something my conscience would bear—for others' sake, less than his. Someone needs to control his

56

worst excesses. And who else would be prepared to take on a task of that magnitude?

"Come on, Edwin." I pull him to his feet. "We'll need to look for a new district to ply our trade."

"Hazel," he says, with some finality.

"Beg pardon?"

"And amaranth. We'll need to find somewhere they both grow wild. Oh, Unwin! Your poems really were awful, you know."

"And yours?" I splutter. "You didn't even hint at the ephemeral nature of the passing seasons half the time. It wasn't much of a spell Father put on us, when all's said and done."

Edwin gives a sad shake of his shaggy head. "He was never much of a charm-weaver."

"And what was all that nonsense about pigeons?"

"I was trying to say," he replies, somewhat stiffly, "that it was obvious Father was behind all this, the blight on the land, our curse. Pigeons always come home to roost, do they not? But you wouldn't listen, would you? Still, I can't be surprised. You never did."

And with that he strides away.

"Wait!"

But he's gone, and all I can do is try to keep pace lest I lose sight of the pest. And so I trail behind him all the way to the rutted highway that leads to the next county—which, I do believe, is known for its hazel groves and amaranth stalks and its plethora of villages whose inhabitants are firm believers in the old magics.

Meet Matt Thompson

Matt Thompson is a London-based experimental musician and writer of strange fictions. His work has been published at Interzone, Black Static, Third Flatiron Publishing, Best of British SF anthology series and many more worthy venues. You can find him online at http://matt-thompson.com.

Hex Messages

STEPHANIE DARE ADAMS

Mia stared at the whirling fan above her bed. Her eyes felt like someone had borrowed them overnight for a rousing game of ping-pong. She squeezed them together tightly hoping to relieve some of the pressure in her head. Grunting, she rolled over to see what time it was: 6:58 a.m. Two minutes until her alarm went off.

Boo! Why do classes have to start so early?

She swatted at her clock like a feral cat after a fish stick. No one likes the sound of an alarm clock—especially when they're hung over. Classes started in an hour, but she didn't even know if she could make it out of bed.

Maybe just a shower.

Mia rolled from one side of the bed to the other, dragging the sheets along with her and turning herself into a human burrito in the process. She untangled the sheets and shuffled stiffly into the bathroom.

The person looking back in the mirror was a mess. Her black hair was now a frizzled ghost of the fancy up-do she had sported the night before. Her perfectly winged liner had flown the coop and crash landed under her eyes. And the glitter, oh heavens, the glitter. It was Sasha's idea to use glitter to "highlight her cheekbones." Now Mia was sure there was not a square inch of her body not covered in sparkles. She looked like she had been trampled by a herd of glitzy unicorns and left for dead.

She hopped in the shower to rinse off the remnants of the night before. She didn't remember much of the party, mostly just a few bits from before she drank the punch.

Ugh. The punch.

Someone had definitely spiked it. Or put a charm on it. Or a hex. Probably a hex. Who knows? Whatever it was, it was enough for her to forget a majority of the night. Thankfully, her two best friends, Sasha and Emily, would help her remember. That is, if they did not abandon her first.

Though foggy, the memory of Sasha and Emily dragging her passed out, lump of a body up three flights of stairs, into her apartment and to bed flashed in her head. They were going to kill her. She should probably get them both a latte on the way to class to smooth things over. But first, she should beg for forgiveness.

After getting dressed, she found her purse and dug around for her phone. Not surprisingly, it was covered in glitter too. She wiped what she could from the screen and skimmed through her contact list. This situation called for a conference call. She dialed Emily first.

"Hey, Em! It's Mia."

"Oh. My. Gawd! You're alive. Sasha and I weren't sure if you were actually going to wake up this morning. I bet you look like crap." Emily laughed loudly.

Mia's face scrunched. She tried to give Emily a not-so-subtle hint.

"Yeah. Head still hurts pretty badly too."

"Well, duh. That's what happens when you drink spiked punch, my friend."

"Yeah, yeah. Hey, hold on a sec. I want to call Sasha too."

"No prob, Bob. I'll be here."

Mia put Emily on hold and called Sasha.

"Oh my goodness, honey! Is that you? How are you feeling this morning? You poor thing. Your first big college party and you get completely smashed."

Sasha's sickly sweet southern accent, though usually endearing, was too much for Mia's aching head. Maybe a conference call first thing in the morning was not the best idea.

"Hey, Sash. I'm ok. I have Emily on the other line. Let me get her. One sec."

"Ok, Love."

Mia added Emily to the call.

"Ok, Em, Sasha and I are here."

Emily mimicked Sasha's accent. "Hey, Punkin'! How you doin' on this glorious mornin?'"

"Oh shove it, Emily," Sasha retorted.

Emily chuckled. "Seriously though. Our girl Mia survived her first college party. Aren't you proud?"

"I think I would be more proud if she hadn't gotten smashed in the first five minutes. What were you thinking, Mia?" Sasha huffed.

"I'm so sorry you had to drag me home last night. I don't know what happened. Whatever they put in the punch must have been really strong."

Given the decibel of her voice, Emily obviously did not take Mia's hint that her head was still throbbing. "Strong? You drank like five huge cups."

Mia whined. "It was raspberry lime! It had lime sherbet in it and everything. Who can resist sherbet punch?"

Emily chuckled. "Dude, my grandma had that kind of punch at her 50th wedding anniversary."

"And I'm sure it was gone before they even cut the cake." Mia sulked.

Sasha interjected. "Ok, you two. Knock it off. The important thing is that Mia is ok. Are you planning on coming to classes this morning, sweetie? Do you want me to come pick you up?"

Sasha was always so thoughtful and caring.

"Awe, thanks, Sash, but I'm ..." Mia turned to grab her books from the shelf, but two black beady eyes staring at her from the bookshelf made her scream.

"Agh! What the Hell-o Kitty!"

Mia always made an effort not to use foul language. Her mother once told her that a lady who curses is like a delectable lava cake with a turd in the middle. That kind of stuck with her.

"Mia! Are you ok?" Sasha squeaked.

"There's a rat on my bookshelf!"

"A rat?" Sasha was still squeaking.

Emily wasn't phased. "Oh yeah! That's Vinny. I forgot to tell you about him."

Mia was finally catching her breath. "Vinny? Where did he come from, Emily?"

"He was in your purse last night. I named him Vinny after my second cousin up in Jersey. He got arrested for selling illegal potions. Isn't that hilarious? Anyway, I didn't see him until we got you home. I figured he was some party goer's familiar that you liked and stole for yourself in your drunken haze. Just bring him to school, and we'll ask around and find out who he belongs to."

"This is seriously the worst morning of my life." Mia sighed. "Anyway, we have a test coming up in Study of Ancient Divination, so I'll be going to school today. And I can drive. Thank you for the offer."

Mia's phone started beeping to alert her another call was coming in. She pulled it from her face to check the caller ID.

"Hey guys, I have to go. I think this is someone from that place I was trying to get an internship at."

Sasha squealed. "Oh, how exciting!"

"Don't let them know what you were doing last night." Emily poked.

Mia rolled her eyes. "Har. Har. Har. Ok, I'll see you guys at school. With lattes!"

"Bye, sweetie. Good luck." Sasha cheered.

"Bye, dork. Don't screw this up."

"See ya!"

Mia hung up and switched over to the new call.

"Hello?"

"Hi. Is this Mia Lockhart?"

"It is. May I ask who's calling?"

"Hi, Ms. Lockhart. This is Diane from Rune. We got your application for the internship and wanted to set up an interview. Would you be available at 3 p.m. next Thursday?"

"Oh my goodness, that's awesome! Yes, I should be free. Let me grab my notebook so I can write down the date."

Mia pounced on her purse and rummaged feverishly through it for her notebook—which, like her phone, was also covered in glitter. She flipped through it until she found a free page.

"Ok, next Thursday at 3 p.m." She recited the date and time as she wrote.

"Please arrive five minutes early so we can see you to the conference room and make sure you're comfortable. We look forward to meeting you, Ms. Lockhart."

"Thank you so much, Diane. I'm looking forward to it as well."

Mia hung up and checked the time on her phone. She only had ten minutes to get to class. She flung her phone and notebook into her backpack.

"Ok, Vinny. You and me are going to be friends, right?"

She tiptoed to the rat who stared at her blankly.

"Into the backpack you go," she said, tapping his behind lightly.

Thankfully, he hopped in without a fight. Mia grabbed her keys and ran out the door. No time to stop for lattes. She would just buy the girls lunch.

The Appalachian Academy of Alchemy and Magic (or Triple A&M as it was known) was one of the few places of higher education that specialized in magic. Only three other universities like it existed in the world. All of them were located in different countries, and all of them were just as difficult to get into. Nonetheless, Mia's family knew she would attend Triple A&M one day. From a young age, both Mia's parents and teachers noticed she was an extremely gifted child, especially when it came to incantations and spell writing. It was no surprise when she got her acceptance letter.

During her first year, she quickly made friends with Emily, a northerner who was blunter than a brick, and Sasha, a southerner who would give you the shirt off her back. Well, only if it went with your outfit. Sasha and Emily could not be more different from Mia (or each other for that matter). While they were outgoing, worldly, and adventurous, Mia liked to play it safe. She knew what she was good at, and she stuck to it. She liked things simple and predictable. She had a list of things she avoided like the plague, and the one thing that topped that list was parties.

That's why last night was not only a big deal for Mia, it was also totally uncharacteristic of her. Sasha and Emily had talked her into it. They assured her it was going to be low-key.

"No alcohol and no loud music, honey. We know you don't like that." Sasha had confirmed.

Mia was sure that was how it started—her friends would never deceive her—but it was not the party she arrived at that evening. People spilled out the door onto the front porch and driveway. She could hear party music thumping from inside Sasha's car as they approached. The only thing that was "low-key" was the absence of alcohol. The only drink available other than soft drinks and water was some sweet, green-and-red swirled, raspberry-lime sherbet punch.

Mia practically pounced on the punch bowl when they stepped inside. She was shocked no one else was drinking it. Oh well, more for her. She had downed three cups by the time Emily caught on to what she was doing.

"Whoa there, granny. Take it easy on the punch. This *is* a college party. You never know what might be in it." Emily gave Mia a weary side eye.

"Whatever, Em. It tastes fine to me, and frankly it's the only thing at this party that I'm actually enjoying."

"Well excuse me, Kathy Killjoy. Maybe if you mingled a bit, you would meet someone interesting to talk to. Maybe even a boy." Emily winked at her.

"I don't have time for boys right now."

Mia was about to break down the minutia of how a long term commitment with a boy would not mesh with her current lifestyle, when a wide-eyed Sasha came power walking from across the room and nearly knocked her over.

"Oh, my stars, Em. Oh, my heavenly stars. Girls, this is not a drill." Sasha panted for a minute, clearly out of breath.

Emily looked both annoyed and concerned. "What is it, Sash?"

Sasha squealed and waved her hands around. "You'll never guess who I just saw. Ahhhh!"

"Spit it out woman! You're killing me." Emily was losing her patience.

"Tom. Polland. Tom freaking Polland, Em. He's here, he's alone, and he's dreamier than I imagined. *And* I'm having the most perfect night ever because my makeup looks really good, and my lucky underwear was clean, and this dress makes my boobs look super perky, and we *have* to go see if we can talk to him."

It wasn't uncommon for alumni to visit the school and drop in on parties to re-live their college days. Sometimes, those alumni were famous. Sometimes, those famous alumni turned certain students into screaming fangirls.

"Dude. That's actually quite awesome. Ok, I'm in. You in, Mia?"

"Nah. I don't even know what I'd say to him."

"Ugh. Seriously, Mia, you have to lighten up. Ok, whatever. We love you, and we'll be back in a few. Please don't drink too much punch."

Emily followed a skipping Sasha into a connecting room. Mia waved as they disappeared out of sight.

Perfect.

Now she was all alone at a party she didn't want to attend. It was like she had never left high school. There were cliques everywhere: the nerds, the jocks, the popular bunch, the pretty girls. Of course, there was also the most popular of the popular girls, Bree Easton. Mia had a few run-ins with Bree in the past, and every one of them was negative. Bree was currently flaunting her body and flirting with the jocks. She must not have gotten the message about Tom Polland. Mia could not help but roll her eyes at Bree's obvious cries for attention. She had the flirting down perfectly: the lash flutter, the hair flips, the accidental brush of her leg against the guy's leg. However obvious and pathetic it was though, it seemed to work. Mia felt a pang of jealousy as Felix, Mia's long time crush, laughed and flirted back. Bree looked over at Mia and smirked. It was as if she knew Mia liked Felix. Mia sighed and poured herself another cup of punch.

That was where her memory began to get foggy. She vaguely remembered walking around the party for a bit before her friends found her. The next thing she remembered was waking up in bed the next morning encrusted with glitter and sporting a horrendous headache.

Mia arrived at school with only minutes to spare. She messaged the girls to let them know she was not able to stop for coffee, but lunch was on her. As she turned the corner to her classroom, she heard a shuffle behind her. She cheerfully whipped around, hoping to greet an equally tardy classmate, but was greeted by an empty hallway.

Were auditory hallucinations part of a hangover? She shook her head and rushed into the room just as the lecture was starting.

Thankfully, class was uneventful, and her headache was finally starting to ease up. She periodically peeked into her backpack to confirm Vinny was still there. She had put a sleeping spell on him so he wouldn't make a break for it in the middle of class. She felt bad for keeping him in her backpack all morning, and didn't want him to suffer. As the professor made his closing comments, one of Mia's classmates sidled up to her as she was gathering her things. The head of the astronomy club, she was a sweet girl, but was hopelessly awkward.

"Hey there, Mia! Top of the mornin'!" She guffawed and pushed her glasses up her skinny nose.

"Hey, Fern. How are you?" Mia gave her a warm smile.

"I'm fantabulous. Know why?" Fern clasped her hands together and stared at Mia excitedly.

"I don't. Please share."

Fern squealed. "The Leonid meteor shower is going to be gracing us with its glorious light show for two straight weeks starting this weekend! Naturally, the astrology club will be going to Blairsville to watch it. We're planning on next Wednesday. Are you in?"

"Uh, why not?" An astronomy field trip was not on the top of Mia's must-do list. However, Fern had always been so kind and sweet to her, Mia didn't want to let her down."Oh, wait! I have an interview next week. I think it's on Thursday, but let me double check."

Mia knew she should remember such an important date, but with all the chaos of that morning—her pounding headache, being late for class, and a random rat in her apartment—she wanted to confirm the date. Making sure not to reveal Vinny, she rummaged through her backpack and dragged out her notebook. She skimmed through it searching for what she had scribbled down that morning. Glitter floated into the air as she flipped the pages. Fern made an "*ohhhhh*" sound, obviously impressed by the majestic glitter cloud her notebook created.

A couple pages were stuck together. Mia carefully pried them open and was bewildered by what she saw. There were three paragraphs of messy notes she recognized as her own, but didn't remember writing. She always had her notebook with her to jot down ideas, phone numbers, dates, etc. so she probably wrote them down during the party last night.

The first paragraph was the easiest to read.

Pretty as a princess doll, boys at your feet do fall.

But what if you they cannot see, would you still pretty be?

The next one was less legible, but Mia was able to make it out nonetheless.

You look like you taste good, you're so handsome to me.

Can you stay with me always, I like you times three.

The last one had a few illegible words.

You suck really bad, your heart's as black as a (unintelligible).

Some people don't deserve life, you're (unintelligible) off as a (unintelligible).

Oh, shi... p.

That last verse made Mia nervous. "Some people don't deserve life." What did that mean? What did she do? How drunk was she?

67

The messages, if you could call them that, were something a five year old would write.

Before turning the page, Mia noticed something else tiny scrawled in the crease of the book. It was easier to read, but was written in Latin.

Obliviscar verba tua. Oblivisci opera tua. Oblivisci hac nocte, et liberari.

Why had she not paid more attention in Latin class?

"Um, hello? Earth to Mia!" Fern chuckled and inserted her head in between Mia and her notebook.

"Oh, my gosh, Fern. I'm so sorry."

Mia flipped a few more pages.

"Here it is. Looks like I'm free on Wednesday. I'll plan on being there."

That is, if she was not having a slumber party in prison, because she had murdered someone. Mia furrowed her brows and wondered which would be worse: prison or an astronomy field trip.

"Wonderful! I'll write you down as one of the drivers. Oh, and I'll ride with you! I have an incredible audiobook on the history of telescopes."

Mia was a pushover for awkward, kind people like Fern. "Oh. Sure. Sounds good, Fern."

The astronomy field trip would definitely be worse.

⁂

After finding the mysterious messages in her notebook, Mia texted Emily and Sasha to fill them in. Neither of them knew what to think, but they all agreed to meet at lunch to read and discuss.

Her next class passed at a glacial pace, but was thankfully uneventful. (Other than hearing more footsteps behind her in the hallway). When the professor dismissed everyone from class, Mia snatched up her books and practically ran out the door toward the cafeteria. She would have made it in record time too, if it were not for someone shrieking her name and stopping her dead in her tracks.

"Mia. Freaking. Lockhart! Stop, *right* now!"

Mia spun around. A few feet in front of her was Bree Easton with her two groupies, Lydia and Millicent. They looked like a bouquet of pink and purple flowers—they were dressed differently, but strangely looked like a package deal. Mia wondered if Bree smelled like a rose or a peony. She probably smelled like one of those Stargazer Lilies that look so pretty, but actually smelled like a rotten dog fart. What could dog fart Bree want with her?

"Celine," Mia stated flatly.

Bree looked confused.

"My middle name is Celine. Not Freaking," Mia clarified.

"Do I look like a give a flying fu—"

"Agh! Don't say it! I hate curse words." Mia interrupted. She was secretly seeing if she could turn Bree's face a darker shade of red than it already was.

"Do you know what *I* hate, Mia *Freaking* Lockhart? I hate mousy little bookworms like you ruining my life. Don't act like you don't know what I'm upset about."

Mia paused for dramatic effect. "I don't know what you're upset about."

Lydia and Millicent's eyebrows simultaneously shot up in an "*oh, crap*" kind of way.

Bree glared at Mia and then slowly started toward her. "Mia... dear...you are testing my patience. Undo the hex, and I won't ruin your reputation at this school."

"Bree, all joking aside, I honestly don't know what you're talking about."

"The *hex*, Mia! The one you put on me in a drunken rage last night. You have to undo it right now, or I will make your measly life a living hell."

Wow, maybe Bree was a Venus fly trap and not a lily.

"I don't remember much of last night, Bree. I'm truly sorry."

"Well, let me help refresh your memory. Lydia?" Bree nodded to the skinny brunette standing next to her.

Lydia locked eyes on a random guy walking down the hall. "Hey, you! Yeah, you. Come here."

The poor soul looked both terrified and excited that Lydia had even talked to him. He strolled over nonchalantly.

"Hey. What's up?"

"How many girls are standing here?"

"Uh...three?" The guy looked like a confused puppy hoping for a treat.

"Thank you." Lydia dismissed him with a wave of her hand. She glared at Mia and cocked her head to the side as if to say "now do you get it, dummy?"

Mia rolled her eyes. "Wow. That was just...so insightful. You proved something I've known my whole life. I'm basically invisible when pretty girls like you are around. Congratulations."

Bree was practically exploding at this point. "No, Mia. No! *I* am the one who is invisible. Me! You have made me completely undetectable to men. They can't hear me. They can't smell my $120 perfume. They can't see my hair I spent forty-five minutes styling this morning or my flawless makeup. They can't see *me*. You understand the difficult situation that puts me in, right?"

So I was drunk hexing last night. Mia pondered.

She felt bad for Bree, but then she remembered Bree smirking at her while flirting with Felix at the party. Then there was the time Emily had finally stepped out of her comfort zone and dressed up for school, only to have Bree trip her in front of everyone at the cafeteria. She didn't feel so bad for her anymore.

"You mean that you're actually going to have to survive a day without the attention of the opposite sex?"

Bree's face had now turned purple. Her eyes seemed to be popping out of her head. It was glorious. She stuck a manicured finger in Mia's face before continuing.

"Mia. I swear to—"

"I'm sorry! Ok? Do you remember anything I said to you?"

"I do!" Millicent finally piped up.

She had been watching the scene unfold like a sordid TV drama. Mia would not have been surprised if she had whipped a bowl of popcorn out from underneath her pink mini-skirt.

Millicent stepped forward like she was going to give a speech, "You said something about her being a doll—I remembered that part because I thought it was so sweet—and then you said something about guys falling at her feet but not being able to see her. "

Holy hot ham and cheese. The writing in her notebook. She pulled her notebook out of her bag and flipped through the wrinkly pages.

"Is this what I said:

'Pretty as a princess doll, boys at your feet do fall.

But what if you they cannot see, would you still pretty be?'"

Lydia scrunched her face in disgust. "Yeah. That was definitely it. That stupid hex along with how sloppy you were, I would be so ashamed if I were you right now, Mia. It was repulsive."

"Yeah, thanks for that, Lydia," Mia sighed. She took out a pen and scribbled in her notebook for a minute. "Ok. Well, I think the ending could be better," she pondered out loud.

"This isn't a book report, Mia. Just say the damn charm," Bree huffed.

"Ok, here goes:

'Concealed, invisible, and unseen; reverse now this unfortunate scheme.

Lovely like a rose in bloom, return Bree now this afternoon.'"

The girls stood frozen for a minute as if waiting for fireworks or confetti.

Finally, a male student walked by and winked at Bree, "Hey, Bree. Looking good today."

"Yes!" Bree shrieked as she pumped her fist in the air.

Her sudden shout, in contrast to the silence moments before, startled the other girls so badly they simultaneously jumped and yelped.

Bree's smiled was instantly replaced with a scowl. "Pull another stunt like this, Lockhart, and I'll make sure not a single boy at this school knows you exist."

"Yeah, ok. Sorry again, Bree." Mia rolled her eyes and headed for the cafeteria. She was annoyed that the little mana available in the world was wasted on such a shallow, sorry excuse for a human being.

As she left the building and started down the hill to the cafeteria, she had the familiar feeling someone was following her. She stopped and looked behind her. No one was there. Was she being paranoid? There was no reason for anyone to be following her. Then again, she did have two hexes remaining in her notebook. Mother of Artemis, what had she done. The only thing that would soothe her soul right now was her friends and the Wednesday Special—buffalo chicken pizza.

Mia quickened her pace. Unfortunately, rain had made the path to the cafeteria slippery. Her grandma clogs (as Sasha called them) lost their traction, and in an instant, her foot slipped out from under her, and she landed with a graceless *thump* on her butt. Before she could stand to her feet and brush the dirt from her derrière, Felix, in all his manly glory, emerged from behind a building and practically sprinted over to her. The scene reminded Mia of the opening credits of Gulf Watch. At that moment, she was sure of two things: 1) he was most definitely running in slow motion, and 2) even while running, he was the most beautiful man she had ever laid eyes on.

Great, now her butt *and* her ego were hurting.

"Mia! Are you ok? I should have been there for you. I'm so sorry!"

Felix ran to Mia's side, took her arm, and gently helped her up.

Mia was equal parts ecstatic and befuddled. "Um...while I really appreciate the help, I think you have me mistaken for someone else."

Felix was visibly hurt. "You...you don't remember me? It's Felix. From the party?"

He paused for a moment waiting for Mia to acknowledge him. Mia was so confused and her heart raced so quickly, she couldn't catch her breath to reply.

"That's ok. But *I* remember *you*. When you first spoke to me, it was like the heavens opened up, and I saw beauty for the first time. I have to admit I've been following you around school today. We talked some at the party, but I've been too nervous to talk to you again. You're just so beautiful, I didn't know what to say. I was afraid I would scare you away. Now you've fallen and gotten hurt. It's all my fault."

Sweet baby Zeus. Felix had been the source of all the footsteps she had heard that day. Why the heck was he suddenly obsessed with *her*? She didn't remember talking to him at the party, but she had obviously made an impression on him. She didn't mind being obsessed over by such a pretty male specimen until he turned her around and started inspecting her back-side for injuries.

"Whoa, slow down there, Romeo. The condition of my rump is neither any of your business or your responsibility. Don't be too hard on yourself. Do you, uh, remember what exactly I said to you at the party?"

"Honestly, I didn't even notice you at first. But then, you walked over to me, read me a beautiful poem you had prepared, and—"

There it was. She had hexed him. "Yep, yep. Actually, I do remember that."

Mia grabbed Felix's arm and started dragging him down the hill to the cafeteria. While having a sexy stalker was nice, she knew she had to undo the hex.

"Hey, why don't you come eat lunch with me and my friends. Yeah? Wouldn't that be nice? They have buffalo pizza today. You *like* buffalo pizza?" Mia was frazzled and out of breath.

"Uh, yeah! Who doesn't like buffalo pizza?"

"My thoughts exactly, Felix. My thoughts exactly."

Emily scowled at Mia, barely blinking her doe brown eyes.

"So explain this to me again, Mia. You got drunk off the punch—"

"Not drunk. Someone put a charm on it," Mia interrupted.

"Whatever. You got drunk-slash-charmed from the punch, hexed random people at the party, wrote down the hexes in your notebook, forgot all about it, and now you need to undo the hexes you did?"

Mia grimaced. "Well... yeah."

Emily glanced over at Sasha. "Sasha, dear, do you have *anything* you'd like to add to this conversation?"

Sasha was too busy ogling Felix to notice Emily. Mia had sent him across the room to pick up pizzas and drinks for them. Sasha hadn't taken her eyes off him since he left the table.

"He really is such a pretty man, Mia. Honestly, doll, I don't know if I would undo this one." Sasha pined.

Emily groaned, "Sasha, my dear friend, you are not helping this situation at all. Actually, Mia, you may want to go ahead and reverse this hex now. It's going to be super awkward if you undo it while he's eating lunch with us."

Sasha whined. "Awe, can we undo it after lunch? I wanna see him up close again,"

"Good Lord, woman. Get ahold of yourself. We don't know what Mia's hexes will do to people long-term. The sooner we reverse it, the better."

Mia agreed. "Emily's right, Sash. I'm sorry. Maybe you can catch up with him later. You know, when he's not under a spell."

"Oh, alright. Do what you gotta do. I'll just sit over here and quietly sulk."

Mia reached for her backpack to retrieve the notebook so she could scribble down a charm. However, as she lifted the bag, she noticed it was lighter than before. Had she dropped some books? She opened it and peered inside.

"Oh fu...dge covered pretzels!"

"What?" Emily looked at Mia like she had grown a third eye.

"Vinny's gone. He was here when I left class, and now he's gone. The sleeping spell must have worn off. "

Emily shrugged. "Eh, I wouldn't worry about it. If he's someone's familiar, he'll probably find them easier than we could. They're bonded to their owners."

"But—" Mia began.

Sasha bolted upright in her seat. "Agh! Mia, Felix is headed this way."

"Crap, crap, crap. Ok, let me think." Mia chewed on her lip as she tried to think of a charm to reverse the hex. Her heart beat faster with every step Felix took toward them. Mia despised awkward exchanges, especially ones with boys.

"Ok! I got it:

'Harder than a rock you fell, for the one who cast this spell.

Now you can go on your way. Perhaps we'll meet another day.'"

Felix stopped dead in his tracks, his hands full of pizzas and drinks. He was obviously confused by the amount of food he was carrying and why he was in the cafeteria. He stood still for a minute trying to process it all. Then, as nonchalantly as he could, he strolled to the trash can, looked around to make sure no one was watching, threw the food away, and made his escape through the cafeteria doors.

"Awe, there goes my perfectly good boy," Sasha grumbled.

"There goes my perfectly good buffalo chicken pizza." Mia's stomach growled.

Emily frowned. "You guys are absolutely ridiculous."

"Em, you're so mean," Sasha pouted. She reached toward Mia's notebook. "Alright, Mia, let me see that notebook. You said you couldn't make out the last hex, right?"

"Yeah. It's really hard to read. It must have been the last hex I wrote."

Mia slid the notebook across the table to Sasha.

"Oh! It's so glittery!" Sasha beamed as she turned the notebook over in her hands and admired the sparkles.

Emily shook her head. "Why are you like this?"

Sasha giggled then mumbled to herself as she skimmed over the pages. Emily peered over her shoulder as she read.

"Uh, Mia. When did you write this spell in the crease of the book?" Sasha looked slightly concerned.

"That's a spell? I don't know. I must have written it last night when I wrote the hexes."

"Well, I think I know why you can't remember anything you did last night."

"What?" Emily perked up. She eyeballed Sasha like she was getting ready to reveal the plot twist in a murder mystery.

"This is an amnesia spell, Mia."

"An amnesia spell?" Emily pondered thoughtfully.

"Yeah, it's in Latin, but this is most definitely an amnesia spell."

"A Latin amnesia spell," Emily mused.

Sasha pointed at the words in the crease of the book, "This particular spell is used for short term memory loss."

"This one is a short term memory loss spell," Emily said as she nodded.

Sasha slammed her fist down on the table startling both Emily and Mia.

"Emily! Sweet butter biscuits, child! Will you stop repeating everything I say? You're driving me crazy!"

Emily huffed. "Geez, I'm sorry. I was just trying to be part of the conversation."

Mia puzzled. "Why isn't the handwriting messy like the rest of the hexes?"

"You must have written it first. Maybe you knew you were about to do a few things you didn't want to remember doing?"

"You think I knew what I was doing when I cast the hexes?"

"No, I think there was definitely something wrong with the punch that caused you to lose your inhibitions. But, I also think that you knew you were going to do some things you would want to forget, so you wrote the spell down *before* you started drunk hexing everyone."

Mia was still confused. "But I don't know that spell? I couldn't even figure it out when I saw it in the notebook."

Emily wrapped an arm around her. "Mia, my friend, I think you may secretly be a genius. You just need to start drinking on a regular basis and free your mind."

"Not helpful, Em." Sasha glared at Emily. "But actually she may be partially right. Somewhere deep down in your brain you must have remembered that spell from somewhere. You know how people who are hypnotized remember stuff they didn't know they knew? It's kind of like that."

Mia took the notebook from Sasha and stared at the text.

Sasha placed her hand on Mia's arm, "What's wrong, honey? You look concerned."

"I want to undo the amnesia spell, but I'm scared. What if I hurt someone?"

"Whatever it is, sweetie, it's better if we confront it head on. Ignoring it won't do anyone any good. Emily and I are here with you. We'll figure it out together."

Mia smiled. "Thanks, you guys." She took a deep breath, "Ok, Sash. What's the reversal spell?"

Sasha took a pen out of her purse and scribbled down the spell. "Here, honey. When you're ready."

Mia stared quietly at the spell for a moment.

Emily was squirming in her seat. "Hot damn, Mia. Just say the stinkin' spell. The suspense is killing me."

"Ok! Ok!

Memento verba. Memento opera tua. Memento nocte, et liberari."

White, hot pain shot through Mia's body. Blood rushed to her head making her dizzy. She thought she was going to pass out and throw up at the same time. Then everything became quiet and clear and the memories flooded back. She remembered the pang of jealousy and anger that bubbled up when Bree smirked at her while flirting with Felix. She wrote down the amnesia spell because she knew she didn't want to remember her actions that night. It would be too embarrassing. She also remembered feeling relieved there was no one there who could identify her.

She cast the hexes on Bree and Felix then spent the evening reveling in her genius. That was until she overheard a conversation between two sleazy-looking guys. She didn't recognize either of them.

"Yeah. I put it in already."

"Why did you put it in the punch though? No one is going to drink that garbage."

"Where else was I supposed to put it? The only thing to drink other than the punch is bottled water and cans of soda!"

"Yeah, but have you ever seen a hot girl drinking sherbet punch?"

"The hell, dude. Why are you giving me such a hard time? The potion was my idea to start with."

They had put a potion in the punch! Mia could only speculate, but she was pretty sure she knew why. She remembered scribbling down the next hex. Then casting it on them both.

You suck really bad; your heart's as black as a cat.

Some people don't deserve life. You're better off as a rat.

Mia felt her face flush, and she was suddenly aware that she was still sitting with Emily and Sasha.

"Oh, no. Oh, no no no." Mia shook her head violently.

"What is it, Mia? Are you ok?" Emily asked nervously.

"Vinny isn't Vinny."

"What?" Sasha looked equally concerned and confused.

"Vinny isn't a rat. Well, he *is* now, but he wasn't always. And he's not the only one. I overheard two guys talking at the party. They put a potion in the punch; like, a bad potion meant for girls, if you know what I mean."

Sasha gasped and covered her mouth. Her southern sensibilities were obviously shaken.

Emily's eyes widened. "You turned two guys at the party into rats... and then stuffed one in your purse as a souvenir?"

Mia was forlorn. "I cannot be held accountable for my actions while under the influence of a potion, *Emily*."

Emily stared at Mia for a second. "You turned two guys into rats."

"Yes, Emily. I turned two guys into rats. No one was around at the time either, so I can't ask anyone where they went. Now I have to find them somehow and undo it, and have *no* idea where to even start looking for them."

"Why?" Sasha had composed herself.

"What do you mean 'why'?" Mia asked dumbfounded.

"Well, those ninnies were obviously after girls. I can only imagine what would have happened if they succeeded. We're able to wield magic for a reason, right? Honestly, I can think of no better reason than to rid the world of scum like that. So I say let it go and relish in the fact that you are a hex throwing, revenge spitting queen."

"Hell, yeah!" Emily shouted and threw her fist into the air. "Sasha, you little minx, I didn't know you had it in you."

Mia paused thoughtfully. "Yeah, I guess you're right."

Emily smirked at Mia. "And look at it this way, now you have something to talk about during your interview at Rune next week."

"Yeah. I mean, I did make up all those hexes on my own, didn't I? And they worked too! And any person who has malicious intent like those guys deserves to be hexed." Mia was trying to convince herself that what she did was okay.

Sasha glanced down at her sparkly, rose gold watch."Oh heavens, girls. It's already 1:54pm. I've got to get to my next class."

Mia stood up. "Me too. Thanks for all the support you guys. I really don't know what I would do without you."

Mia still felt a little guilty for not pursuing the rat boys, but knew Sasha was right. What would have happened if their scheme had been successful? She hugged Emily and Sasha as they gathered their belongings.

Emily took Mia by her shoulders and looked her straight in the eyes. "You learned a valuable lesson today. Right, Mia, my dear?"

"Don't drink the punch," Mia giggled.

"No. Next time a famous celebrity shows up at a party, you come with Sasha and me to flirt."

Mia laughed and nodded. "See you all after class. Let's go grab dinner. I'll pay."

Emily poked at Mia. "Yeah, yeah. You keep saying that, but I have yet to consume any free food,"

Emily and Sasha disappeared out the door with two big smiles and a wave of their hands.

Mia slid her bag on her shoulder and started toward Building C. Halfway there, her phone started ringing. She pulled it out, but didn't recognize the number. Maybe it was someone from Rune again?

"Hello?"

"Hi, is this Mia?" A male voice asked.

"Yes, this is Mia. Who is this?"

"Hey, Mia. It's Tom."

"Tom?"

"Tom Polland. From the party? Are we still on for our dinner date tonight?"

Mia froze.

Oh, he... x.

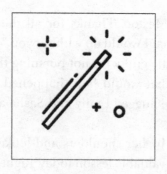

Meet Stephanie Dare Adams

Stephanie is a pharmacist turned stay-at-home mama with a love of organizing all the things. She has too many hobbies, one of which is writing, but not enough time to do any of them consistently. When she's not following everyone around cleaning up their messes, she can be found reading web comics or painting animals in fancy clothes. Stephanie lives in North Carolina with her talented husband and hilarious six-year-old son.

Sight Unseen

MATTHEW A.J. ANDERSON

D o you think anyone will see us?" Manny asks, nervously taking off his glasses and cleaning them for the fifteenth time that afternoon.

"No. Why would anyone be watching the church this late? Stop worrying, will ya?" says Lucas. He places a calming hand on Manny's shoulder and looks him in the eye. "We can do this. Trust me."

In the afternoon light, Lucas's eyes stood out brightly against his dark, Aboriginal skin tone. Manny nodded and replaced his glasses.

"Okay, let's be quick. Grab it and get out," he says.

The two boys quickly cross the road to the church garden. They head past the main church toward the meeting hall behind. The two boys walk right past the front door, to the kitchen door around the back. Lucas heads over, and pushes it open easily. "Ta-da!"

Lucas quickly takes the small pebble out of the door latch which he'd placed earlier, and puts it in his pocket, then heads inside.

"Did you bring a torch or something?" says Manny, as he slowly treads into the darkness.

"Dude, you're overthinking it," says Lucas. With a click, the fluorescent light flickers to life. "Nobody else is here. Just chill."

Lucas heads straight for a small, metal cabinet in the back corner of the room. It had a small keyhole in the middle.

"How are we going to unlock that?" asks Manny.

"With magic," says Lucas, rubbing his hands together. He holds his hands in front of himself as though he were praying. Then he places both hands against the cabinet, right on the seam beside the keyhole. He lets out a slow breath, and slowly parts his hands. As he does, the doors warp, bending unnaturally outward, as though they were made of rubber. The small, thin gap spreads wider, as Lucas opens his hands wide and starts panting. Behind the door, the small latch holding it closed is revealed.

"Okay," he grunts, "push the latch, Manny."

Manny reaches over one of Lucas's arms to twist the simple locking mechanism. As soon as he does, there's a loud *pop!* and Lucas falls onto his back as the doors slap open from the force, hanging slightly ajar.

"You did really good that time," says Manny, offering his hand to Lucas. "I've never seen you bend metal before."

"It doesn't matter what it's made of," says Lucas, trying to catch his breath as he's helped back to his feet. "It's space magic, I'm bending the space *around* it."

"Whatever," says Manny.

Lucas takes the book from the top shelf of the cabinet: *Advanced Rites and Sigilisms by Angela Goodchild.*

"But how are we going to lock it again? If we leave it open, they'll *know* we stole the book."

"Okay, first of all, I keep telling you, nobody will *assume* we're stealing, they'll think it was left open by mistake," says Lucas, opening the book and turning several pages. "And *second* of all, we're just gonna take a *picture* of the symbol, we're not stealing anything."

Lucas flips through the pages carefully. The book is quite old, and he doesn't want to damage it. He stops after a few pages.

"Holy crap, look! We can *fly* if we do this one!" says Lucas.

"No, no, no, Lucas. *Please*, we both agreed that invisibility was the best one."

"A photo costs nothing," says Lucas, taking out his smartphone.

"Yeah, but we're both *new* to this magic stuff, Lucas. I mean, what if you fall out of the sky or something? Invisibility is safe, man."

"True..." says Lucas. Finally, he continues turning pages, until he stops on the page they're looking for titled "Invisibility Spell - Rite and Magics."

Lucas holds his phone above the book, and taps his screen until it focuses clearly, then the phone flashes and makes an artificial camera shutter sound.

"Okay, we've got it," says Lucas excitedly, putting the book back. Manny comes over to try to shut the doors and gasps.

"Look, you left a big dent in it," says Manny.

"That was there before," says Lucas. "I *can't* bend matter."

Manny frets over the door, trying to straighten it, as Lucas turns off the light.

"Come on, let's get out of here," he says.

After a few moments, Manny sighs and joins his friend as they head out of the door, closing it behind them.

Lucas has a few brothers and sisters, so the two boys go to Manny's house. His parents had gone out for dinner, so they have the house to themselves for the moment. Manny wipes down the kitchen bench, while Lucas sits on a stool, looking at his phone. He scrolls and zooms in on the words.

"Yeah, it's all here," he says. "And look, you don't have to take your clothes off. It specifically says that all 'adornments on the target' will become sightless as well. So, anything you're wearing."

"Thank goodness. I don't like the idea of running around naked," says Manny.

"What are you doing?" says Lucas.

"I'm cleaning up the kitchen. If we're doing the ritual here, I don't want to make a mess."

"Then why not wipe up *after* we do the spell?" asks Lucas.

Manny just shrugs and throws the cloth in the sink. "Okay, what do we need?"

"Well, something to draw an unbroken line, so I'm thinking a marker pen. You just need to draw a symbol on the floor, and a few on your body, and then add some magic through it all."

"What kind of magic?" asks Manny

"It doesn't matter. Sorceror, psychic, whatever," says Lucas, gesturing between the two of them. "This spell comes from the symbols; they transform the magic the way we need it. See, I *told* you, you don't need to be an expert wizard to do this kind of stuff, Manny. And we can use this to get into the movies for free, or sneak into the girl's locker room."

"*And* get back at Jared Creed for bullying us," says Manny.

"But we still have to decide if we think we can convince him that his bag is *haunted*, or if you just want to mess with him."

"I just *don't* think he's superstitious," says Manny.

"*Anyone* would be superstitious if they were being haunted by a ghost," says Lucas, laughing.

"I wouldn't," says Manny. Suddenly, he frowns. "Wait, would you *seriously* go into the girl's locker room?"

Lucas's smile drops. "...no."

"You hesitated."

"What? No, I didn't. And even if I did, I mean, you *can't* tell me you haven't *thought* about it."

"Yeah, I thought about it. And what I *thought* was 'Gee, that sounds really creepy, even for me.' I'm not a Peeping Tom."

"Dude, you overthink *everything*. Who would it even hurt, if we did?"

"The *girls*, Lucas. It's an invasion of their privacy."

"Look, whatever man... let's just try this out, alright? Where's a marker pen?" says Lucas.

Manny heads into the study. After searching for a few minutes, he comes back with a large marker.

"Permanent marker, just in case," he says. Manny joins Lucas in the middle of the kitchen. "Okay, who goes first?"

"Uh, I mean, it doesn't really matter, does it?"

"I mean, you can go first if you want to," says Manny.

Lucas sighs.

"Look, you *know* I want to, but now you're thinking I'm a creep, and I just want to spy on naked girls."

"What? I don't think that."

"You do! I see how you think," says Lucas. "I don't need to be a creep to spy on girls. I've seen a girl naked before."

"No you haven't."

"I *have*. At Tracey's last Halloween party. We were playing truth or dare in the pool, and we dared Cassandra Heathers to show us her boobs, and she *did*."

"Were *you* the one that dared her?"

Lucas opens his mouth, then closes it again and snatches the marker pen out of Manny's hands. "Y'know what? You go first."

"I'm just saying it's a *little* creepy. Daring a girl to—"

"Look, I get it, alright? You're going first."

Lucas draws a semi-circle on the ground and writes strange symbols around the edge. It takes him almost five minutes to draw all the connecting lines, letters, symbols, and runes. Finally, he stands up and checks his phone again.

"Okay, now stand in the middle of the symbol and take off your shirt," says Lucas.

"Do you want to dare me, first?"

"Manny, I swear to god, I will hit you." Manny laughs as he takes his shirt off. As he steps barefoot into the circle, Lucas draws some lines and shapes over his arms. These were much simpler, some connecting lines that ran across his chest, down his arms, and up to his chin, as well as a large circle with more writing on his back.

"Okay, maybe let the ink dry for a minute, then put your shirt on."

"Do you need to do my legs?"

"No, the symbol just goes across your torso."

"Are you sure?"

"Check for yourself," says Lucas, showing him the photo on his phone.

After a moment, Manny nods, satisfied. "Okay, hand me my shirt."

"Y'know, you look kind of cool. Like a biker with a massive tattoo."

"I'm excited," says Manny, smoothing the wrinkles out of his shirt. "What's next?"

"Well, you have to turn yourself invisible by directing the magic through your body into the symbol at your feet."

"How do I do that?" says Manny.

"Well, y'know, you just *bring it forth*, y'know? Like..." Lucas makes a weak gesture that looks like vomiting from his chest.

"What the hell does that mean?"

"How do you usually focus your magic?"

"Well, I have to target a person's mind. That's how I make a psychic connection."

"Okay, well, do that... at your feet."

Manny raises an eyebrow at Lucas, but eventually looks down at his feet and breathes slowly.

"Okay, focus," Manny mutters to himself. He slowly closes, then opens his eyes, looking straight down at his feet. After a few seconds he sighs.

"Look, I can't target if there isn't a mind I can empathize with."

"Well, think of the spell as alive," says Lucas.

"But it *isn't* alive," says Manny flatly.

"I *know* that. But, imagine it's like a mind, it's a thinking thing, and you're connecting to it. Look at the image on the ground as though it's looking back up at you."

Manny nods, and looks at his feet again. As soon as he does, the black lines on his arms start to glow, bright red.

"Oh my god, it's working!" says Lucas. The symbol on the ground glows the same deep, bright red, and the light intensifies until the symbols seem to meld together into one circle of light, shining up under Manny. Manny closes his eyes as the light glares up at him. Just as quickly as it grew, the light disappears, but Manny disappears with it. In his place is nothing but a skeleton, picked clean. The light fades away to nothing.

"Oh no, what have I done?" says Lucas. "My best friend..."

"Did it work?" asks the skeleton.

"Aah!" screams Lucas, jumping back.

"Am I invisible? That was *so* cool! Did you see how bright that light was?" says the skeleton, in Manny's voice.

"Manny?" says Lucas.

"Yeah?" says Manny's skeleton. "Can you see me?"

"Uh, sort of," says Lucas.

"What do you mean?" says Manny, looking at his hands. "Gah! What the hell! I'm all bones!"

Manny pats his hands over his body. As he does, his hands seem to stop just an inch above his ribcage, but it still makes an obvious patting sound.

"My body's still here, but I can't see it. Lucas, my body's invisible, but my bones aren't!"

"Yeah, I can see that," says Lucas, rubbing his hands over his short hair.

"This is okay. We can figure this out," says the skeleton, gesturing with bony hands. "Lucas, show me the spell."

Lucas unlocks his phone and hands it to Manny. It's strange to see the phone floating just above the bones of his hand, not actually touching them. Then again, the whole sight is strange.

"I can't read this, where are my glasses?" says Manny.

"Aren't you... *wearing* them?" asks Lucas.

Manny reaches for his skull.

"Oh no, my glasses are invisible. Lucas, I can feel them, but I'm looking right through them," says Manny, sounding panicked. "Lucas, I can't see!"

"Hey, you can still see, you just can't *read*, okay? It's gonna be okay, man," says Lucas, holding out his hand. "Give me the phone; I'll read it for you."

Manny gives the phone back, and Lucas reads over the spell.

After a minute, Manny asks. "Well, what does it say?"

"Just give me a minute, I'm reading through it again," says Lucas.

"Why are you reading over it again? Did we do something wrong?"

"No, we did the *spell* right; we followed every step. But, Manny, it doesn't have a 'way to undo it' section."

"What do you mean? Are you saying I can't undo it?" asks Manny, frantic.

"I *mean*," Lucas looks up, "I think we only took a photo of the spell page, not the *dis*spell page."

"Do we need to get the book again?" asks Manny.

"We can't," says Lucas. He takes a small pebble out of his pocket. "I put this in the strike plate to stop it from latching, but I took it out. The door's locked."

"Well, can't we open it with magic? You opened the cabinet."

"I can't, the door's too thick. I'm not strong enough," says Lucas.

"No, no, no," says Manny, stepping forward. Lucas couldn't stop himself from backing up from the advancing, panicking skeleton. "*You* said that you don't move matter, but space. Just move the space *around* the door!"

"The door *occupies* space, Manny!" says Lucas. "Please, calm down. We can fix this."

"How can we fix this?" Manny paces back and forth in the kitchen, breathing in shallow, panting breaths. "I'm a walking skeleton. We can't get the book back. We don't even know what went wrong."

"Manny, you're panicking."

"Of *course,* I'm panicking! I'm a bloody skeleton!" shrieks Manny.

"I mean, you're having a panic attack. Breathe, Manny. Center yourself. I know what to do to fix this. Just *calm* yourself, okay?"

"Okay, okay," says Manny. "Calm."

The skeleton walks into the dining room and sits down in a chair, staring straight ahead as it sits there, breathing.

"Lucas," says Manny the skeleton.

"Yes, Manny?"

"Y'know I'm... I'm *definitely* calming down." Manny sounds stressed. "But it's *kind* of hard to meditate when my eyelids are invisible."

"Look, we screwed up, okay? This isn't what we wanted," says Lucas, walking over and placing a calming hand on Manny that floated a centimeter above his shoulder blade. "But, we can fix this, okay?"

Manny looks up into his friend's deep, caring eyes as Lucas stares into the skull's hollow eye sockets.

"Okay," says Manny. "How can we fix this?"

"We have to talk to Father Jake," says Lucas. "It was *his* book, so he should know a way to fix this."

"Doesn't that mean we have to admit we stole his book?" asks Manny.

"Firstly, we didn't *steal* the book, we... I mean, yeah. Yes, we will."

"Damn," says Manny. "But I mean, it's our own fault."

"Yeah," says Lucas. "Look, I'll take all the blame when I talk to him."

"How are we going to get there?" asks Manny.

"Well, *we* won't. *I* will. You stay here so no one sees you."

"Lucas, my parents will be home in half an hour," says Manny, standing up from the dining room chair. "I *can't* let them see me like this."

"You can't go outside," says Lucas.

"Sure I can. If, uh... if I wear a hoodie and jeans, I'll cover most of it up."

"Then wear a hoodie and jeans *at home*!" shouts Lucas.

"Oh yeah, I'll lie in bed, wearing a hoodie. That won't look weird or suspicious at all."

Lucas sighs heavily. "You have a point. Okay, it's just a thirty-minute walk to Father Jake's place and it's late. If we cover you up well enough, maybe we can pull this off."

"Okay," says Manny. "Either way, I'd rather scare the crap out of some stranger than my own mother."

"Yeah, but we'll try to avoid that no matter what, okay?"

"Of course," says Manny, nodding. "It's a shame, y'know? I was really looking forward to being invisible."

"Really?" says Lucas, smiling. "I couldn't see myself doing it." Lucas quickly walks off to grab Manny a pair of jeans, chuckling to himself.

"Ha! You're hilarious," grumbles Manny, mirthlessly. "Y'know, that's as funny as the *first* time you said it."

After a minute, Manny is dressed in jeans, boots, and a hoodie.

"Put your hands in your pockets," says Lucas.

Manny the skeleton puts his hands in the pouch on his hoodie, and looks at his friend.

"How do I look?" asks Manny.

"I dunno... can we put something on your face? Sunglasses, maybe?"

"I can't put sunglasses over my glasses," says Manny.

"Then take them off," says Lucas.

"They're invisible, Lucas. If I take them off, I could lose them forever."

"You took your invisible *pants* off."

"Those are just pants. Glasses are expensive," says Manny. "Look, let's just go. We're wasting time."

Manny the skeleton opens the front door, then puts his hands back in his pockets and steps outside. Lucas follows close behind. After a minute of walking, Lucas looks over at his friend.

"Does it *feel* weird?" asks Lucas.

"No, I feel the same as always. Besides not being able to blink..."

"Yeah, but, I mean... it looks like it would feel weird."

"I'm in*visible*, not in*feel*, uh, intouchable? *Un*touchable?"

"Intangible?"

"Yeah, that... I think," says Manny.

"Okay. It's just freaky, man. I mean, it's your *voice*, but you look like a videogame enemy or something."

"Yeah, it's a real shame," says Manny. "I was looking forward to getting back at Jared. Scare *him* for a change, y'know?"

Lucas stops walking. "Manny..." he says.

"What?" asks Manny, turning to look at his friend.

"*Manny*," says Lucas again, with a smile growing on his lips.

"*Lucas*, what?" asks Manny mockingly.

"Dude, you look *freaky*. Why can't we scare Jared like *this*?"

"No—"

"Manny, come on! This is *so* much better than haunting him, or messing with his stuff. He'll think a goddamned *monster* is chasing after him."

"No, Lucas. I liked invisibility because it's safe. He can't fight us if he can't see us. But he can see me like *this*. If I scare him, he'll punch me in the face."

"You don't *have* a face."

"I do have a face, you just can't see it," says Manny.

"Dude, he's not even going to get that close. He's going to crap his pants and run away."

"No, he's not. None of that is going to happen, because we're *not* doing it."

"Manny, be honest with me, do you really want to give him a good scare?"

"Of course I do. I hate Jared; he's a jerk. But not like this."

"Why not? Look, we've come *this* far, and we'll never get this chance again. When we tell Jake we took the book, he'll put it somewhere that we *can't* try to steal it."

"True, but I don't feel safe like this," says Manny.

"Dude, I'll be with you. If you think he's gonna hurt you, I'll get you out and distract him or something."

Manny sighs, looking down the street, trying to convince himself he didn't want to do this, but he fails.

"Okay, let's do this quick," says Manny. "Where does he live?"

⚡

It was just a ten-minute walk to Jared's house. Manny waits on the curb, whilst Lucas sneaks over and checks it out. After a quick scout, Lucas comes back, practically hopping with every excited step.

"Oh my god, this is *perfect*," he whispers. "He's in his room, on his own, and the *window is open*."

"Yeah, so what?" says Manny, flapping his hoodie to get some cool air.

"*So*, you can *climb in* and scare him."

"Alright," says Manny. He takes a few steps closer to the neighbor's fence, then takes his hoodie off, so he's a skeleton in jeans and boots. "Where is his room?"

"Dude, you have to take the shoes and pants off too. You look kinda silly."

"I can't take the pants off, then I'll be naked."

"You *are* wearing underwear, right?"

91

"Of course I'm wearing underwear, but I took my invisible pants off. My legs will be bare."

"So what? He won't see that."

"I'll *feel* it, though."

"Come on, skeletons wearing pants aren't scary, dude."

"*Fine.*" Manny the skeleton takes off his jeans and boots, and hands them and his hoodie to Lucas.

"Okay," says Lucas, dropping the clothes on the lawn. "His room is the second-last window on—"

"Dude, I handed them to you so they *didn't* fall on the ground."

"How can I help you if I'm busy holding your clothes?"

"Whatever," says Manny, with a sigh.

"Now, like I was saying, it's on the right side, just there," says Lucas, pointing. "Just go in and scare him."

"Okay, how do I scare him?"

"I dunno, do like a scary voice and be like," Lucas crouches slightly, and holds his hands out by his side, "*I'm here to eat your flesh, Jared.*"

"You look ridiculous," says Manny.

"Yeah, well, I'm not a skeleton."

"Shush! Don't let him hear," says Manny.

"But, seriously, do this," says Lucas, and he opens his mouth and holds his hands out.

Manny copies him, opening his jaw and holding out his bone hands.

"Awesome," says Lucas.

"I dunno, this feels silly. What if instead I make him think I'm the grim reaper or something? Man, if I had a cloak and a scythe."

"*Where* are we gonna get a *scythe*?" says Lucas, straining to keep his voice down. "Come on, let's just do *this*."

"How will I know if he's really scared?" asks Manny.

"I mean, he'll probably yell and scream. But, dude, you're a psychic. Read his mind or whatever," says Lucas.

"I still can't *read minds*, just emotions," says Manny.

"Fear is an emotion," says Lucas. "Now come on, the longer we hang around here, the more likely someone will spot us. Let's *go*."

The two head toward the backyard of the house. As they approach the second-last window, Lucas leans against the wall, puts a finger to his lips, then points at the window frame. Manny nods, heads over to the window, and peeks his skull inside. Jared's room was pretty clean, except for a pile of socks and discarded clothes by the door. Jared himself was tall and kind of lanky, but still with enough muscle to rough up kids shorter than him. He sits on the side of his bed, cutting his fingernails with a nail clipper, and flicking the cuttings toward the bin in the far corner.

Manny takes a breath, then grips the bottom edge of the window, and tries to lift himself up. After a few seconds, he falls back to the grass. He tries again, struggling as quietly as he can. Seeing that he's having trouble, Lucas kneels down, grabs his feet, and gives him a push.

"Ohhh, *crap*," says Manny, as he suddenly rolls forward through the window, his heels slapping the glass as he rolls in and onto the floor, lying on his back.

"Jesus!" screams Jared, jumping off his bed.

He turns around to look at the intruder.

Manny groans as he gets up to his feet.

"What the hell," mutters Jared, staring at the skeleton rising to its feet.

"Uh... *Jared*," says Manny, putting on a forced, raspy voice. "*I am death... I'm here for you, Jared Creed.*"

"Agh!" screams Jared, and he pegs the nail clippers at Manny.

Manny flinches, raising up his arms, but the clippers bounce harmlessly off where his stomach would have been.

"*F-forcefield*," stammers Jared.

"Hey," says Manny angrily.

"No, no, don't kill me!" screams Jared. He jumps back and crashes into his dresser, making it rattle, then scrambles toward his bedroom door, racing into the hall.

"*Run, Jared!*" Manny yells, trying to rasp his voice, which makes him cough from the effort. Then, quickly, he heads back to the window. "We did it!"

"I heard the whole thing. That was *awesome!*" says Lucas, excitedly.

"Now, quick, help me out of here," says Manny. He holds out his arms, and Lucas helps him step up and jump down from the window. Lucas heads toward the street, but Manny looks back in through the window.

"*What* are you doing?" says Lucas, in a stage whisper.

"Do you think we could get him again?" asks Manny, turning back to his friend. "He was scared for his *life*."

Suddenly, the glass of the window shatters, spilling over Manny as the end of a baseball bat smashes out, but gets caught in the sliding frame.

"*Get away!*" Jared shrieks, in a surprisingly high-pitched voice.

"Oh, crap!" says Manny, running away, as fast as he can.

"I'll fight you, Death!" yells Jared. "I'm too young to die!"

Manny catches up with Lucas, who grabs his clothes from the lawn, and the two run onto the road.

"Ow! Ow! *Boots*, Lucas! I need my boots."

Lucas scrambles with the pile of clothes and hands Manny his boots. He hops on one foot as he puts each boot on, then they keep running down the street. They get around the corner before they stop, panting heavily.

"Oh my god, did you see that? I'm *shaking*," says Lucas.

"Am I bleeding? I felt some of that glass scratch me," says Manny.

"Where?" says Lucas.

"Here," says Manny, pointing at his neck, then his arm. "And *here*."

"I don't see anything," says Lucas.

"It's *invisible*," says Manny. "I think I'm bleeding."

Lucas puts his hand around Manny's arm, and it feels wet, so he brings his wet hand to his nose, and sniffs. Salty.

"Dude, it's just sweat. You're fine," says Lucas. "You got lucky."

"Yeah," says Manny. "That last moment aside, that was pretty awesome, right?"

"Hey, I will never forget how high-pitched he screamed. He sounded like a toddler!"

"Alright, give me my pants back. I feel naked out here," says Manny.

When they finally arrive at Jake's one-story, little house, the two fall silent. They walk up to his front door, but neither is prepared to knock.

"Knock on the door," says Manny.

"I will, just give me a second," says Lucas.

After about fifteen seconds, he reaches out his hand and taps his knuckles on the front door.

"Louder than that," says Manny.

"It's fine. He'll hear us."

"What if he's asleep?"

"Who goes to sleep *now*?" asks Lucas. "It's barely seven o'clock."

Manny just pushes the doorbell. They hear a loud *ding-dong* from inside the house. After a minute, a short, middle-aged, bald man opens the door.

"Hello? Oh, Lucas? What brings you... Aaagh!" suddenly, he slams the door shut. After a few seconds, the door opens a crack. "Lucas?"

"Hey, Jake. It's Lucas, and this is Manny."

"Herman? Herman *Dendy*?" says Jake, opening the door wide.

"Yeah," says Lucas, and Manny nods.

"What happened?"

"We tried an invisibility spell, but it didn't work," says Manny the skeleton. "We need your help."

"Alright, come in, come in. Before someone sees you," says Jake. "Come on, this way, let's have a look at you."

They head into the study, a small, square room with bookshelves and a small, cheap desk, chair and laptop. Jake spins the study chair around and sits in it.

"Alright, what was the spell you used?" asks Jake.

"The invisibility rite from *Advanced Rites and Symbols*," says Lucas.

"And how did you get your hands on that spell?" asks Jake.

95

"We broke in," admits Manny, "And, we took pictures of the spell."

"Ah, I see," says Jake. "You boys realize that I don't invite *everyone* from my flock into my inner circle, don't you?"

"Yes, Father Jake," says Manny.

"Lucas?" says Jake.

"Yes, Father Jake," Lucas repeats.

"Magic is powerful, and our god wants us to have it. But, it's dangerous, so I can only have people that I *trust* in my Sunday school magic lessons. This makes me *seriously* question that trust, boys."

"Look, we're sorry," says Manny. "We just wanted to prank Jared Creed with it."

"He's a bully at school," says Lucas. "He picks on Manny all the time for being small, and he beats me up... I think that's because he's a racist dick."

"*Language*, Lucas," says Father Jake.

"For real, though," says Lucas. "We just wanted to pay him back."

Father Jake sighs. "It's been a long time since I was in school, but I understand where you're coming from, boys. But we don't need magic to fight our enemies, if we're smart. And we *especially* shouldn't be using spells that are beyond our level. That's just asking for trouble."

"Can you fix it though?" says Manny.

"Of course, it's simple," says Father Jake. He stands up and places his hands on Manny's shoulders. He closes his eyes for a moment and nods his head. He opens his eyes and sits back down.

"Alright. You should be able to release this yourself," says Jake.

"How?" says Manny.

"Well, do you remember what I said about how magic is like a muscle?"

"No," says Lucas.

"Although it comes from within, it starts off small and needs to be grown with time and use. There's nothing wrong with your invisibility spell, it worked as it was supposed to. But your magic was too weak, Manny. It could penetrate your skin, but not your bones," says Jake, clearly switching to sermon mode. "See, bones are hard for magic to penetrate, because it tries to flow around—that's why some

96

magic-users make their wands out of bone. Your magic was too thin to get all the way through."

"Then *how* do I deactivate it?" asks Manny.

"Well, you tell me," says Jake. "How did you engage the spell?"

"I focused on the symbol and connected with it,"

"Exactly. I haven't covered sigils with you boys, yet. But a sigil is a lot like a circuit. To switch it off, you need to sever the connection—break the loop, as it were. You need to actively *un*focus the connection and disconnect."

"Okay, how do I do *that*?" asks Manny

"Find that focus once more, and break it. Like when you disconnect from a target you're reading, Manny. You can do this..."

Manny looks down at his feet, and concentrates. After almost thirty seconds, as quick as a flash, his flesh re-appeared.

"Oh my god! I'm blind!" yells Manny.

"Open your eyes, Manny," says Jake. Manny does and looks around. "Oh, wow... I can blink again! Did it work?"

"Yes, Manny, it worked," says Jake, smiling. "Now, what have we learned?"

"That deep down, we all have a skeleton," says Lucas.

Father Jake chuckles, but Manny gives his friend the side-eye.

"No, boys. Magic is a *step-by-step* process. When we try to rush into more advanced spells, our *reach* exceeds our *grasp*."

"Yes, Father Jake," Lucas and Manny say in unison.

"Alright, now, before you go, the subject of punishment."

"Come on," says Lucas. "Isn't this punishment enough?"

"I'm sorry, but fair is fair," says Father Jake. "You'll both be on kitchen clean-up duty for three weeks."

"Three *weeks*?" says Manny, sadly.

"It could be much worse. If anyone had seen you, you might have the authorities after you. I've told you about the men in green suits, haven't I?"

"Yes, Father Jake," says Manny.

"Alright," says Father Jake. "Now, you two better get home. Do I need to call your parents to come pick you up?"

"No, we can walk home," says Manny.

"We'll be safe, together," says Lucas.

"Alright then," says Father Jake. "Manny, you're sweating in that thing, do you need a glass of water?"

"Oh, right," says Manny, taking off his hoodie and handing it to Lucas. Underneath, his hair's a mess, his shirt's damp with sweat, and the marker on his arms is badly smudged. "Yeah, I could use a drink."

Father Jake heads to the kitchen, and Manny follows with Lucas not far behind. After a glass of water, Manny sighs heavily.

"Thanks, Jake."

"Alright, you two, get home," says Father Jake. "I'm disappointed that you were playing with dangerous spells, but I'm glad you came to me for help."

"Of course," says Manny. "We trust you."

The boys head out of his house. With a final wave, Father Jake closes the door. The two head back to Manny's house. Manny holds out his sweaty arms to dry off in the warm breeze, but Lucas just walks alongside, carrying Manny's hoodie in both hands.

"Three weeks," says Manny. "Well, I guess it *could* be worse."

"Yeah, it's actually kinda cool, all told," says Lucas with a smile.

"What are you so happy about?" asks Manny.

"Okay, don't tell anyone, but..." Lucas reaches into the hoodie, and pulls out a book.

"What's that?" asks Manny. Then his eyes grow wide. "You *stole* one of the books from his study?"

"Hey, no, I *borrowed* a book from his study."

"Did you listen to *anything* he said?"

"Yeah, he said it's real easy to disspell symbols for yourself."

"And all that stuff about trust, and magic being dangerous?"

"We already *knew* that. Besides, *read the title*," says Lucas.

Manny takes the book and reads the cover, "*Summoning for Beginners*." He slowly lowers the book from his face and glares at his friend. "*Lucas*."

"Come on! Maybe we can summon a demon, or an *angel*. What if she's hot?"

"What would we do with an angel? Play truth or dare?"

"Come on, Manny, stop worrying, will ya?" Lucas places a hand on his friend's damp shoulder and looks him dead in the eye. "We can do this. Trust me."

Meet Matthew A.J. Anderson

Matthew A. J. Anderson was born in Queensland, Australia. A daydreamer and avid reader in his childhood, he grew up to love horror, mystery and speculative fiction; he most enjoys writing stories that disturb, inspire and intrigue. He is now living in Albury Wodonga, New South Wales and in his free time is working on short stories as well as larger fiction projects that he hopes to publish. Matt also posts some of his shorter writing, as well as non-fiction pieces on his blog absurdwordnerd.blogspot.com.au.

Plants and Prophecies

JM JORDAN

P archment and sweet treats don't mix." Agnes plunged her gloved fingers into the dark soil, ignoring her young companion as she settled red geraniums into the planter at the entrance of the Royal Gardens.

"And why exactly not?"

"Decorum, my dear, begins there." Agnes looked at Calliope with an affectionate smile. "Records of that nature are quite priceless."

With a wrinkle of her button nose, the young woman put her snacks back in the satchel at her feet, her frown deep as she fixed an unpleasant stare at the unfurled scroll on her lap. Calliope was discontent, bored, and without an immortal classification which left her vulnerable to the uncertainty surrounding the problem.

"I resent the idea of going without snacks while reading the drudgery contained upon this scroll." Calliope's dark corkscrew curls bounced with the firm tilt of her head as she held the parchment up so that it would catch the sunlight. "Sweet treats should always be allowed."

Agnes could feel the lines near her eyes deepen, though she tried to suppress her smile. There was something infectious about this girl, in spite of her irregularity.

Calliope's tan skin glistened in the mid-day sun. She had returned to the Realm of Reason with no memories of her *Pneuma Mortalis*—more commonly known as a mortal journey—or her premortal years as a souling. Agnes considered her for a long moment. Missing memories didn't happen in the Taeron Cosmos.

"Is this the same portion you were reading to the children before they fell asleep?" Agnes mused with a glance at the twin grand-soulings sprawled out beneath the large oak at the center of the garden.

"Yes." The response was soft. Calliope had lowered the scroll, already lost in the words of the aged parchment despite her protest.

She was pretty, this lost girl, in her yellow chiffon dress the color of a daffodil. Her round cheeks flushed just enough to make her look excited though she clearly wasn't. Agnes turned back to her geraniums. "At least read aloud," she said. "There are bits of this story I'd like to hear again."

"Hmmm?" Calliope looked up.

"The words." Agnes pointed her spade at the parchment. "Read them to me."

Calliope blushed, her thick black lashes batting as she cleared her throat and began.

"*Near the Heart, Mirk, High King and Lord Steward, was accompanied by his chosen few to tend the needs of the growing Realm. The Heart pumped waters of life to feed the surface. From this, the seas filled and the land blossomed with vegetation. An expanse of rivers crawled across the plains and into the mountainous spine which split the Realm in two great halves. It is there that the tributaries rushed down in a great waterfall to join the Heart again. In a continuous cycle, the Realm of Reason found its balance within the Taeron Cosmos.*"

Calliope looked up from the parchment. Agnes watched an inquisitive expression creep across the young immortal's face.

"Where is this place with the waterfall?" Calliope mused. "Surely not anywhere near the Royal Cove. I've not heard a single immortal or souling speak of it."

They wouldn't. Not since the Dyvisioun had split the Realm and cost many souls their existence. Immortals who had lived through the affair were bound by vows of silence. Enough time had passed that the soulings who had survived the experience had long since left for their mortal journeys. All remnants of the event had been purged from the histories; at least the ones that new soulings had access to.

"It is forbidden," Agnes said, voice flat.

Calliope's eyes grew wide. "Why?"

Agnes shook her head. "That is a story for another scroll. First, you must get through the creation of our home and then we will move on to the more complicated parts of inhabiting it."

"Oh, but forbidden lore sounds much more exciting," Calliope whispered as she bent forward, her face expectant. "I won't tell if you don't."

"Hmph." Agnes ignored her and glanced to the shaded area beneath the oak where Huldah and Samy slept. Calliope would understand soon enough if those memories of hers would return. "The children didn't seem to think this current bit so boring."

"That's because I was play acting to try and get through it." Calliope frowned and sat back. "They'll be bored when they really have to learn about it."

"Don't let their mother hear you say that." Agnes shook her head with a wry grin.

Naptime had come after mid-day play and full bellies. Huldah and Samy's cheeks were flushed even in the shade.

"Emmet is late today," Calliope noted.

Agnes wasn't shocked. "He will arrive in time, have some patience. We won't be left beneath the afternoon sun for too much longer."

Calliope frowned.

"No need for an argument. Those scrolls are your focus while the twins sleep. You must prove to the Assembly of Lord Stewards that you merit the immortal classification of Creator. The alternative is to work as a Sylph and possibly be required to return to the mortal worlds as a souling conscience. It's honorable, mind you, sylph service work. But a girl with your talents should put her energies elsewhere."

"Grandmother is not without prejudice," Emmet's voice rang from behind where Agnes sat. She turned and saw her oldest grand-soul, his broad frame filling the archway as he looked over the merry garden scene. He had long-since earned his immortality, and now worked alongside his parents in management of the Realm.

"She keeps me on my toes." Calliope smiled up at him.

"As she does us all," Emmet responded just before taking a stride to where Agnes sat. He pecked her cheek with a kiss. "We're all better for it."

"You young souls do too much kissing." Agnes swatted at his shoulder. "But who's complaining?"

His laugh was deep and warm as he tucked his chestnut-colored hair behind his ears. "Looks like they played themselves out." He smiled at his little brother and sister.

"Truly," Calliope agreed. "But wouldn't we all if we were still only four?"

There was no need for a response as play was something every soul, no matter the age, could do a little more of. Agnes had taught Emmet the principle long ago. She watched the older souls gather Huldah and Samy in their arms. Calliope struggled for a moment with Samy's dead weight. Huldah was the lighter of the twins but never seemed to settle unless transported by Emmet. Sleep was hard on the wee thing. Agnes had never seen a souling struggle quite like this one did. It was a cause of deep concern.

Agnes made quick work of collecting the personal items while leaving the rest of the picnic items for a servant to gather. The walk from the garden to the main stairwell was quiet. Emmet's broad, strong frame was quite the contrast to Calliope's slight build and bouncing curls. She would miss these souls when her time came to join the other Ancients in the Court of the Taeron Emperor. The thought brought on a frown.

"Come along you two," Agnes whispered as she scurried around Emmet and Calliope with their slumbering packages. Agnes took the railing and began to move swiftly up the stairs. "Comfortable beds and a quiet afternoon await."

The nursery would house the twins until their fifth natal day. By then Agnes would be gone. She shook her head, hardly able to imagine the twins growing up with her so far away.

Agnes pushed through the nursery door with Calliope on her

heels and watched as the slip of a girl tucked the sound-asleep Samy into his bed. The boy rolled right over with a heavy sigh. Huldah was another matter. She clung to Emmet, her little fists full of her brother's hair. With a whimper, she looked up at him.

"It's scary to sleep," she shuddered.

Emmet stroked Huldah's golden locks as Calliope hurried to help pry her fingers loose.

"Huldah," Emmet whispered. "Remember your Moonsinger, it's here to protect you when I am not."

The scared little soul turned her gaze to the dancing vine with the large purple bloom that swayed in her windowsill. She pointed at it, and Emmet nodded. "Yes, it's going to watch over you as you rest, and tonight when the moon comes out, it will dance for you."

"Awe." Huldah's frown turned into a slight smile. "For me?"

"Yes, for you. Now time to nap. Calliope and Nana will be right here."

"I'll sing to you," Calliope added, taking Huldah from Emmet's arms. "You'll like that. Come now, let's tuck you in."

Once Huldah settled, Emmet stroked her cheek and gave her a wink. Agnes took a seat in the rocking chair between the beds which gave her the perfect view of both her grand-soulings and the door. She knew Emmet wouldn't linger for fear Huldah wouldn't go back to sleep. Instead, he headed out with a brief wave to each of them.

As Agnes rocked and Calliope hummed, the Moonsinger swayed above them. Samy's Lightbringer, the cousin to Huldah's plant, spiraled around his bed pole and cast a slight glow on his face. Agnes would miss these moments bitterly.

It didn't take long for Huldah to settle as Calliope's sweet melody urged the souling back to sleep. The lullaby was just finished when a quiet knock at the nursery door interrupted the calm reverie. With quiet ease, Calliope hurried to the door to greet the souling who rolled a small wooden cart into the room.

"I was instructed to bring this to the nursery as stealthily as possible," the young souling whispered to Calliope who ushered him inside with a finger over her lips. "Time to fertilize the, er, plants."

Agnes watched as the souling's sylph flew in behind him. The little man with colorful wings hovered near the souling's shoulder. His long black hair was tied with a ribbon that matched his tiny green tweed vest. He had a studious air about him and took scrupulous notes on the scroll in his hands.

Calliope schooled her eyes on the items the cart held, pretending she couldn't see the small, winged figure. It took some practice around premortal soulings to ignore their sylph, but it was necessary since the souling himself couldn't know it was there. Calliope was obviously still uncomfortable with the ruse.

When she'd returned from her assigned Mortal Realm, Calliope's own sylph had worked with her for some time, reviewing the life scrolls. Their attempts to spark Calliope's memories were to no avail. The work was abandoned, which was when Calliope had joined Agnes.

"Thank you," Calliope whispered. "Are there instructions?"

The young souling nodded, producing a small piece of rolled parchment from his breast pocket and unfolding it.

"Will you be assisting? Um, what's your name?"

"Mathius." The young man nodded. "And yes, I will stay and then return with the cart once we're finished."

"Lovely." Calliope smiled and then moved to collect the Moonsinger from Huldah's window.

Agnes continued the steady rhythm of her rocking with a watchful eye on her grand-soulings as Calliope bustled about. She hurried back to Samy's bedside and gingerly unwrapped the Lightbringer which took a long moment as the vine was not fond of being moved. Agnes chuckled. She'd always been fond of plants and these two creations were something special.

"How about you tend the Moonsingers?" Mathius suggested as Calliope deposited the unhappy Lightbringer into his hands. "And I'll manage this one."

"Works for me." Calliope shivered as she watched the coiling vine constrict around Mathius's arm. "Just to be clear, I've not done anything like this before. At least, not that I remember."

"Oh, I didn't know that." Mathius's throat-knot bobbed up and down at the unexpected pressure.

Agnes doubted this little chore had been just an errand. Emmet was good with his students as he eased them into higher learning through demonstration without them suspecting. From the looks of it, this young soul felt like he'd been tossed into deep waters.

"What's first?" Calliope asked in a nearly inaudible whisper.

"The poultice." Mathius stuck his free pointer finger down on the parchment which was held in place by the Lightbringer's pot. "It's the most important part. Gives these beauties their speciality. Neither are grown in any other Realm and certainly not on mortal worlds. From what I know, Emmet created them just for the royal twins. A proto-type, I think, one of a kind."

"Yes." Calliope nodded. "Grandmother Agnes told me that too."

"Right then." Mathius swallowed hard. "We must be diligent not to cross contaminate or spill the contents."

The young souling was only too right. Agnes sat forward in her rocking chair and considered joining the two.

"What is it? If you don't mind me asking," Calliope whispered as her fingers traced the tops of the wooden boxes sitting on the cart.

Agnes knew Calliope's fingers touched a sun and a moon carved delicately into the boxes. They had been her gift to Emmet upon his return from the mortal worlds some centuries ago. It had pleased her to see him put the contents to good use.

"Extract of star oil and moondust." Mathius breathed slow and steady as he removed the lids of the enclosed beakers to reveal a slight glow coming from them both. "The Lightbringers will take the star oil, of course."

Calliope and her curls bobbed in agreement as Mathius took a small syringe from the box in preparation to withdraw the oil.

"Once I apply this to the prepared teabag, settle it at the base of the Lightbringer's stem. You must try to wrap it around, then I will tie it in place with twine."

Agnes observed from the edge of the rocking chair. The boy had done this before or at least something similar. His movements were precise, not wasteful as the shining oil filled the syringe and imme-diate area with warmth and bright light. He'd do well in a specialized training of the Laboratorial Arts. Mathius was quick to dispel the oil on the teabag.

Calliope moved with haste and Mathius, having sealed the syringe in a bag for cleaning, came behind her with the twine and tied the poultice in place. With great affect, the Lightbringer relaxed as its bulbs pulsed from the nourishment it drew in.

"That was fairly easy." Calliope beamed. "Now my turn?"

Mathius nodded. "You will have one additional step. There are two vials we'll draw from. The first of course is the moondust. Take out the tiny spoon in the case. Your poultice will only need one scoop and be sure to level it off."

"Oh, it's so fine," Calliope observed as she spilled the soft silver particles into the small bowl Mathius held between his hands.

"Yes, it is," he whispered in a tone of appreciation. "Now stow the spoon back in the case. We clean as we craft, that's what Emmet says." He smiled before his face turned grave. "The serious part is upon us. We must mix the moondust with the elixir of life. It gives the Moon-singer just enough will to charm the soulings. Extract of star oil already has a high enough content in it. Too much elixir and the little dancing thing would act an awful lot like us."

"How is that possible?" Calliope stared incredulous at the second, smaller vial in the case.

Mathius shrugged. "Don't know yet, above my skill level."

"And yet you're trusted to do this alone?" Calliope struggled with the idea.

"We aren't exactly alone." Mathius dipped his head in Agnes's direction. "I doubt I'd have been sent otherwise."

Agnes chuckled and nodded back. Emmet had known the souling would be in good hands under Agnes's watchful eye.

"Remove the last syringe. Good. Time to uncork the vial. Hold it steady, yes, that's it. Now pull on the syringe only to where the basin begins."

The clear vial had a colorless syrup consistency. Agnes cocked a brow as Calliope shook her head and took a deep breath. With her hands trembling, she tried once and then again to insert the syringe and extract the elixir.

"Something's wrong," she mumbled.

Agnes jumped to her feet too late. Calliope's body shook with a sharp snap and slammed forward into the cart. The plants and feeding ingredients crashed to the ground with her. Mathius jumped back, startled by the sudden collapse.

"Get behind me and keep a close watch on the children," Agnes ordered as she rushed to Calliope's side. "If they so much as stir, shield them from whatever is happening here."

"Yes, Queen Regent." Mathius yelped as he scrambled past Agnes who bent with an effort to obscure Calliope's convulsing body from view.

"A sylph will bring my daughter, the High King, Emmet. Whomever can be found first, without delay." Agnes didn't say more knowing one of the three sylphs in the room, which Mathius could not see, would zip on her orders.

"Excuse me, Queen Regent? Did you say—" Mathius was confused. He had a right to be, but there was no time for it.

"I did say. Keep your eyes on those babes and don't disturb me or make a move unless I call your name directly."

"Of course, Queen Regent."

Agnes held Calliope's hands in hers. The quaking slowed but her skin felt hot to the touch. Not a good sign. The star-oil's cork had come loose in the fall and was seeping into Calliope's dark curls which had begun to shine in a blinding platinum white. To make matters worse, both the Moonsinger and Lightbringer lay in a puddle of the life elixir which had broken in the fall.

"Won't be able to fix any of this." Agnes hissed to herself.

"Nor will you need to," a deep voice spoke through Calliope's lips.

Agnes jumped and then calmed almost at once. The voice held her fixated as Calliope opened her eyes. What were once a brilliant green now shown as silver as the moon on a dark night. Agnes had seen this once before. As a young immortal, she'd witnessed the awakening of a Seer. Rare it was to witness once; twice was unheard of.

"As with all things, Queen Regent, time and memory has a way of arriving when it must."

"Of all the Realms in the Cosmos ... " Agnes struggled to push the words from her chest. Both remaining sylphs fluttered into view, equally flabbergasted though their quills wasted no time in recording the event.

"Yes." The young immortal once called Calliope sat up. "Awakened by need and so the mystery of memories lost is now solved. The life I once knew was removed to make room for all that will be."

Agnes dipped her head in reverence. Only three Seers existed at any time within the Taeron Cosmos. All were housed at the Cathedral of Conscious. This would mean that one had been cleansed. The remains of that vessel would be taken to the Void of Matter in a great ceremonial procession to be recycled and birthed again at the will of the Cosmos. Entire Realms could be born and extinguished during the lifespan of a Seer and here was Agnes, witnessing an awakening for the second time.

"You will bring me to your grand-soulings. There are words to be spoken." Calliope's delicate hand extended itself to Agnes who helped the Seer to her feet. This too was unprecedented. Had words ever been spoken over souls so young?

"But first, Mathius," the Seer beckoned. "Come."

Agnes watched as the young soul turned toward them. Alarm danced across his features. "Be still, boy, there are less than ten throughout all the Cosmos to have witnessed a thing such as this. It is well."

The Seer held out her hand for him to take which he did. "One such as I must have two guides, an Ancient and the other pure. Agnes and Mathius, this will be your task."

Mathius was tall with a good build but shook like a leaf in the breeze in the presence of the Seer.

"Explain this to him," the Seer instructed. "He must calm himself before I speak the words."

Agnes swallowed hard. She knew, of course, all Ancients did. "To accompany a Seer requires service at the Cathedral of Conscious until the Seer is cleansed. There are two posts, a Warden and Wardeness. One to record the words of prophecy spoken before the departure of souls to mortal worlds, the other to tend to the needs of the Seer."

"I don't understand," Mathius stammered. "What about my training and advancement?"

"Your mortal journey will be delayed," Agnes explained in soft tones, hoping to alleviate shattered expectations. "My soul will be tied to the existence of the Seer. Yours will simply be delayed. Upon our cleansing you will take up your existence."

"And so it is," the Seer whispered. "At this very time, the pure soul who served for two Realm cycles will soon know his mortality."

"There's a soul who has been waiting 20 millennia to become mortal?" Utter disbelief washed over Mathius as the gravity of the situation registered. A circle of faint blue light began to spin around his hand held by the Seer. His circlet, once silver, transformed to the turquoise blue of a summer sea.

The Seer turned to Agnes and extended her hand. This appointment would take Agnes from her home, away from her grand-soulings and daughter for the rest of her existence. Agnes sighed as her eyes rested on Huldah and then Samy. Her heart ached as she took the Seers hand and watched her own golden circlet turn the same turquoise blue that Mathius now wore.

"We are three. One final detail remains."

"The quill and parchment," Agnes breathed.

It was a sad affair to see the abrupt end of a sylph and souling relationship. Mathius of course was more perplexed, having never seen his sylph, but the little man who floated at his shoulder frowned in deep sorrow. With a quick tug to his vest, the tiny sylph flew to Agnes with Mathius's life scrolls.

"I have extra," he said. "And am honored, Queen Regent, to give you my quill and ink." With a curt nod of respect, the tiny man handed over his tools "If you don't mind, I have resizing droplets with me."

"Of course not." Agnes gestured for him to perform the work and watched with interest as he opened his vest and revealed a series of pockets filled with vials. He selected one and gave Agnes the slightest of smiles before placing one drop of blue liquid on each of the items in her palm.

"Do not go, Sylph," the Seer commanded as she turned toward Samy's bed. "You're more a part of this than you know."

The Seer took a few steps and then lifted her arms, palms out over the bed where Samy began to stir. "These are the words. Courage radiates. Capable of greatness while quiet in the knowing. Shield and protector of the Daughter Heir, his life will be lost in her service. You, Sylph, will be his guide. The souling will need you as his sister requires him. The Realm will need them both. These are the words."

Agnes watched as the quill moved across the parchment recording the words but also images of what it saw. This was part of the mantle bequeathed upon her with the binding circlet. Every detail Agnes witnessed, the quill would now record.

The little man with colored wings watched the quill and its work in great interest, then shook to reality at the last of what the Seer had said. He flew to Samy whose silver bond had faded from his wrist. Samy stared up at the soul he'd once known as Calliope. The Seer smiled in return and knelt beside his bed. In loving strokes, she pushed his unruly curls away from his eyes. "You have a good mind, use it for the purposes of light as your days grow dim."

Samy nodded in youthful innocence.

"Hold out your hand now," the Seer urged. "I will leave you with a new friend who you cannot see but will always be with you."

Agnes felt her heart pierce with a myriad of emotions as the little soul did as asked without question. The long-haired sylph placed his hand on Samy's and with an approving nod from the Seer, began the bonding rite.

"I am Bentrius, descendent of the Second Prince Immortal, born in the Realm of Reason and charged with the Keeping of life scrolls. I claim you, Samenthrius, last born of the line of Mirk, our High King of the Realm of Reason and Lord Steward of the Taeron Cosmos. From now until our bond is severed, I will watch and warn, guide and follow, and always keep what must be kept."

"May the Keeping be kept," Agnes heard herself say, along with the Seer and Huldah's trembling sylph.

Bentrius sat down on the bed next to Samy and opened his satchel for what Agnes knew would be another roll of parchment and likely a spare quill kept within. To the astonishment of all who watched except the Seer, Samy draped an arm over the little sylph as if he knew his bond holder was there.

The Seer wasted no time, turning ever so slightly toward the bed where Huldah, with her golden hair shining in the afternoon light, continued to sleep. Agnes watched Huldah's sylph gulp as she steadied her quill. No doubt she wished it had been her who went for help with the way her eyes kept going to the door and back again. The Seer raised her arms and quaked as if she pushed against an opposing force.

"These are the words," she declared with authority. "This soul's existence will be treacherous. It hangs by a thread. Innocence will be eaten away by the vile enmity of a soul. The blight is centered in power and rooted in family. Darkness will shroud. Her people will suffer. Huldah will be forced to choose. I sense despair and yet hope will rise from a bond un-foreseen. These are the words."

Anxious pressure built in Agnes's chest. She stared at the angelic face of her grand-souling, frozen in fear of the words that had been spoken when the bedroom door burst open.

The Seer turned, arms open and silver eyes wide as her aura grew and filled the room. Mirk and Magdalena, High King and Queen of the Realm of Reason, paused at the threshold. "These are the words. Your babes inherit a sickness you cannot cleanse. Surrender your lives and they will win. These are the words."

It was wrong. All of it. The plant feeding, the prophecy, the look on Magdalena's face. Agnes was old, her time spent. It was all terribly, terribly wrong.

Emmet burst through the door just as his parents hurried to their babes and pulled them into their arms. On trembling knees Agnes fell just as Emmet neared and was able to catch her.

"Grandmother, what has happened?"

Agnes couldn't seem to piece it all together. The day had started so bright, been so full. Now all she knew seemed lost without a thing to change it.

"Oh, Emmet." She clutched at his shirt, her knuckles white. "You must protect them. Hide them. Do something so they will not bear the weight of our choices in the Dyvisioun."

"Slow down, Grandmother. All will be well." His confused face broke Agnes a bit more.

"No." She shook her head. "What's been sealed away will come. For the love of the Cosmos, Emmet, do not let him have them."

There in the nursery, with the Seer at the center, two large vines crawled across the floor and stationed themselves like sentries. Small plants meant to sooth were now as large as the man who had created them. Agnes shook her head in disbelief.

In a Cosmos as large as Taeron, with all the power they possessed, the prophecies would prevail, and the Darkness would come.

Meet JM Jordan

Novelist JM Jordan lives in Houston, Texas, with her sons and spoiled fur babies. She loves spending free time at the beach, reading fantasy novels, or playing card games with friends. Feel free to keep up with her events and blogs on www.jmjordan.net. Ms. Jordan can also be found on the following social media sites:

Facebook: @JMJordan15
Twitter: @JMJordan_15
Instagram: @JMJordan_15

Last Rite of the God Heist

GREGORY D. LITTLE

B *lazings don't belong in the Pit.* The thought had repeated endlessly ever since Casey had been roughly hauled from her precinct cot by Sergeant Roscio and told she'd been chosen to go on this insane expedition, never mind that she hadn't asked for the honor. It drummed through Casey the entire barge ride down through the planet's crust and mantle. None of the polistraat in this group, Blazings all, belonged in the Pit. Worship of the imprisoned gods was forbidden in all places, but most especially in the Pit, the very site of that prison.

Casey's first view of the great, hollow space at the center of the world didn't ease her churning stomach. Miles in diameter, the Pit was spherical, almost entirely empty, and bounded by a shell of molten rock which glowed orange with heat and had nothing visible holding it back. Knowing there were wrighted fields holding the magma back did not soothe Casey in the slightest. Wrightings were fine as tools, but she wasn't comfortable with the idea of the unnatural objects being the only things preventing her painful death.

The barge opened onto a platform at the Pit's edge, one of the rare disruptions in that otherwise unbroken stretch of fiery glare. Turning her head in any direction showed her a field of molten rock gently curving upward. And directly above her head... Well, Casey didn't want to look directly upward. It was too much of a reminder of why she didn't belong here.

Major Gnaeus gathered them, his several dozen polistraat officers, but he held off speaking until the cylindrical barge had begun threading its way back up the shaft that would return it to the surface.

"All right, listen up," Gnaeus said as the barge's noise faded into eerie echoes. His hatchet face took on a ghoulish cast, a special talent of his. "This is what you've been preparing for."

Except, of course, Casey hadn't.

"I know it's tempting to think only of the prize," Gnaeus said, "but we've got some time yet. Complete First and Second Rites when you safely can, but wait for my explicit order before beginning Last Rite. We're in hostile territory. You have to have each other's backs until, well, you don't."

Several others joined in his dark laughter. Casey frowned. She'd heard barely any details about this secret competition for the gods' favor. The others seemed to know exactly what it entailed.

"Above all else," Gnaeus continued, "remember why we're here." He visibly steeled himself to speak the unspeakable. "Our gods have been imprisoned for too long by our own government. We are here to set them free." This part, Casey knew, but she still had to lock her knees to keep from collapsing. Gnaeus was not much better. Whether from fear or fervor, he struggled to get his shaking voice back under control. "It's a dangerous mission. I can't promise the first person to break our cover down here will be the first to die. But I promise they will be the first to *start* dying."

Above his head, at the exact center of the Pit, the gods' prison hovered, shadowed in backlit glare, a massive sphere of iron and a malevolent promise all its own.

⚡

First Rite, as explained hastily to Casey on the way down, was: "demonstrate that you serve your god."

She hoped to be first to visit Ashavid's temple. Not because she believed this would convey some advantage, but because she wanted the temple of her erstwhile god to herself. A last-minute replacement for an acolyte who had fallen ill, Casey was the lowest ranked of all the supplicants, even the alternates. Her unasked-for bid was doomed to failure, but she could at least try to minimize humiliation.

The temples were dotted along the Pit's magma wall at regular intervals. This was by necessity, for they collectively maintained the invisible energy field that held back the unthinkable pressure of all that molten rock. There could be no Pit without the temples, forbidden as they were.

Travel in the Pit was accomplished by launching oneself from designated platforms studded with wrightings for the purpose. A few feet above any walkable surface, the false gravity vanished and all things became weightless, so once Casey launched, only air resistance served to slow her down. Her landing at Ashavid's cruciform temple was undignified at best. Rather than risk vertigo from staring back—up, rather—to the place she'd just launched from, Casey headed inside the structure.

It was a grim place, gray metal that gleamed wetly with wrighted light. The central chamber housing Ashavid's artifact was a straight shot down a corridor, and Casey hadn't even cleared the chamber's threshold when she realized that her hopes had been in vain.

Victus was already here.

She almost left, but he'd spotted her. *It's all right. He's a competitor, not a predator.* Reasoning was useless, however. The man had frightened her ever since she'd been assigned to his precinct. *You're an officer of the polistraat,* she told herself. *Act like it!* But the only thing she normally policed was a clerk's desk.

"Pontus!" Victus said, smiling toothily. "You're early. Our confrontation is still some way off. Some little way."

"I didn't mean to disturb you," Casey said automatically.

"Of course not," Victus said. "You've never meant to disturb anyone. That's probably why I find you so *fascinating.* You're just here to do as you're told, like a good little girl." He drew closer, emphasizing his size advantage. "Well," he said, gesturing at the glass-encased pedestal in the room's center as though he wasn't blocking the path. "By all means."

Slowly, trying to edge around him without touching him, Casey moved as he bid. The moment she broke eye contact, he lunged. She felt a spike of animal panic as his grip closed around her throat, and she was driven painfully back against the cold, unyielding chamber wall.

"I want you to know," he said, his Blazing silver eyes on hers, "that the only reason I don't kill you right here is that it's too early. I haven't finished Second Rite, and we mustn't skip to Last Rite just yet. But I promise you it will be me."

He's just trying to scare you, Casey told herself. *If he wanted to kill you, you wouldn't be able to breathe right now.* But another part of her stoked her panic, wondering how killing entered into this at all.

"Wh-why?" she asked plaintively. "Last Rite is 'demonstrate the force of your belief,' and I—" She cut off at his startling, wheezing laughter.

"By all the gods, Pontus, are you really that naïve? I can't believe my plan worked this well. You being here instead of Balerus, can you imagine it? If that isn't proof that I'm to be Ashavid's chosen, I don't know what is. You needn't worry right away. It'll have to be Roscio before you. She represents an actual threat."

Abruptly he released her, his laughter redoubling. Casey almost bolted, but remembering just in time, she darted first to the pedestal, encased in unbreakable nifeglass, which supported Ashavid's mask. There Casey knelt and uttered the prayer she'd been taught as a child.

"Belief brightens as bones burn." It would have to do for First Rite. Prayers to the gods had to be quick when the Pit was always watching for illicit worship, ready to administer the Godbane to the devout. She'd watched the Godbane used against her mother, and neither had ever been the same. As Casey rose and made for the door, her relief felt like a powerful rush inside her as if it came from somewhere else entirely.

"I'm glad you're so stupid, Pontus," Victus called into her retreat. "You might actually get to enjoy your last few days alive."

Whatever else he said was lost as Casey broke into a run.

✦

Major Gnaeus will help me, Casey decided during the harrowing flight back to the barracks. He was in charge of this operation. He could order Casey home, substitute in one of the others, or curb Victus's impulses. Victus had all but admitted being responsible for the formidable Captain Balerus being sick and Casey being substituted in, though she wasn't even an alternate.

Major Gnaeus had taken over the office of the deposed head of Pit Operations, removed on some pretext severe enough to allow Blazing polistraat into the Pit. Despite its stature, the commandeered office was a cramped space, and the major's legendary self-regard seemed to press at its edges. But Casey had handled people like him before. Her own self-effacement served to soothe their inflamed egos.

"Officer Pontus," Gnaeus said. "To what do I owe this interruption?"

Casey swallowed. "I'm terribly sorry to bother you, Major. But I think there's been some mistake. I shouldn't be here. I'm the only one with a rank lower than sergeant. I've barely been polistraat a year, and just now, Victus—"

But the major was already irritably waving her to silence. "You are a polistraat officer and a practicing believer in Ashavid." Casey restrained herself from flinching. "Those are the only qualifications required." His Blazing, sapphire eyes flashed at the affront of her insinuations.

But I'm not practicing! Casey wanted to shout these words, but doing so here would be a surer path to death than taking her chances with Victus. *This is all a huge misunderstanding. I'm a lapsed follower!*

It had been so easy to go along with her parents' worship as a child, feeling safe and protected, letting them think for her. But then Casey had seen her mother writhing on the ground in agony, unable to help, victim of the punishment that eventually found all worshipers. And Casey, as it turned out, was not brave. That sense of being a coward had shamed her. But it just meant she couldn't trust her own feelings.

What Gnaeus would hear if she tried to explain this would be different. *I'm not actually part of your conspiracy. I might spill my guts to save myself at any moment.* She prickled with sweat. If she admitted her apostasy, she might not leave this *office* alive, much less the Pit.

"More importantly," Gnaeus said, oblivious to her suffering. "I'm not part of your god's clergy." He pointed to his Blazing blue eyes to indicate that, yes, they were the wrong color for worship of Ashavid. His ancestors had followed a different god. "The rest of your silver-eyed fellows would not appreciate my interfering in their decision to elevate you. If you didn't think you could handle this, you shouldn't have applied. You were told the risks—"

"Apply?" Casey said, exasperated. "I didn't apply. I was *told* to join this. I didn't even know what this mission entailed until just before leaving. And then I still didn't *really* know until Victus told me an hour ago!"

"Control yourself, Officer Pontus," Gnaeus said, but he looked shocked. "You truly didn't know what this was, that the acolyte that goes on to become their god's avatar will be the last surviving acolyte of their group?" He did not wait for an answer. "That changes things. What idiot would be so reckless as to..." He trailed off.

"Very well. I will reach out to your clergy." The words sounded dragged from him by hooks, but he said them. "Explain the situation. Having you here, unwitting and unwilling, is a risk to the entire operation. There should be time. First Rite will be done by day's end, but even those eager enough to finish Second Rite won't dare begin Last Rite until I give the order." And for once, his harsh confidence comforted Casey.

"Thank you, sir," she said.

"Go and get some rest," he said, his voice kindly for the first time Casey could remember. "We'll sort this out."

She felt better the rest of that day and, despite the unfamiliar bed, slept soundly. She'd scarcely left the barracks the next morning, though, when she learned that one of their own had been murdered in the night.

The omnipresent warmth in the Pit's air was suddenly chill with menace as a lockdown and curfew were instated. As bad as the tenor had been upon their arrival, it was ten times worse when the apprentices were glaring at the officers and the officers glared right back.

Despite Gnaeus's suspicions, Casey doubted any of the smiths were to blame. There were always too few of the gods' jailers for all the forging and repair work needed to maintain the prison, not to mention monitoring for illegal worship on the surface above. The smiths' apprentices, meanwhile, were just teenagers. Now that she knew the truth of this ritual, surely the simpler explanation was an overeager officer. Casey had half-expected the victim to be Roscio, given Victus's unseemly eagerness. But it was one of the gold Blazings, those followers of Blessbite, who had met his untimely end. With nothing to gain from killing outside his clade, Casey doubted that Victus had been the perpetrator.

Yet her fragile inner peace was shattered. As Gnaeus conferred angrily with another member of the gold contingent, Casey wondered how long until she could safely approach the major for an update on her situation. She noticed Victus staring at her then. While the rest of the officers were fixated on the unfolding scene of the apprentices and the covered body, Victus had eyes only for Casey Pontus. His smile was lupine.

When Gnaeus barked a dismissal with an order to meet an hour hence, Casey shook free of that stare and hurried away. Footsteps came up behind her too fast to avoid, and the whisper in her ear was rancid.

"Second Rite," Victus whispered. "'Demonstrate that your faith is to your god alone.' What better way to swear off any other god than to kill one of their disciples?"

Casey's breath caught.

"I mean, that fellow might have been Blessbite's favorite son," Victus went on with a little giggle. "I might have robbed a rival god of his chosen avatar. I can't believe I'm the first to think of it."

"They shouldn't be rivals," Casey hissed back without thought. "It's not Ashavid's way." She blinked in surprise at herself. The flash of outrage on her god's behalf, an outrage she had not thought she still possessed, had momentarily blotted out the fear. "I'm going to tell Gnaeus what you've done."

"Try," Victus said, unperturbed. "I'd be happy to kill you before Roscio. The prospect really does excite me. I mean, this fellow was just someone I decided had to die, and even still, the feel of his blood on my fingers..."

He gave a rapturous little shudder, and Casey fought the urge to be sick.

"I just thought you might appreciate a few more days," Victus said after he'd recovered himself. He shrugged. "I'm not really sure how long Roscio will take me. But I'll see you soon."

When he kissed her cheek, she thought the skin of her face might peel away as he withdrew.

Casey couldn't concentrate at all during the meeting, the collected officers crammed into a storage room to avoid prying ears. She'd made sure to keep as far away from Victus as possible, a difficult feat in the cramped space.

Against the rising drone of Gnaeus delivering new orders and threats, she scanned the room for Roscio. Allying with the woman, as distasteful as the thought was, might be her only fallback plan.

Gnaeus promised to get me out.

Casey didn't see Roscio anywhere, which did nothing to calm her still-pounding heart. *Was Victus just playing with me? Is she already dead?* Or maybe she'd taken Casey's place with Gnaeus and gone home. *Stop it.*

Riling Gnaeus was unwise, but Casey cornered him immediately after the meeting.

"No," he said.

"But—" she began, but he cut her off.

"Things have changed. I need all officers here and active, controlling the situation. And as mediocre an officer as I perceive you to be, at least you won't try to make things worse. The matter is closed. Don't ask me again, or your fellow silvers will be the least of your worries." Then he pushed past her and was gone.

Roscio, then. No other option. Steeling herself, Casey set about searching. She searched, and she searched. For days, she searched entirely in vain. All the while, more polistraat turned up dead.

Hands gripping Casey's shoulders shook her roughly awake. Her eyes shot open upon the haggard face of Pellenea Roscio stooped over Casey's bed. It was so like the morning she was informed of her "selection" that Casey wondered if she was reliving the past.

"If you want a chance to stop Victus from killing us both," Roscio said, "get up now, and follow me."

Barely giving Casey enough time to dress, Roscio led her from her commandeered quarters in the barracks and to a familiar launch platform at the edge of the complex.

"We're going to Ashavid's temple?" Casey asked dubiously as they positioned themselves to launch.

"Where's the one place Victus wouldn't think to look for us?" Roscio responded by way of explanation, sounding like she was explaining to a child.

"What's the plan, then, Sergeant?" Casey asked, hoping her use of rank would placate the woman. Roscio hated her, and coming to her for help would be a blow to the sergeant's pride.

"Launch first," Roscio said. "Talk later."

The flight between platforms gave Casey too much time to think. Thinking meant anxiety, so she focused on studying Roscio surreptitiously instead. The sergeant looked haunted, as though she hadn't slept in a week. Which, based on how long she'd been missing, might not be so far off.

"Why are you looking at me?" Roscio demanded.

"I've been looking *for* you for days," Casey said.

"I had no desire to be found with Victus finally unconstrained.

I'd hoped he'd never be selected for this. Don't forget I've worked with him for years. I knew what would happen the moment that rabid dog slipped his leash. I had a run-in with him the night of the first death, but I managed to get away mostly unscathed. I've been hiding out since. No offense, but I knew he would come after me first."

Casey managed a decent landing at the temple and followed Roscio, whose head swiveled in every direction but into the temple itself. Why the other woman felt so safe in the temple, Casey very much wanted to know.

"There's something inside I have to show you," Roscio said as they navigated a turn in the corridor. Casey frowned, remembering no such turn on her first trip to this place. Perhaps they'd come in through another entrance. The temple had four arrayed in its cruciform shape, but Casey could have sworn it was symmetrical.

Another turn, and the central chamber came into view. Casey could see the pedestal with its eerily moving mask encased in nifeglass at the chamber's center. Roscio gestured her through the archway first.

Then she gripped Casey's right forearm from behind and twisted, forcing Casey to double over or have her arm popped from its socket.

"Me," came the voice of Victus from ahead as he entered from another doorway. "She wanted to show you me."

※

If Casey expected an apology from her sergeant, none was forthcoming. On the contrary, in short order Roscio attached binder wrightings to Casey's wrists, cinching them tight behind her back.

"You lied to me," Casey said, more numb than angry.

"You should have known better," Roscio said. "When have I ever given you the impression that I cared whether you lived or died?" She forced Casey to her knees then, apparently satisfied, moved off to stand with her co-conspirator, who beheld his new prize with a gloating smile. He cradled something, an odd wrighting, in both hands, holding it as lovingly as a normal person might an infant.

"Nicely done, Pellenea," he said, eyes burning. "You've earned your reprieve."

"You know he'll just kill you too," Casey said leadenly. "He could kill us both whenever. He's just playing with us."

"I'd rather be killed last," Roscio said, shrugging. "And I was tired of being held captive here." She massaged her wrists with her hands, and Casey saw marks there, evidence that Roscio had been the last person to wear these binders. Then her movement changed. Roscio's hand become a blur, streaking toward Victus's throat and flashing in the cold light of the wrighted sconces.

Then came a clatter of metal, and Roscio doubled over with a surprised grunt. It happened so fast it took Casey several moments to process what she'd seen. Victus had dropped his strange wrighting. He now held Roscio's wrist, the one that had thrust the hidden knife toward him, caught in an iron grip. Her hand was empty now, and Victus's grip was the only thing holding her up. Roscio's own knife lay buried in her belly, twisted from her grip and driven there by Victus's free hand.

"And there you go and waste your reprieve," Victus said, but he didn't sound disappointed. "I see Pontus wasn't the only thing you picked up at the barracks."

Casey rose on unsteady legs and rushed for the wrighting he'd dropped, some sort of ceremonial dagger with a pyramidal, stabbing blade. Any weapon would be better than none. Victus pulled his gaze reluctantly from Roscio's messy, prolonged death and timed his kick to take Casey under the ribs just as she tried to fall on the dagger-thing, sending her sprawling, landing painfully on her bound hands, gasping around an explosion of pain.

Casually recovering the strange dagger, Victus approached. "Always in such a rush to reach your end. I predicted it from your very first day in the precinct. 'She'll end young and badly,' I said. You can ask Pellenea—well, you could have. But here's a secret. I always knew I'd be the one to kill you. You were just too innocent to live."

He hefted the strange dagger above Casey's heart, pinned her shoulder with his free hand. With her own hands bound, she had no leverage to roll.

"It's your honor as my final rival to get *very* acquainted with this dagger. It's how we break the so-called unbreakable nifeglass, you see. This is the Last Rite. Soon my god and I will be one." He leered. "Then I will kill every single person in the Pit. Our people. Theirs. The only god that will be free will be *my* god. And once I put on the mask, I will be that god."

"That's not her way!" Casey shouted, surprising herself. Even a lapsed worshiper of Ashavid knew as much. "The other gods loved strife and conflict, but not her. She's a peacemaker. She would never want you to kill everyone!"

As she spoke the words, Casey felt something, that heady rush from elsewhere, the same as she'd felt after First Rite. This time she recognized it for what it was. *Demonstrate that your faith is to your god alone. The Second Rite.*

"Once she and I are one," Victus said, "she'll do whatever I tell her to do." He raised the dagger high. "Goodbye, Pontus."

The binders around Casey's wrists sprang open.

She whipped her hands around to catch Victus's wrist as it descended. Catching him off-guard, Casey managed to throw him aside and rise to her feet. Adrenaline sang in her veins. The blood pounding in her ears formed staccato words.

Run. Run. Run.

Casey obeyed. She had no plan beyond getting back to the barracks to get help. She took the first turn at speed, then the other, preparing to break into a full sprint toward the exit.

Instead, she was faced with yet another turn.

She paused just long enough to hear Victus's pounding footsteps behind her. Casey made that turn, then the next.

And the next.

It's different. It changed. It was no longer a corridor, but a maze. Casey came upon a fork of three options. She went left, then left again at the next fork. Twelve more forks she took, covering more distance than was possible for the interior of the temple. The pounding blood in her head urged her onward.

After what must have been an hour, she reached an exit, but

instead of opening onto the launch platform, she emerged into the central chamber.

Aside from Roscio's dead body, which Casey tried not to look at, she was alone. She felt desolate. To go back into the maze was risking Victus would find her before she found a way out. She glanced at the other three doorways, but saw only walls and turns, no straight shots to the outside.

Wait.

Casey heard the word in her own exhalation, but it was not hers. Casting a furtive half-glance at the mask, she waited. Her blood subsided as she stood there, listening. She'd begun hoping he'd left when Victus emerged. Casey froze, tensing and ready to run for one of the other exits, but hesitated at his behavior.

His eyes darted about as he swiveled his head left and right. She was ten paces away, and he didn't acknowledge her existence in any way.

"How can this be?" he muttered to himself. "The hallway was straight. Straight! She'll be back with help soon. I've got to get out of here!" All his icy self-control gone, Victus looked like the animal he was. He lurched to a stop, turning sharply on his heel and heading to his right.

He still sees a maze, Casey realized, wondering if that had been true for her as well. Had either of them really left the central chamber?

Now. That voice again, formed of her exhalation.

Casey almost responded aloud, but feared it would break the illusion trapping Victus.

Now?

The Last Rite, said the scuffs of Victus's boots upon the metal floor.

I... I can't.

The sensation Casey felt then was too complex for halting words to convey. One of them had to perform the Last Rite, and Ashavid would prefer it be Casey.

"He's a monster," she whispered to herself. "He means to kill them all. And... and my god wills it."

She approached Victus, who still couldn't see her, with trembling purpose.

The nifeglass surrounding the mask turned matte gray in an expanding circle as the strange, sacrificial dagger wrighting did its work from where it lay buried in Victus's heart. The center of that slate-gray circle upon the glass had already crumbled to dust, and the crumbling ring was expanding outward.

Ashavid's mask, metal like everything else here, shone with prismatic color, like light upon an oil slick. The face was featureless aside from eyeholes. A cowl surrounded it, and it whipped in an imaginary wind like a corona.

The way was open, yet Casey still hesitated.

"Hurry." Victus muttered this word, but he was nearly gone. It was not *his* word. It carried a resonance no human voice ever could.

"Why me?" Casey asked. "I wasn't even supposed to be here. That was his doing."

"Are you so certain of that?"

"But I stopped worshipping you."

"Yet here you are. Lapses can be forgiven."

"Because I remembered a basic fact about you?"

"Because you will serve me well in the struggle to come." The otherworldly voice grew stronger. "You, who carries no false pride. You, who will sacrifice for the comfort of others. It is through you that I will weld the gods together and avoid the mistakes of the past as we remake this world."

Tired of worry, of imagining the worst, Casey's will gave out. She reached in and grasped the mask. As her fingers closed about it, the world fell away. She stood upon a promontory of rock above a vast abyss. There was a presence behind her, one she dared not behold.

"You were correct, child, that I am not like the others." Ashavid's voice rang like bells in this non-place. "They crush life and soul both from their avatars, leave them nothing but a shell, the better to allow more of the god into them. I will not do such."

127

Casey felt her worries drop away. A rush of relief and gratitude welled up in her. All her life she had not trusted her own judgment, and here was the final proof of why. She had not believed she should be here, and she had, once again, been wrong.

Then her god spoke again.

"You have shown me your true self today, but once-forgotten truths can be forgotten again. Lapses can be forgiven, but they must not be forgotten. Thus, your life will be spared, but your soul will not. This is my judgment. I cannot brook a willful avatar. Perhaps fate shall see you in command of your body once again, after my true freedom is achieved, but it will not be the you that I speak to now. For this, I am sorry."

There was no time to respond. The shove was feather-light, yet Casey possessed no weight in this place. She went hurtling from the promontory's tip, falling into endless black. Looking back on her short life, she struggled to form a final thought before the oblivion below could claim her. Final meaning, understanding, eluded her, but mercifully, she was no longer aware of this failure.

Meanwhile, wearing Cassia Pontus's body like a glove, the god Ashavid rose and placed the mask upon her head.

Meet Gregory D. Little

Gregory D. Little is the author of the *Unwilling Souls* epic fantasy series (the same series "Last Rite of the God Heist" takes place in) and the forthcoming science fiction novel *The Last Humans*, arriving in 2022 from Cursed Dragon Ship Publishing. His short fiction can be found in the *A Game of Horns*, *Dragon Writers*, *Undercurrents*, and *Eclectically Scientific* anthologies as well as *The Colored Lens* ezine. When not writing or reading, he's usually playing video games while thinking about writing or traveling while thinking about writing.

Everything Poops

KEVIN DAVID ANDERSON

The floorboards creaked just enough to roust Casandra. She could see the closet door reflected in her full-length mirror. Although closed when she went to bed, it was now open. She tried to stay still as the sound of suction cups gripping the floor echoed in the tiny bedroom, and she knew it was dragging itself toward her. Then it became quiet for several moments. She felt its presence at the side of her bed. Even in the dark, it was like a shadow moving over her. When the air turned cold, she knew after weeks of work and spell research, the closet monster had finally left its interdimensional confines and made its way to her bed.

Casandra grinned. Her summoning incantation had worked perfectly. She rolled over, sat up abruptly, gazed into its many eyes and said, "Are you planning on eating me?"

The closet monster stared down with at least three sets of yellow pupils, set very close together. "Well, yeah. That's the general idea," it said through a massive slit of a mouth. "You must've known that when you summoned—"

"Then what?"

The monster tilted what can only be described as a head. "What do you mean, then what?"

"I mean," Casandra said, "after I'm eaten, what happens to me. You know, biologically?"

"Well, I..." A tentacle reached across possibly a chin. "Not sure."

"It's a real curiosity of mine. I've watched you move about in my closet from time to time." She reached over and turned on the lamp on her nightstand.

The closet monster recoiled from the light; tentacles covered its many eyes as it slid back toward the closet.

"No, please, don't go. I've waited so long to meet you."

"Why?" The monster stopped and lowered a tentacle.

"It's my inquisitive nature," she said. "I want to know more about you. Call it scientific curiosity."

"You summoned me from my closet for scientific curiosity?" The monster moved back close to the bed. "I don't know. This doesn't feel right."

"Can you just tell me? Do you defecate?"

The monster laid a tentacle on the pillow. "Do I what?"

"Defecate," Casandra repeated. "You know, evacuate waste."

"I'm not following."

"Poop. Do you poop?"

"Oh. Uhm...well, no."

"You must," Casandra countered. "Everybody poops. It's basic biology. Even for an interdimensional being. Let me show you."

"I really think I should get on with it and just eat you."

"Yes, yes," Casandra said, reaching under her pillow and pulling out a stack of books. "We'll definitely get to that, but take a look at this." Casandra waved him closer.

A thick row of pustule welts that served as eyebrows composed a frown.

Casandra scooched over and patted the space next to her.

The closet monster shrugged what might have been a shoulder, then hopped up on the bed.

The bed frame creaked under the stress as Casandra flipped through the books. "Freud, Nietzsche, Carl Jung, Gray's Anatomy, ah here it is." She moved a picture book to the top of the pile. "See. I read this when I was four, but it still applies." She held the book out to the monster.

"*Everybody Poops* by Tarō Gomi," the monster read.

Casandra flipped through the pages. "It attests most emphatically that every living animal poops. I researched the subject thoroughly, and except for Demodex mites, microscopic animals distantly related to spiders, which only live two weeks, everything poops." Casandra met the monster's gaze. "You do live longer than two weeks, correct?"

"Oh, yes, much longer." The monster sort of smiled. "I like the pictures."

"I thought you might," Casandra said. "If the hypothesis in this child's book is correct and you live longer than a Demodex mite, you must poop."

"Well, I don't. At least I don't think I do."

She looked him up and down. "Besides your mouth, which is very frightening by the way."

"Thanks."

"Do you have any other orifices?"

"What?'

"Orifices, openings in your body."

The closet monster held up a tentacle displaying its tip. "Does this count." The end of the tentacle split open like a Venus flytrap, needle-like teeth extending outward.

"Hmm," Casandra leaned close. "It's very interesting, but I surmise it is designed to acquire material not expel it." She sat back. "Curious."

"Well, this has been interesting," the monster said. "But I'm not really supposed to engage, just eat. If you don't mind—"

"So, we must be talking about total absorption," Casandra said, her voice raised. "I mean, a complete and utter consuming of all biological material, which is then used to..."

"To what?" The monster sounded generally curious.

"Well, I mean that is the question, isn't it?" She turned to him. "Do you, I'm sorry I don't know your name."

"Todd."

"I'm Casandra, pleased to meet you. Do you get any bigger after you eat?"

"Not really. I've always been this size."

"Do you feel particularly energized after you eat someone?

The closet monster seemed to consider that for a moment. It put two tentacles behind its head and leaned back on the headboard. "No ... no, I don't. In fact, I'm a bit lethargic afterward."

Casandra leaned back. "So, it doesn't appear that you need to eat children to support your body, perhaps to feed your mind."

"My mind?"

Casandra considered for a moment. "When you absorb a child do you feel their emotions."

"Uh, well, yes. There is lots of screaming and trying to get away, so I assume fear, terror, horror, that kind of thing."

"Beyond surface emotions, do you absorb their emotional thoughts, their sense of being, wonder?"

"Are you talking about memories?"

"Perhaps, yes. Do you acquire their memories?"

"I sometimes dream that I'm learning to ride a bike or play a video game. Once I walked on a beach with my parents, when our dog ran into the water ... no wait." The monster looked down. "Never been to a beach. Not really. So maybe, yeah."

Casandra sensed it felt unease, maybe even shame. "I wonder, does it ever become too much for you? The absorbing, the constant emotional intake, I mean."

"Whatcha mean, too much? Like eating twins or something? Because I've eaten triplets once—"

"No, no, I mean absorbing the feelings, the thoughts, the dreams," Casandra said. "How can you ever be sure that what you're dreaming is your dream or just something you ate?"

"I don't really ... "

"I mean seriously, what about you?"

"Me?"

"What does Todd dream of?"

Half of the creature's many eyes seemed contemplative. He held up three tentacles pensively. "What do I dream about?"

Casandra seized the handle hidden underneath the stack of books.

"I never gave it any thought really. I just do what I do."

She pulled the knife from its sheath and plunged the seven-inch blade deep into the top row of the monster's eyes. Casandra sliced downward, laying the closet monster's head open. It fell from the bed, tentacles knocking the lamp off the nightstand.

The closet monster spasmed on the floorboard it had recently traversed, creating loud thumps only slightly muffled by a throw rug. After ten seconds, the thing lay still.

The bedroom door flew open.

"Cassey!" her dad said and turned on the main light. He stepped inside, making a beeline to the bed but stopped suddenly just short of the bleeding two-hundred-pound closet monster carcass.

"Are you alright?" he said.

Casandra, on all fours, grinned. "You were right, Dad. They are stupid."

"I thought we agreed that you'd practice the incantation with us before you tried it on your own. It can be tricky to get it just right."

"Dad, you're such a worrywart. I can handle it. See." She pointed to the large ex-closet monster.

Her dad smiled. "Did you remember to slice downward?"

Casandra sat back. "I did."

"I'm so proud of you, honey. I can't wait to tell your mom." He beamed at her with pride, then turned back to the door. "I'll go get the cleanup kit." He paused at the door. "Are you sure you did it correctly? I mean you got the cadence right. If it's off just a little, it might leave the door open—"

"Dad, I got this. You and Mom taught me well."

"Okay. So proud," he said, then disappeared into the hall.

Casandra gazed down at her first kill. She wanted to grab her smartphone and take some pics, maybe even a selfie with her first slaying. But that was against the code. She still had a lot to learn, but the monster-slaying code wasn't one of them.

What was that he said about cadence? How could that affect any—

The bed vibrated slightly. She sat still, wondering if it had been her imagination. Then after a beat, she peered over at the monster corpse. Perhaps it wasn't all the way dead. She gazed down. No movement. The vibration came again, and Casandra distinctly felt it emanating from the other side of the bed. She rolled over and peered off the edge.

A pair of tentacles, thin and dark shot up from underneath the bed. One wrapped around Casandra's wrist, the other her neck. A gelatinous form slid out from under the bed frame. One bowling ball-sized eye, yellow and bloodshot, glared up at her.

Casandra struggled to speak. "Who are you?"

A horrific slit of blood-colored lips parted. "I'm the monster that lives under your bed." Its eye narrowed. "My good friend Todd got summoned. He's never been summoned before so he asked me to check up on him." The creature pulled Casandra's face closer. "Now tell me, what happened to my friend?"

Fighting against the tentacle constricting her throat, Cassandra managed to whimper, "Oh, poop."

Meet Kevin David Anderson

Kevin David Anderson's debut novel is the cult zombie-romp, *Night of the Living Trekkies* and his latest book is the horror-comedy *Midnight Men: The Supernatural Adventures of Earl and Dale*. *Night of the Living Trekkies* was required reading in college courses, most notably the class designed for incoming freshmen, *How to Survive Your Freshman Year by Studying the Zombie Apocalypse*, at Mansfield University in Pennsylvania. Anderson's fiction has appeared more than a hundred times in different publications from anthologies, magazines, podcasts, radio dramas, and award-worthy publications like the British Fantasy Award-winning *Murky Depths*, and the Bram Stoker nominated anthology *The Beauty of Death*. Anderson's stories have been turned into audio productions on Parsec Award-winning podcasts like Pseudopod, Drabblecast, and on the popular No Sleep and Horror Hill Podcasts. When not writing horror-comedy, Anderson spends time at the beach with his family, attends horror conventions and book festivals, and writes and tells bad, corny, nerdy jokes. Dad jokes with a geeky twist are his specialty, and under the pen name Giggles A. Lott and Nee Slapper, he has published such works as *JURASSIC JOKES: A Joke Book 65 Million Years in the Making* and *STAR WARS: The Jokes Awaken*. www.KevinDavid-Anderson.com

The Hidden Language of Flowers

LAUREL BECKLEY

I sn't that *pretty*?"

Edith turned, glowering at both the youth and the bouquet shoved against her register, a step away from the trash bin. Her green-stained hands continued working her pestle, churning rosemary, thyme, pink rose petals, cilantro, and a single droplet of belladonna with half a dash of water into a slushy, chunky goo.

"It doesn't look like one of yours, though," Katherine continued, oblivious to Edith's irritation. "Too...spiky? But so elegant. Very haute couture." She beamed at her pronunciation, face illuminating with a new realization. "Why, Miss Edith, do you have a *beau*?"

Edith's lips pinched together as she strained the solution through a stained square of cheese cloth. Liquid dripped sullenly into a glass bottle. One drop. Two drops. Three. All the way to seven. There. That would do. She twisted the cap on and placed it on the counter between them, eyebrow raised.

"Do you want your tincture or not?" There would be no speculation on her private life in her shop, not now, not ever.

The girl colored and slid two crumpled dollars across the counter, parting with a week's pay slinging ice cream at Dutch Girl's for three months of assurance against pregnancy. Edith handed over the bottle with the instructions to consume a drop with her morning drink every day of the week of the coming waning moon.

Edith sighed as the youth left, shop door tinkling behind her. A cold, deep fury burned within Edith's chest as she took in the bouquet for the thousandth time that afternoon.

Rosemary sprigs showed *she* remembered. Accents of purple fountain grass spiked at random intervals, indicating this was the initial salvo. Purple columbine, out of season, displayed double resolution in this fight. And a purple focal point of autumn crocus signified nothing more than a spark of memory. When Edith tentatively touched one of the violet petals, she had been transported to a hazy farewell in a field of flowers that ended in a kiss and continued into decades-lasting silence and heartbreak.

Do you have a beau, Miss Edith?

The innocent question echoed throughout the half-empty shelves lining Bisbee's flower shop. It ricocheted across the remnants of the V-J victory bouquets—still fresh thanks to a little magic and water—and bounced into the near-empty register. It seemed to hover over the bouquet, directing Edith's attention and ire. Delicate petals wilted from the force of her glare, revealing the note—plain, cream paper fresh from Seattle and neatly folded in half—tucked between two sprigs of rosemary.

Two words were scrawled in precise cursive, hidden until seen by the intended recipient.

I'm back.

There was no accompanying signature save the lingering tingles of the reveal charm.

Alice LaVelle née Dolores Hartley remembered the last Friday of August.

Edith's fists clenched.

It wasn't enough for *her* to return to Cottage Grove after all these years of *nothing*, with a new name, a rich dead husband, fancy city manners, and big ideas. It wasn't enough for her to set up a rival flower shop practically overnight across the street from Edith's family-run store, in a town still recovering from the after-effects of the Depression and four long years of war rations and belt-tightening. It wasn't enough to peddle fantastical mutations of plants from Hawaii and New York City, to bring a sense of much-needed glamour and sophistication and freedom.

No. Dolores-turned-Alice opened her store on the last Friday of August, sent her assistant to Bisbee's armed with a loaded floral arrangement, and declared war.

Edith shoved the bouquet—purple vase and all—into the trash bin and locked the register. She didn't bother counting the till. Katherine's purchase had been the only one over the past week. The work day was effectively over, with all potential shoppers saving their money and attention for the new florist in town instead of Bisbee's. No one wanted the same flowers they'd seen throughout the war. Adding insult to injury, Edith had overheard a rumor at the grocer's that Mrs. LaVelle sold tinctures even more potent than hers.

The comment bit deeply.

Her *solutions* had resolved a lot of potential problems over the years. She was the best earth witch in Lane County, better even than her grandmother. Despite her rough manners and sharp tongue, she was discreet. She kept their secrets and only asked for discretion in return.

And how it was repaid.

The sky was overcast as she walked to her car, grey clouds hiding the brilliant blue of summer that was the Willamette Valley's greatest secret. She fumbled with her keys as the sky opened up, the first sprinkles hitting the top of her head and dampening her curls. Curse her for forgetting her hat today of all days.

It *always* rained the last Friday of August in Cottage Grove.

Had ever since *that* last Friday, over twenty years ago. Damn reporter from the *Oregonian* had been in town just yesterday to write a piece on the meteorological phenomena.

"Edith?"

Edith's shoulders tensed. She knew that voice anywhere. The heel of Edith's sensible T-strap sandals crunched along the sidewalk as she turned to face her enemy.

Alice LaVelle stood just outside The Flower Shoppe, hanging on the door like a circus monkey. "It *is* you! Did you get my bouquet? Oh, it has been *ages*."

It *hurt* looking at her, the bone-deep ache of a half-healed wound scraped anew. A white apron covered her linen purple suit dress and an amethyst ring sparkled on a silver chain about her neck. An autumn crocus and rosemary arrangement was shoved artfully into her lapel, mimicking that spiteful bouquet. She wore a ridiculous purple curvette and black half-veil that hit mid-cheekbone, revealing perfectly applied red lipstick.

The juxtaposition between Seattle high-fashion and Edith's faded floral rayon dress and limp hair was stark. The Flower Shoppe's fresh coat of mint green paint was a stark contrast to Bisbee's faded brick façade—it represented the new versus the old, the triumphant reinvention against the worn-out workhorse.

Edith's teeth ground. "I got it."

"And?" Alice's eyes glinted through the veil.

"Message received." Edith opened the door to her car and threw herself inside. Her knuckles whitened as she flung the car into a wide turn, nearly t-boning Mr. Jefferson as he pulled out from the hardware store.

She didn't release her death grip on the wheel until she was well on the way to Hebron. Her tension eased further when she passed the last house of the tiny town and entered the tree line and the wards surrounding her house. Her driveway was empty, the dry packed dust growing dark brown speckles as the rain picked up, as if the cloud was her own personal rainstorm.

Her latest visitors had left that morning, scurrying into their car at the first light of dawn on their migration south to Los Angeles and a new beginning. They always arrived late in the night, bodies tensed and scared and aching with exhaustion. She gave them discretion and a safe harbor in a country filled with sundown laws and hatred, knowing it wasn't enough. It was never enough.

Edith leaned her head against the steering wheel, trying to find some sense of equilibrium, not wanting to bring her foul mood into her home. The engine of her Studebaker ticked in time to the rain pattering against the metal roof of the car. The rain turned from drizzle to downpour, droplets tinking harder, and the tan driveway transformed into mud.

It was time to go inside.

Edith scrounged about the passenger side for an old newspaper to cover her head as she scrambled the several steps across the dirt driveway and onto her porch.

There was a new letter shoved into the doorjamb; the paper crinkled as though it knew it was not welcome. She took a deep breath. The eviction notices were a minor insult twirling within the greater swarm of anger in her chest.

The letter fluttered to the ground as she opened the door, joining a sad pile of wrinkled notices, all stamped with officious seals ranging from the Army Corps of Engineers to Lane County Government to the mayor of Cottage Grove. She would deal with *that* mess later.

Another deep breath and she was through the tiny house, kicking off her shoes as she entered her true domain—her garden.

Tension melted, but resolve remained, along with bittersweet memories of two girls kissing on a field of purple flowers. A secret promise transformed into permanent silence and rejection.

Until now.

So Dolores-turned-Alice wanted a war, did she?

Edith's lips curved as she gathered her supplies, half-chuckling under her breath. Never enter a flower war with an earth witch, especially not when pride was on the line.

She'd send her own declaration of war.

There was only room for one witch in town, and that witch was *her*.

✦

Alice sent her reply a month later, on September twenty-third.

The blue box sat at Bisbee's front step, and Edith would have stepped on it save she'd been watching her storefront for hexes for the past month. The box was decorated with purple and pink ribbons. Inside, wrapped in pink tissue paper, lay a corsage.

Edith retrieved her faded copy of *Interpreting Flowers* from its hiding place under the loose floorboard below the front counter.

Pink carnations. *I'll never forget.* Clearly, Alice remembered Edith's boldness so many years ago and wasn't going to let her forget it either.

A lavender rose. *Capriciousness.* There was no need to interpret that one. Pulsing intent roiled off that magically imbued flower, so thick Edith practically tasted it.

Blue hibiscus, grown out of season. *I agree.* Alice had accepted Edith's challenge and would go to extremes to win.

The message was all twisted into a corsage to wear the curse at the wrist and sent on a Sunday for extra insult.

Edith returned fire October eighth with a boutonniere hex of orange and yellow carnations for disdain, garnished with reversed red chrysanthemums for hatred, the stems wrapped with aloe to showcase her deep bitterness of Alice's long-past silent rejection. Pink ribbons dangled in pretty twists, because Edith might be engaged in a battle for the fate of her business and her life, but she wasn't a monster.

On October eleventh, Alice stepped out into a town hall meeting discussing the upcoming Christmas Bazaar wearing Edith's boutonniere on her lapel and bright red lipstick underneath her black veil. Subtly embroidered flowers matching the colors of the boutonniere lined the brim of her black pillbox. Her amethyst ring was nowhere in sight.

"Where'd you get those gorgeous flowers, Mrs. LaVelle?" was the question of the night, asked over and over as Alice smugly patted the flowers on her chest and invited everyone to a soiree at the Cottage Grove Hotel after the meeting. She'd arranged a private room, no doubt to further bind the gullible townspeople into doing whatever it was she had planned. Already the tendrils of a spell stretched and wove about them. A thin green vine reached toward Edith, and she slapped it away, garnering looks and whispers as the people she'd supported murmured over *poor, strange Edith.*

"Oh, just somewhere." Alice's gaze flicked to Edith as she continued to stroke those damn flowers like she had *won* something.

And she had—she'd effectively stolen all business away from Bisbee's with her hocus pocus and scientifically mutated flowers and fancy citified self. She wore Edith's hex like it was a victory banner.

Edith could no longer take the insult lying down. "This town is not big enough for two florists, Dolores." Her voice echoed across the room, rebounding and bounding.

The mayor stopped preening over Alice's boutonniere. "What did you call our dear Mrs. LaVelle, Miss Bisbee?"

Mrs. Smith, the baker's wife, put a hand to her mouth at Edith's rudeness. Two other women—old classmates, but *who wasn't*—tittered in delight at a possible scandal. A couple soldiers wearing Army Engineer insignia paused mid-drink by the punchbowl, and honestly who had even invited them to a town hall meeting?

"Dolores," Edith repeated. Two spots of red burned on her cheeks. "That's her name. Not *Alice LaVelle*. You should remember her, Billy. She went to elementary school with us and moved the summer before sixth grade."

Eyes swiveled between Alice and Edith, trying to reconcile fashionable Alice LaVelle with vague memories of a skinned-kneed girl child who flitted like a ghost along the riverbank near her grandmother's house, catching frogs and playing in the mud instead of acting a lady. The girl Edith remembered, because she had been in the mud beside her.

Dolores laughed. "You misremember."

"I do not."

Unspoken between them, the accusation of foul spellcraft. Because it had to be a casting. Surely everyone remembered Dolores Hartley, even if they'd forgotten her long-deceased grandmother.

"So this town isn't big enough for the both of us?" There was something in Dolores's eyes, something in her expression Edith couldn't decipher beyond a fierce hunger.

Edith's chin lifted. She would not back down. "You heard me."

The entire town—and the entire green-clad complement of 2-162's headquarters and headquarters company—seemed to have packed into the high school gymnasium for this meeting, and they were now silent, hanging on each word. The vines of Alice's spell continued to stretch and bind, weave and coax.

Whispers rose between the tendrils of magic as the two women faced off.

Whispers Edith had heard her entire life but ignored because that's what it took to survive in this town—just as her mother and her grandmother and her great-grandmother had endured, stretching all the way back to the first white settlers in this small pocket of the Willamette Valley. Her hands clenched into fists.

"Well, we'll have no bickering among hens here," the mayor said. He eyed Edith up and down, warning her into silence. "This is a triumphant autumn. A return to normalcy and a chance to let our town grow. A time to welcome our heroes back from the war!"

"I don't know what normalcy we want to fall back to," Dolores murmured. Somehow, they'd drifted until they were an arms-length apart. The cloying scent of Tabu by Dana tickled Edith's nose with top notes of orange and coriander, while the middle notes of ylang-ylang and jasmine reminded her of the dangers of getting close to Dolores Hartley turned Alice LaVelle.

"The one where you *stay* gone," Edith snapped.

"Now, now, ladies." The mayor waved his hands to lower their antagonism. "How about a contest to settle this little spat?"

"What kind of contest?" Edith locked eyes with Dolores, daring her to mention their *other* history, to reveal her deepest, darkest secret.

"Why, a friendly flower contest." The mayor flushed, clearly warming to the idea. "It'll be held during our Christmas Bazaar—see our talented florists and celebrate the birth of Christ and American might. We won the war, and we'll beat that rival Christmas celebration in Eugene. Exercise your creativity, ladies."

Dolores pursed her lips. "All contests have stakes."

Edith crossed her arms, stiffening in resolve. The woman just wouldn't stop hurting her and then doubling down on that hurt. Two could play that game. "I win, you leave town."

"Now, Edith, I'm sure Mrs. LaVelle didn't come to our fair town to push you out of it," the mayor said. "There's room for two."

Dolores ignored the mayor, her focus on her enemy. "And if I win?"

Edith grit out, "Then I leave."

"Ladies, this is just a friendly competition," the mayor said. "No one actually has to go anywhere. Edith, I'm sure people still love your little bouquets."

Something glittered in Dolores's eyes. Her smile faltered, and she batted her lashes quickly before turning toward the mayor, her smile set once again in demure pleasantry. "It's a deal. I win, she leaves. She wins, I leave."

"Perfect." Edith spun on her heel and stormed out of the hall. Townspeople, folks she'd grown up with, gone to school with, sweated through the Depression and the War and made sacrifices alongside, healed and birthed and laid to rest and everything in between, stepped out of her way, their noses upturned in disgust.

She didn't need them.

She had never needed them.

But they had always needed her, even if they hated to admit it—even if they could never admit it bound as they were by the vines of Dolores's spell.

"Edith..." The word wafted after her, whispered from Dolores's lips and swallowed by the clouds breaking over Edith's shoulders.

*

Edith would show them just how much she was a part of this town, how deep her roots grew.

Dolores left them all and came back with her big city ideas and fashionable notions and pretty dresses and exotic flowers and a new name, just like her wild great-aunt Opal. She'd traveled the world and returned to town with a score to settle.

Edith *was* the town.

She was Oregon and Cottage Grove and Lane County. Her family had been there from the beginning of the pioneers colonizing the land of the Winefelly peoples. Her family had spoken Chinook jargon, married magics among the Douglas Firs, sung for gold in the

145

Cascades, battled the rising winter floods along the Coast Fork, healed where they could even as the peoples native to this land were driven from it—hidden folk caught in the middle of a sundown county at dusk.

Her mother and her mother before and her mother before that and on and on had sunk their lives into this part of the Willamette Valley, had stood strong despite the rumors and the side-eyed glances at the long line of unmarried women of sin who refused to step into a church on Sunday. They had survived flood and famine and sickness and ignorance and heartbreak.

She would not be the one who ended that legacy.

But as the leaves on the deciduous trees changed color and fell, leaving the great firs standing tall and green and alone against a gray sky, business shifted almost entirely to The Flower Shoppe. Townsfolk gasped over tropical ice blue calathea, tittered over the scandalous orchids resembling women's secrets, and oohed over the marvelous widow's tragically fashionable self. Dolores ate up the attention, wearing a rotating display of black suits nipped in at the waist and black veils to mourn the husband lost at Iwo Jima.

After two weeks of no sales and no visitors, Edith rotated Bisbee's sign to closed—not for the first time in recent years—with a note of her grand reopening on New Year's Day, and focused on her plan.

She gathered cow parsnip and cat tail from the Row River.

She snuck into the Army Corps of Engineer's construction site under a full moon and stole mud from the base of Cottage Drove Dam.

In the middle of November, she received a simple pot of white, blue, and pink flowering cacti from her enemy. The thorns were prominent. One pricked her, sending three droplets of blood into the sandy soil.

She sent back a tin of chamomile to show her patience in the face of adversity.

She found trilliums blooming months ahead of season by following a deer trail to a hidden grove deep among the Douglas Firs along the Coast Fork.

She stole warped boards from Dr. Pierce's Pleasant Pellets barn.

She drove south, along the Umpqua River in rain so heavy she could hardly see out the windshield, walked through miles of old growth and wet ferns, and scrambled down boulders and over fallen logs to gather water from the base of Toketee.

A single poppy on her doorstep marked December first.

Edith did not respond.

She continued her trek, driving along winding switchbacks until she arrived at the vast blue of Crater Lake. She dug through the accumulating snow two miles from the lodge and collected five orange-red rocks. In between two boulders facing Wizard Island, she found a lone white skyrocket. She left it there. It was just the one, after all.

She went north, collecting moss from an old-growth forest in the foothills of the Coastal Range near Lorane, ferns from the old Bohemian Mining site, and lichen from the Oregon white oak behind the elementary school playground.

By the Christmas Bazaar, she had assembled her creation and bartered her prized blackberry pies for the use of her neighbor Henry's truck to transport it through the drizzling rain into the Armory, newly converted into a winter wonderland by eager high schoolers and young soldiers fresh from Europe.

Two seniors in varsity sweaters helped maneuver her triumph into place. They stayed, curious, as she gently peeled away the protective covering. Their jaws dropped, and she smiled. She dared Dolores try to beat this.

The mayor had opened up the contest to whoever wanted to participate, but only one other booth in this corner of the gym was occupied, its offering covered with a battered military canvas, a single cream card tucked into its folds.

Slowly, the gym filled with revelers. Edith waited behind her booth, fingers tapping. The judging would end at seven, the prize a ten-dollar check donated by the grocery store.

She ignored the townsfolk oohing and aahing, their appreciative nods.

Edith wanted their respect, but she hadn't made this for *them*.

She had poured her heart and soul, her anger and bitterness, her love and everything else she possessed, into her floral arrangement.

Her flowers and findings woven into her most powerful hex of binding and warding and banishing all twisted into the shape of a covered bridge—just like the many dotting the landscape of her town.

Her finger tapping increased to leg bouncing as the night drew on, as the clock on the wall ticked toward seven and the official judgment of the contest.

Dolores didn't show.

Her booth remained bare, with just that canvas covered lump and that blank card crying for attention. Edith knew it meant her spell had worked, but dammit the woman was a witch and the spell didn't go into effect until moonrise anyways.

At 6:55 p.m. Edith could take it no longer.

She pushed past the admirers, strode over to Dolores's booth and whipped away the canvas.

A simple heart formed from blue roses lay on the wooden surface.

Soft gasps of disappointment came from the crowd, who obviously thought the impossible petals had been dyed instead of perfected over time, crafted with science and magic and patience. At a distance it was so simple compared to the complex masterpiece of Edith's perfectly created covered bridge pulled from natural elements. But up close, the edges of the petals darkened to a brilliant purple.

Edith stared, shaking her head. Before the heart lay a parchment-covered square bound in twine. Her name was written in the upper left corner. She unwrapped the twine and removed the parchment, revealing a book titled, *The Language of Flowers*. Many of the pages were folded over.

There was no accompanying note.

Edith's jaw worked. *What could it mean?*

Outside of her daze, the mayor announced Edith's win and wondered aloud where Mrs. LaVelle was. Edith ignored him, scrambling about for the note that had fluttered to the floor when she'd removed the canvas.

There had to be *something*. There had to be an answer, a key, *something*.

She found the note, fallen into a corner and half hidden. Her hands shook as she unfolded the card.

You win.

No. Not like this.

She needed a battle, a dramatic showdown, a great *triumph* to show Dolores that *she* belonged here, that she was in the right, that she should never have been abandoned like that, not after revealing her most secret self to the person she loved over all others and continued to love even with her heart broken into a million lost promises.

She flipped through the book, searching for answers, and turned to the first dog-eared page.

Rosemary: a sign of memory and remembrance. Can be used for tinctures and potions to pull away the memory of pain and induce healing. In floral arrangements, indicates remembrance of happier times.

Handwritten in the margins, next to the accompanying illustration of the herb: *You might not remember the field of crocuses where we kissed before I left for Seattle that summer, but I did. I never forgot you.*

Edith shook her head. She flipped to the next folded corner.

Purple Columbine: resolution of intent.

"No, no, no," she whispered, heart sinking as she scanned the note.

I came back to show you all I had learned. That I was worthy of you, my beloved witchling. My resolve is so strong I grew these out of season. They bloomed from yearning.

Her world was ending.

All preconceptions shattered.

History was overwritten.

The next page was a blank buffer separating chapters and covered in handwritten annotations. Unlike the other three pages, this one had been written long before, the pen strokes faded. Alice's notes to herself as she planned the second arrangement, the corsage sent on September twenty-third.

Carnations—because they're pretty, and even though they are standard they have set meaning. Pink to show that I will never forget her. Roses are the signs of love, with lavender petals because this is the love that was my first, despite lavender roses being the most fickle to develop and first love being so difficult to continue or overcome. Blue hibiscus for delicate beauty, and out of season as we had to hide our feelings for so long. But no longer. It needs to be something dramatic, something to show her I am no longer scared and will no longer hide. Something to wear, perhaps? To let the world know? A corsage, to wear my feelings on her sleeve. Perfect.

"No."

She had had it all wrong.

All wrong.

So, so wrong.

A tear hit the page, smearing the last word.

Perfect vanished into nothing but the suggestion of ink on paper. The wound that had festered so long inside Edith bled anew, for the loss of what had been before her this entire time. What she could not see was now gone, banished due to her own arrogance.

She clutched the book to her chest.

"Edith, are you—"

She pushed the person away and fled toward the door, ignoring the well-wishers, the mayor, and everyone else who had held her apart for so long.

Rain cascaded as she burst into the parking lot, changing from a drizzle into a torrential downpour that soaked through and chilled her to the bone. She tucked the book underneath her sweater to protect it and ran. She had to know. She had to find Alice.

The streets were deserted, everyone at the Armory, as she raced through Main Street toward the river and their stores.

The Flower Shoppe was dark.

She still ran to the door, tugging and pulling at the handle. It didn't budge. Everything closed so early in December, and today all shops had locked their doors to prepare for the Bazaar. She slapped her hand against the pane, trying to get someone's, *anyone's*, attention.

"Dolores!"

Edith pressed her face to the glass, struggling to see inside. The shop was empty.

Not the emptiness of a closed store, but barren, stripped of everything that had made it a flower shop in the first place.

"Dolores, answer me! I know you're in there. You have to be in there."

Magic tingled at Edith's fingertips, the tinges of the spell she had cast in her covered bridge creation. The biggest mistake she had ever made.

"Alice ... " The grief she had crammed down over the years took over. Her knees buckled, and she fell to the ground, pressing herself against the door as if she could melt into the shop, could find her in the bare floorboards, capture her essence in the lingering scent of lavender and lemon.

The rain fell forever into the night, swelling the river with her heartbreak. She curled her knees up to her chest and rested her head, back pressed against the empty shop, rear growing cold and wet from the sidewalk.

"I must say, this is a new low for you."

Sniffling, Edith looked up.

Dolores stood several steps away, an umbrella clutched in both hands. She was dry and beautiful and *there*, impossibly there.

Edith blinked.

"Well, are you going to just sit there wallowing in misery?" In the dimness of the streetlights, a corner of Dolores's red-painted mouth quirked up. "You won."

Edith rose to her feet, shaky and bewildered. "But I banished you."

Dolores snorted. "Please. You never were any good at hexes."

Edith rushed forward and wrapped her arms around Dolores.

"I see you got my note. I had a feeling some things were lost in translation with the flowers." Dolores pressed her forehead against Edith's, sobering. "I'm sorry," she whispered, cupping Edith's cheek with a bare hand, "it took me so long to come back."

They stared at each other as the rain pattered down on the umbrella, lost in a cocoon of warmth and shelter. The hurt of the years, the completely misinterpreted declaration of war and the battle of the flowers, the different language of flowers books, the contest, everything was just too much and too miniscule.

"I'm so, so sorry. I didn't—"

"Just kiss me. I've been waiting long enough. We can work out everything else afterwards."

She did.

And they did.

Meet Laurel Beckley

Laurel Beckley is a writer, Marine Corps veteran and librarian. She is from Eugene, Oregon, and currently lives in northern Virginia with her wife, fur creatures and a collection of gently neglected houseplants. Her debut novel, THAT DISTANT DREAM, is available from NineStar Press and Amazon. She can be found on twitter @laurelthereader and her blog, The Suspected Bibliophile (https://thesuspectedbibliophile.home.blog/).

Wish Upon a Star Pearl

CITLALIN OSSIO

Carina's rumbling stomach seemed to echo in the small waiting room. Bright sunlight from the window opposite her coated her in gold warmth. Too much warmth. She looked to the double wooden doors of Doña Matilde's office and wiped sweaty palms on her long knit skirt.

Doña Matilde was the Patrona of the local gang, and Carina's ticket out of the cold bleak room she lived in since Abuela succumbed to her illness. To pay for her grandmother's hospital bills, Carina sold the panaderia she had dreamed to inherit. Unfortunately, the money had been in vain. After burying the precious woman who raised her, Carina rented a small rooftop room above a vendor in the fish market. It was a roof overhead so she didn't complain until the potent smell of seafood seeped into her clothes and skin. No job she took since being on her own lasted long. Eerily silent nights and dwindling savings pushed her to seek refuge with a criminal family. At least they *were* a family.

A blond middle-aged man with an axe strapped to his back exited Doña Matilde's office and towered over Carina, who shifted on the hard wooden bench. "The Patrona will see you."

"Muchas gracias." She rose and stood before the tall, decoratively carved, wooden doors. *This is the last time. If you're truly in heaven*

153

Abuela, if God is really listening, then ask Him to let me have a family again. She took a deep breath and pushed the creaky door open.

An older woman with wavy hair that was almost all gray save a few streaks of black hunched over a weathered map and a clutter of papers. Without a glance to her guest, Doña Matilde waved Carina forward. "Sit."

Carina obeyed, taking a seat in a soft green upholstered armchair. The matriarch said nothing, her focus remaining on the work in front of her. Carina glanced around at an eclectic array of wood furniture. The hint of citrus flowers filtered in through an open window. She breathed it in deeply. *Like Abuela.*

When the Patrona finished her note and looked at Carina, the older woman's warm smile reminded Carina of her grandmother. It could've been her desperation tricking her. "How can I help you, corazón?"

She was taken aback. It had been a long time since she had been called corazón. She missed it.

"There's no need to be afraid. What can we help you with? Do you need a loan, or—"

"I want to join your family," blurted Carina. Her cheeks burned at her mistake. "I-I mean I want to join your group."

Doña Matilde relaxed into her purple-cushioned chair, a smirk on her lips. "You seem like a good girl. Why do you want to join us?"

Carina debated telling the truth. She settled on a less personal answer. "Guaranteed room and board."

"We're no charity. You want that, you have to work."

"I will."

Doña Matilde studied Carina who tried hard not to squirm. Then the Patrona said, "If you truly wish to join us, bring me a star pearl. The closest one is in a shop in the next town."

That was it? Carina's shoulders relaxed. "I'll buy it right away."

Doña Matilde laughed a little. "If you could buy it, you wouldn't be asking me for help." She leaned forward. "I want you to steal it."

Steal? Carina pushed away her grandmother's reprimanding voice sneaking into her mind. Abuela was gone. So was the faith she had given her.

"Oh," Carina's voice cracked so she cleared her throat. "Okay."

Red brick poked Carina's back as she leaned against an alley wall, across from the oddities shop the star pearl was in. Her nerves hadn't faded since arriving. The nearby church didn't help. Every bell toll sent Carina's heart and conscience racing. And every time she reminded herself God had left her no alternative. She had asked numerous times. He hadn't listened.

Her stomach gurgled, and her eyes moved to the neighboring panaderia. The sweet smell of fresh bread saturated her lungs. She groaned. Abuela always teased her big appetite, in a loving way, and Carina prided herself on it as a baker's granddaughter. Her nervous hunger though, not so much. *Maybe one pan—* She shook the thought away and entered the oddities shop, escaping the mouthwatering scent.

Inside, the shelves were cluttered with a variety of curios, from glowing charms to shining metal accessories. The owner paused his inventory check to greet her. "Buenos dias. Looking for anything in particular?"

"I'm just browsing." She moved through the aisles looking for her quarry.

A trio of small, colorful, fuzzy creatures in a terrarium watched her from the counter as if they knew her ill intentions. After a thorough search, Carina found no star pearl in the entire store. *Oh no, does he keep it behind the counter?* She grabbed a glass jar with flowers floating in glittering liquid, hesitating to inquire about the rare item. She kept her eyes on the bottle as a bell jingled signaling a new customer.

A soft and delighted voice spoke behind her, "I still wish I could buy one of everything. He has such a wonderful assortment. Don't you think?"

"I think you should get what you came for quickly so we can leave," answered another, his voice deep and warm.

"Very well. Don Inigo, we've returned to purchase the star pearl."

155

Carina's ears perked up. She faced the counter where a beautiful young woman, a few years older than her, with lavender and pink hair in a bright dress and gold-rimmed glasses stood beside a man with russet brown skin in a forest green cloak embroidered with gold leaves on the edges, a holstered sword at his waist.

The clerk said, "You're lucky, I have just one left. Do you have what I asked for?"

The young woman placed two velvet pouches from her leather bag onto the counter. "Three rubies, seven diamonds, and an ounce of gold."

Carina almost dropped the glass jar. It was worth that much?

The clerk said, "Ah, it's *two* ounces of gold now." He held up two fingers.

The cloaked man said, "We agreed on one last week."

"You said it, last week."

"You arrogant—"

The woman interrupted, "Oh just give him the extra gold. I'll pay you back."

As the cloaked man set a leather pouch on the counter, Carina's stomach rumbled, causing the former to glance in her direction. She turned away before their eyes met. Then Carina exited as calmly as she could and retreated to the alley, keeping an eye on the shop.

Now what do I do? That star pearl was her only chance at securing her future. Carina watched the man hold the door open as the young woman exited the building, her face beaming as she cradled a small silver box in her palm, no doubt holding the star pearl inside.

Carina remembered the dim room above the fish market. Alone, with nothing but shadows and bitter cold for companions. A shiver ran down her spine. She had to take it, whether from a store or a person.

She took a step forward when the church bells rang. Her heart lurched. *Those darn bells.* She frowned at them. Maybe God was listening, maybe He was warning her. Well, just as He had ignored her, Carina would ignore Him.

She trailed the pair to the zocalo. Carina had never stolen more than the occasional pan, fresh out the oven, when Abuela wasn't looking, so she had no idea how to swipe the silver box, glistening in the sunlight, as if teasing her. *I just have to wait until they're distracted, then take it and run.* She scoffed. *What a wonderful plan, self.* It was her only plan, so it would have to do.

The young woman pulled the man toward a crowd watching a water mage performance, and Carina caught up with them. The woman put the box in her leather bag which—to Carina's relief—she forgot to clasp. Panic or hunger made Carina's stomach complain as she stood behind the pair. Both the woman and man were focused on the spheres of water floating in the air so Carina glanced around to make sure no one was watching and as stealthily as possible reached into the bag. Her sweaty hand hugged the small case. As Carina began to pull her arm out, her victim stepped back and collided with Carina.

The woman turned apologizing, "I'm sorr..." She gasped.

Carina tightened her grip on the box and ran, pushing innocent bystanders until she broke through the crowd. She glanced back, and her heart jumped. The man was chasing her. If she made it to the street market, she could lose him in the maze of stalls and people. She turned into an alley that led straight to her haven and picked up her speed. The sunlight at the end grew larger. She was almost there.

Something—worse—someone yanked her back so hard she tumbled to the ground, hard cobblestone digging into her arm. Her captor pulled her up and a pair of eyes like glimmering peridot gems glared at her.

Carina marveled at the beauty in those eyes. Coming to her senses as her predicament overcame her temporary fascination, Carina struggled to free herself. The man clutched her arm tighter. "Release me!"

"Not until you return what you stole, thief."

The accusation hit her like a poisoned arrow. She was a thief now. Abuela would be heartbroken.

"You've got the wrong person. I don't know what you're talking about." She cringed internally. It was a pathetic defense.

Her captor held up her left hand still holding the silver box. "We'll let the authorities judge." When he tried to pull it from her,

Carina clenched her hand so tight her knuckles turned white. She shoved into him, and he released her. To her horror, the case slipped from her grasp. It opened, sending a glittering marble-like gem skipping across the cobblestone. Its colors shifted in a rainbow gradient.

Carina and her captor dived for it. She stretched her arm and relief washed over her when her hand wrapped around the smooth orb. Why she thought to do what she did next, she had no clue. Maybe it was desperation or pure hunger. Or the first led to the second. She popped the star pearl in her mouth where the man couldn't possibly get it. To her surprise, it tasted...sweet.

His green eyes widened. "Why you!" He grabbed her face and tried to make her spit it out while she pushed away from him.

In the struggle, gravity did its job, and Carina accidentally swallowed. The star pearl slid halfway down her throat and stopped. As did her breathing.

Oh my God! I'm choking! She gasped, and the man released her, staring at her with confusion. She slapped her chest and tried to swallow but the star pearl wouldn't budge. *I can't believe this is how I die! I'm sorry! I don't want to die! Not like this. Not as a thief.*

She hit her chest hard, and this time the star pearl went down. Tears blurred her vision while her throat burned as she sucked air in long, deep gasps, her lungs hungry for oxygen. *I'm alive!*

The man's face was aghast. "You...you ate it!"

She answered between coughs, "It was an accident, and it's your fault."

"Mine?" He scoffed, then grabbed her arm and spoke into a sapphire pin on his cloak. "I caught her. Where are you?"

"I returned to the inn," answered a woman on the other end.

"Let's go." He pulled Carina to the fancier of the two inns in town and entered a room on the third floor. Two guards, a female human and male camafol with green scales and a gold cuff on his coiled tail, saluted him before exiting, then he shoved Carina in front of the woman with glasses.

"Gilberto! Don't treat a lady so rough."

"She's no lady; she's a thief."

"It doesn't matter." She turned to Carina and smiled softly. "Did he hurt you?"

Carina was surprised by her kindness. Why did she care if the person who stole from her was hurt? She tried her luck. "Well, he pulled me to the ground and squeezed my face."

"You insolent thief!" shouted Gilberto. "You dare accuse me after stealing and eating what isn't yours?"

The young woman furrowed her brow. "Eating?"

He sighed and rubbed his temple. "She ate the star pearl."

Her jaw slackened. "You—"

"Not on purpose," said Carina. She glared at Gilberto. "If you hadn't squeezed my face so hard, I wouldn't have swallowed it."

"You're blaming me again, when *you* stole—"

The young woman burst into laughter, surprising both Carina and Gilberto.

"Iris?" said Gilberto.

Her laughter subsided. She said to Carina, "I'm impressed. How did you think to do that?"

"I didn't plan to, it just happened."

"Don't encourage her, Iris," Gilberto said. "Thievery is not impressive."

"Beating you is."

Carina's stomach grumbled loudly, and her face grew hot when their eyes shot to her.

Iris smiled warmly. "What's your name?"

"Carina."

She shook her hand. "It's nice to meet you, Carina. I'm Princess Iris."

Carina was suddenly sick. *Oh, I'm dead.*

"Will you join Gilberto and me for lunch?"

"What?" Gilberto asked, annoyed.

Carina was equally dumbfounded by the invitation. This woman, this *princess*, treated her extremely well despite the fact Carina had stolen from her. Could she have an ulterior motive?

"Do you plan to poison me?"

Gilberto started, "You—"

"I promise I won't poison you," answered Iris, smiling.

Behind her gold frames, her dark brown eyes reminded Carina of Abuela. Her stomach complained softly again. "What's there to eat?"

✼

Carina's spoon clinked against the fine talavera as she scooped the last bit of broccoli cream. She wanted to scrape what little remained with her torta but didn't think her captors shared her table manners. Not only were their appearances and clothes elegant, they ate and sat gracefully.

"How did it taste?" asked Iris, tucking a strand of pink-purple hair behind her ear.

Carina answered, "Delicious, thank you."

"You're welcome." She paused. "So...how did the star pearl taste?"

Gilberto shook his head. "Only you would ask that."

"I'm curious."

Carina answered, "Um, it was sweet."

Iris laughed. "Really?"

Gilberto said, "Of course it tasted sweet. She didn't pay for it."

Carina's stomach tightened.

Iris frowned at him then turned back to Carina. "Do you live here?"

"No."

"Where are you from?"

"It doesn't matter." If Carina traced herself back to Doña Matilde, prison would be the least of her worries. The thought made her stomach hurt more.

The princess paused, trying to come up with a new topic of conversation. "Have you been to the Capital?"

"Once." Carina winced, the pain growing. "Twelve years ago when I was five, so I don't remember much."

Gilberto said, "We have an excellent prison system."

"Stop scaring her," chided Iris.

He shrugged. "I'm just making conversation."

160

The pain in Carina's abdomen sharpened, and she doubled over clutching her stomach.

Iris asked, "Oh, it's taking effect already?"

Carina's heart sank at the betrayal. "You...you said you wouldn't poison me."

"I didn't, but I did add a few drops of laxative."

"Laxative!" Carina shouted.

Gilberto smirked, and Carina glared weakly at him.

"I'm sorry, Carina. The bathroom is over there."

Carina jumped out of her seat and raced to the door, certain she heard Gilberto chuckling.

Even after a dozen trips to the bathroom, the star pearl never appeared. For four days, Carina waited in vain for it to leave her body. Despite Gilberto's opposition, Iris upgraded to a double suite to share with her, and the two wore magic links that prohibited Carina from escaping. Thankfully, she got along with Iris. Gilberto (who, Carina was horrified to learn, was Iris's cousin) on the other hand always seemed displeased with her.

"Hmm..." pondered Iris, twirling a silver boomerang in her hands. "I wonder if we have to raise her body temperature?"

"What do you mean?" asked Gilberto.

"Well, it is a star pearl. When it fell, it lost its heat and became dormant. In order to activate its magic, it needs to burn."

Carina stopped putting her dark brown hair in a braid. "B-Burn?"

"Not you, the star pearl."

Gilberto said, "I suppose throwing her into Mount Volumbrá is out of the question?"

An image of him throwing her into the active volcano made Carina shudder. He noticed and smirked, which annoyed her.

The corners of Iris's lips quirked up as she shook her head. "I think the hot springs south of here may do the trick. Hopefully."

"We're supposed to return to the Capital in two days," Gilberto said.

"You know my parents won't mind if we extend our vacation."

He sighed. "Very well. If this doesn't work though, we're throwing her in prison and that's final." He paused. "Unless you change your mind about Mount Volumbrá."

Carina resisted the childish urge to stick her tongue out at him.

***

Fields of wildflowers passed by in hazes of color, and the forested mountains in the distance rolled across the land like waves. Carina rode with Iris in her private coach, while Gilberto and the two guards travelled by horseback. Carina couldn't believe she was traveling in a cozy carriage instead of a corroded cell. She wondered if God was playing a trick on her.

Iris yanked her from her thoughts. "What are you thinking, Carina?"

"I was thinking how fortunate it is that my captors are good people. Not many would feed the person who stole from them or let them travel so comfortably."

"Do you enjoy stealing?"

Carina lowered her gaze. "No."

"I had a little sister. She would be about your age, if she hadn't passed away a few days after her birth. If she had lived, like my siblings and I, she would've learned to sit without slouching, been taught three languages, and worn fancy clothes. She would've eaten delicious food as often as she pleased and slept on the softest of beds. She would've never had a need to steal. I understand not everyone has that choice. People do bad things, but God doesn't make bad people. I think you're a good person who made a mistake, so I've forgiven you."

A lump caught in Carina's throat that reminded her of when she choked days before.

"Besides, now I get to enjoy a day at the hot springs," smiled Iris. "That's something to look forward to, don't you agree?"

Carina returned her smile. "Sounds wonderful."

***

"Abuela, you promised we'd go to the nevería." Ten-year-old Carina pulled on her grandmother's arm. "It's going to close."

Abuela rubbed her granddaughter's hair. "We have plenty of time, corazón. I'm almost finished."

"But if we don't hurry, Don Sebastian will sell out of mango nieves."

"Very well, let's go."

Carina hurried ten paces ahead and excitedly urged, "Come on, come on!"

Abuela laughed. "This abuela of yours can't run as fast as you."

She stretched out her hand. Carina took it, forced to go at her grandmother's pace.

"Abuela, when I'm older and stronger, I'll carry you everywhere, okay?"

"You'll do that for me?"

"Mm-hm, and I'll run."

Laughing, they arrived at the nevería. To Carina's horror, it was closed. "You see, Abuela, I told you we'd be too late," she pouted. "Why didn't you listen to me?"

"I did listen to you, but you're as impatient as ever."

"What do you mean?"

"Have patience, corazón, and you'll see."

Faint voices woke Carina.

She turned to sleep again when Iris said, "Carina is a good person, Gil."

Carina's eyes shot open.

"It's not her fault her situation caused her to commit a crime."

"Suffering is no excuse for bad actions."

"Says the one who ran away from home when his father died."

"I was a child, and I didn't hurt others. *She* is nothing more than a thief. Don't let her fool you. The moment she has a chance she'll try to escape or cause us more trouble. The sooner we're rid of her the better."

Carina pulled the covers over her head to muffle their voices. She didn't care what Gilberto thought of her. His appearance was his only charming quality, and as kind as Iris was, her opinion didn't matter either. She couldn't stay with them, and she didn't want to.

She didn't want to.

⁕

The resort was a few hours east, but a renovation of the bridge halted their journey. The only other path took longer and was more dangerous, so Iris and Gilberto chose to wait in town. Carina dragged herself out of bed, less than eager to spend the day under Gilberto's suspecting watch. His words from the night prior were still fresh in her mind. He already waited for Carina and Iris in the hallway alone, as Iris had given the other guards the day off. Carina didn't look at him or greet him.

"Oh, I forgot something," Iris said. When Carina moved to follow, she added, "Wait here. I'll be quick."

Carina leaned against the opposite wall and stared away from Gilberto, toward an open window that let in cool air and birdsong.

"Plotting an escape?"

She faced him. His peridot eyes, alert and frowning, studied her. It was petty but instead of easing his worries, she mustered as mischievous a smile as she could. "If I were, I wouldn't tell you, would I?"

Before he could respond, Iris returned with the key to the magic links. "I think we can take these off now."

Gilberto nearly shouted, "What?"

Iris ignored him and unlocked the cuffs. Was she trying to prove Gilberto wrong? Carina couldn't leave until the star pearl was out of her body so there was no chance she'd escape. Gilberto didn't know that though. The temptation to taunt him was too strong. "You sure you want to do that?"

Baited, he stepped forward. "Iris, this—"

Iris smiled wide. "I'm positive. Let's go." She linked arms with Carina and pulled her outside.

After a few hours of shopping, Iris asked to rest and sat on a wooden bench.

"If you're tired, we should return to the inn," suggested Gilberto.

The princess refused. When she felt better, she jumped up. Gilberto extended his arm for her to take. She accepted then linked with Carina.

Carina joked, "I don't see the point of removing the magic links. You've had me on your arm all day."

Iris laughed. Carina didn't mind, it reminded her of walking arm in arm with Abuela on the way to Mass. The sweet scent of frozen fruit entered her nose, and Carina turned her gaze to a neveria across the street.

"Do you want something?" asked Iris.

Carina's cheeks warmed. "I'm craving a nieve."

The princess beamed. "I haven't had one in a while." She pulled Carina and Gilberto to the end of the line. "What flavor do you two want?"

Carina answered immediately, "Mango." Gilberto remained silent which didn't shock her. It was her craving, of course he wouldn't—

"Lime."

Carina's eyebrows shot up. What a surprise.

"I think I'll ask for strawberry." Iris smiled.

The line advanced when a commotion broke out behind Carina. A cloaked man pushed a dark-skinned elderly man against a shop window then yanked him by the collar. "Where's your proof, old man?"

An elderly woman wept to the side. "Let go of my husband." She reached to pull on the man's arm but a woman held her back with a spear, a vicious smile on her lips.

Her husband shouted, "I'm sorry. Take what you want, just don't hurt her, please!"

Without thinking, Carina unhooked her arm from Iris and ran toward them. "Hey! Leave them alone."

The man in the cloak turned to Carina. "This is none of your concern, girl. Get lost."

She stood her ground. "Release him."

"He said beat it," echoed his accomplice, still blocking the elderly woman whose tear-filled eyes shifted between her husband and Carina.

Carina's eyes searched and landed on a crate of apples. She clenched her fist and swallowed hard then grabbed a glistening fruit and threw. It hit the blue-cloaked man in the back of his head.

His expression when he faced Carina was as frightening as a roaring lion. She instinctively stepped back when he released his victim and advanced toward her. He moved lightning fast and had his sword unsheathed before Carina knew how to react.

Someone pulled her away as his blade hit stone. Carina looked up and met Gilberto's frowning eyes. He released her and parried the assailant's next attack while Iris threw her silver boomerang at the woman who blocked it with her pointed spear, sending it clattering to the ground far from Iris's reach. The woman lunged at Iris. The princess dodged and wrestled for the spear.

Carina came to her senses and retrieved Iris's weapon, the shining wing cold in her hand. How was she supposed to throw it? When the cloaked woman took hold of the spear and struck Iris's arm, Carina forgot her hesitation and ran forward, striking the woman on the shoulder with the boomerang. The woman cried out, and her weapon clattered to the ground. Iris took possession of the spear, aiming it at the woman's neck. Carina hurried to her side as Gilberto disarmed his opponent and picked up the fallen blade.

Carina stared at the line of blood dripping from Iris's arm. "Iris—"

"Halt!" Town guards appeared and surrounded the storefront. "Lower your weapons." Soldiers moved to arrest Carina and Iris, but the shop owners stopped them.

"No," said the elderly man. "They saved us. The ones you want are these two." He pointed to his attackers. "I caught them stealing so they attacked us."

The guards took their word and bound the assailants and shoved them into an iron cage cart while the shopkeepers thanked the trio.

The elderly woman cupped Carina's hands in hers. "Thank you for helping us."

Carina smiled.

"Please take this," said her husband, handing Gilberto a paper bag full of fruit.

When Iris grabbed at the cut on her arm and winced, Gilberto said, "Let's hurry to the inn to treat your wound."

After Iris's arm was bandaged, Carina apologized. "I'm sorry. I didn't mean for you to get hurt."

Gilberto said, "Then you should've minded your own business and let the town guards solve the situation. What were you thinking provoking them when you can't even fight?"

"They were hurting them; I couldn't watch and do nothing. My abuela taught me to help others. I'm surprised you didn't step in first. Isn't it your job to defend others?"

"My only duty is to Iris."

They stared each other down.

Iris said, "Enough you two. Ev—"

He turned on her. "And you. You should've stayed put instead of risking your life for her. How do you think your parents would react if you died saving someone like *her*?"

A pang in Carina's chest burned into a fiery rage. "Oh, that's right because I'm just a lowly thief. All I do is cause trouble. The sooner you're rid of me the better, right? If you hate me so much, why did you protect me?"

"I protected you because I had to not because I wanted to."

His answer was like ice cold water dousing her anger down to a flickering flame. The flame was enough. "Then you should've let me die instead! Then you could cut me up and get your precious star pearl and finally be rid of me."

She crossed to the bedroom, slamming the door behind her before hiding under the covers. Tears pushed behind her eyelids, but she held them off. She didn't care what Gilberto thought of her, much less if he hated her.

Hours later, Iris sat at the edge of Carina's bed. "It's time for dinner. Aren't you hungry?"

"No."

"Gilberto didn't mean it. He—"

"He's right about one thing. The sooner we get this star pearl out of me and part ways the better."

Iris sighed and left without another word. Carina couldn't hold her tears anymore. She sobbed into her pillow until she drifted off to sleep.

Even though her body begged for food, Carina skipped breakfast the next morning, eager to postpone seeing Gilberto. The bridge renovations were complete, so she stared at the ceiling from her bed, ready to go at a moment's notice. Her stomach wasn't as strong as her resolve and gurgled.

Iris knocked and opened the door. "Ready to go?"

Carina followed her outside the inn where Gilberto was waiting by the carriage. "Ready?" he asked Iris.

"Almost." Iris signaled to the camafol guard who approached Carina, then took Gilberto's hand. "You'll thank me later." Iris slapped a magic link on his wrist and her guard put the matching pair on Carina.

Her heart sank. *Oh no.*

Gilberto mirrored Carina's annoyance, "What are you doing?"

Iris beamed. "Giving you two a chance to be friends."

"We don't have time for this."

"The star pearl's not going anywhere, and this tension's going to ruin my vacation."

"I don't think this is a good idea."

"Me either," said Carina.

"See, you two are finding common ground already." The princess grinned. "We'll wait in the zocalo. Have fun!" She left with her guard before Carina or Gilberto could protest further. They stood, without facing each other for a minute then Carina's stomach roared.

Gilberto sighed beside her. "Let's go."

He walked forward, and Carina waited as long as she could before the links worked their magic forcing her to follow. He stopped at a street vendor selling gorditas. Carina's mouth watered at the smell of masa and the sound of bubbling oil.

"Order what you want."

Her pride and hunger warred. Hunger won. "Two gorditas with salsa verde, please."

"Three," added Gilberto.

Carina finished the last bite of gordita, the warm cheese melting in her mouth while the salsa burned her tongue. The delicious food improved her mood and she smiled. "Thank you for the meal."

"You're welcome."

Carina took a swig of horchata as an awkward silence passed between them.

Gilberto cleared his throat. "I'm sorry for hurting you last night." His apology surprised Carina. He continued, "While you did act recklessly, it was wrong of me to speak so cruelly to you."

"It's okay." She paused. "I'm sorry for putting you both in danger too. Truthfully, I've gotten used to doing things without thinking of others. Although, Abuela always said I was impulsive."

"You said she taught you to help others. So, why steal instead?"

"It was the first time I stole anything," Carina admitted. "Why do you think I was caught so easily?"

"I thought you were just a sloppy thief."

"You've made that very clear."

"So, why choose that life?"

Carina played with cheese crumbs on her plate as she answered, "I was tired of eating alone."

Gilberto raised an eyebrow, so she elaborated. "Abuela told me all food, even the food you don't like, tastes better when you eat with others, but your favorite food loses its flavor when you eat alone. I didn't understand what she meant until she was gone."

"You don't have anyone else?"

She shook her head. "Abuela was my only family, and the few friends I have are off on their own adventures or have their own families. I didn't want to burden them. The patrona of a gang in town said I could join if I got her a star pearl. Joining guaranteed me a home, food, and family. It meant the food I ate would taste good again, at least that's what I hoped."

Gilberto didn't respond, and Carina wondered if he even believed her.

Finally, he said, "I'm sorry I misjudged you, Carina."

Her heart skipped a beat. It was the first time he called her by her name. When she looked up at him, he was smiling. His peridot eyes sparkled.

She returned her gaze to her empty plate as her face warmed. "I-It's okay."

"I don't agree with your actions, though I understand now why Iris trusts you." He took her plate and his and gave them back to the street vendor. When he returned, he asked, "Do you want desert?"

Carina smiled. "Sure."

✧

Carina could still taste the sweet mango on her tongue as she walked beside Gilberto in silence. The zocalo came into view, where Iris waved them over.

"Um, Gilberto? Thank you for the food and for listening."

"You're welcome." A cloud blocked the sun behind Gilberto at the same time he smiled making it more radiant. Thankfully Iris called their names and drew his attention.

Carina chided her racing heart. *What are you thinking, calm down!* A breeze cooled her flushed cheeks, and she willed the wind to carry her fascination away. She would never fall for him. Ever.

"Are you two friends now?" Iris asked, hopeful.

"That's a stretch," answered Gilberto. "However, I think we'll tolerate each other from now on. Would you agree, Carina?"

She shrugged. "I can always try."

Iris's face lit up. "This is certainly an improvement. I always have brilliant ideas." She unlocked the links. "So, what did you do?"

Gilberto answered, "We ate gorditas and nieves."

170

"You two had nieves without me?" She pouted.

He laughed. "I'll buy you one now."

After Iris enjoyed a strawberry nieve, the party set out and a few hours later arrived at Corona Hot Springs. Steam rose from the tree-tops, and waterfalls roared in the distance. Inside the main building, a burgundy-scaled camafol stopped sweeping to greet the guests. She had three white bands on her coiled tail.

"Bienvenidos! Are you looking to enjoy some time in our hot springs?"

Iris answered enthusiastically, "Yes!" She failed to convince Gilberto and the guards to enjoy the resort so only she and Carina followed the camafol to the female-only hot springs.

There were a few other patrons, including a mother with her three daughters. Iris ventured in after testing the water with her foot, while Carina hesitated. She wasn't sure Iris's idea would work and if it did it meant her time with Iris and Gilberto would end.

"What's wrong?" Iris asked.

"Nothing," Carina answered, shaking her head, then she dipped her toes in the steaming water. The heat traveled up her body as she submerged completely. "Now what?"

"Now we relax," laughed Iris.

The young women were silent and only the giggles and splashing of the girls playing filled the space. Carina concentrated on her body and if anything felt off.

Then Iris said, "I'm really happy we met, Carina. I've gotten to experience what it would've been like if my baby sister lived. I was always curious." She looked up to the sky where clouds drifted slowly.

Carina closed her eyes and sank deeper into the water. She was grateful too. What began as a stressful week turned into one she never wished to forget. She had enjoyed her meals again. She would miss Iris, and even Gilberto, when she was alone.

Her body got warmer, and she was enjoying the water when one of the girls shouted from the other end of the hot spring, "Hey, lady, you're glowing!"

Carina's eyes shot open.

Iris gasped beside her. "Carina, you...you're..."

"What?" She looked down at her body. "Ahhh!" She was glowing! Her face, arms, hair, everything! "What's happened to me?"

Iris's female guard rushed in. "Lady Iris, are you hurt?" Her eyes widened at Carina's new look. The burgundy-scaled camafol appeared behind the guard and her scales paled to near invisibility.

Iris answered, "No, we're fine. Carina's just..." She tried and failed to stifle her laughter.

Carina frowned at her, annoyed. "This isn't funny, Iris. I'm glowing!" She touched her skin emanating a rainbow shimmer like a diamond.

The princess had one last chuckle then cleared her throat. "I'm sorry. Are you in pain?"

Carina shook her head.

"That's good." She grabbed her chin in thought. "Did the star pearl actually fuse with you?"

"Fuse? Why?"

Iris slapped the water, splashing Carina with warm droplets. "I was right! The water's heat activated its magic. I had no idea this would be the result though. This is amazing!"

"How is this amazing? I look like a—"

"A star?" offered Iris with a giggle.

"You're very annoying right now."

"Okay, don't worry. We'll figure this out, together." A smile flashed across her lips. "First things first, do you have magic now?"

Carina frowned. She didn't want to indulge Iris but her own curiosity made her extend her hand out, imitating what she had seen mages do. Nothing happened.

"Too bad," said Iris.

They exited the hot springs and a collective gasp from the guards and employees made Carina cringe. *I must look so odd.*

"What happened?" Gilberto asked.

Iris answered proudly, "The heat activated the star pearl's magic just as I said."

"Does it hurt?" he asked Carina.

"No."

The employees had spared no time in alerting the owner of the resort, a violet-scaled camafol, who approached Carina and studied her shining appearance. "So, it's true."

"Do you think something's happened to the waterfalls?" asked the burgundy camafol.

Iris said, "Actually..." She explained Carina's situation with the star pearl, leaving out the fact that she stole it.

The owner laughed. "For a moment, I thought we had a new marketing campaign. 'Corona Hot Springs leaves you glowing, literally.'"

"Do you know anyone who could help her?" asked Iris.

"I'm afraid not."

Carina twiddled her fingers.

Iris noticed and grabbed her hands. "Don't worry. We'll return home and find someone who can."

"Do you still have hope of getting the star pearl somehow?"

"No."

"Then why do you still care to help me?"

Iris smiled. "Because you're my friend."

Carina's chest filled with warmth and she blinked away tears. "Thank y—" Her stomach roared, ruining the moment. Carina's cheeks burned.

Iris chuckled and even Gilberto couldn't stifle his laughter.

Iris said, "Let's eat first."

Carina tried her best to ignore the curious looks and whispers of other patrons in the resort cafeteria as she ate. Then a small boy gathered courage and approached her and asked, "Are you an angel?"

Carina choked on a strip of bacon. "N-No."

"She's a star," said Iris.

Carina frowned.

The boy beamed. "If I make a wish, will you grant it?"

"Um..."

"Damian!" His father hurried to his son's side and grabbed his hand. "I'm sorry my son bothered you."

The boy pulled against his father. "But she's a star! I want to wish for Abuela's back to stop hurting."

His father's expression saddened. "Let them eat in peace."

"Wait," Carina said. "What do you want?"

The boy's smile shined almost as bright as Carina. "I want Abuela's back to stop hurting so she won't be tired anymore and she can play with us again." He pointed to an elderly woman seated across from a woman and two girls younger than him.

Carina looked down at her glowing hands. Unsure if it would work, she gave it a shot and prayed. *Diosito, I'm sorry I stole and I'm sorry I was angry with you. I know I don't deserve to ask You for anything, but I hope this boy's abuela can be cured of her ailments and that he and her share many happy memories like Abuela and I.*

To her amazement, Carina's body shone brighter until the whole room was covered in blinding light. Carina shut her eyes. When she opened them, the light was gone.

Iris said, "Carina, you're not glowing anymore."

Carina looked at her body. Sure enough she was back to normal. *Could it be?*

"Abuela!" The boy ran to his grandmother who picked him up easily and spun him in a circle. The boy and his family thanked Carina and paid for her meal.

"Carina, that was amazing!" Iris surprised her with a hug. But the greatest shock came next.

"That was pretty impressive," said Gilberto smiling.

Carina ignored the skip in her heartbeat his words caused. "It wasn't really me. It was the star pearl." She turned her hands over— the glow from before most certainly gone—and felt a pit in her stomach. "Looks like we don't have to go to the Capital anymore, unless..." She looked at Gilberto. "You still plan to put me in prison?"

"It's up to her." He looked to Iris who flashed a grin.

"I never planned to imprison you."

"Then, I guess this is where we part ways. I'm sorry for all the trouble I caused you."

Gilberto asked, "Will you still try to join your town's gang?"

She shook her head. "I don't think that life was really for me. I'm not scared anymore though. I'll find a place."

"How about living with us?" Iris asked.

Carina blinked. She must've heard wrong. "What?"

"Come work at the palace, oh, I know! Become my companion and eat with our family every day."

Ask Him to let me have a family again.

Carina's heart raced. Abuela was right; she *was* impatient. Tears rolled down her cheeks.

"What's wrong? I thought you'd be happy." Iris bit her bottom lip.

"I am."

"So, you'll stay with us?"

Carina smiled. "I'd love to."

Iris hugged her, and even Gilberto flashed a quick smile.

Thank you, Diosito. Thank you, Abuela. I won't be sad anymore. I'm going to make you proud.

Meet Citlalin Ossio

Citlalin Ossio is an avid fantasy writer and reader, whose work is heavily inspired by her Catholic faith, her Mexican heritage, and Nintendo's *Legend of Zelda*. Her short stories were featured in the anthology *Eclectically Magical* as well as previous installments of *Legion of Dorks Presents*. Her fantasy short story, *She Has No Voice*, won second place in the Prose category for Rehumanize International's 2021 Create | Encounter. She lives in Houston, Texas with her family and enjoys creating art, playing video games, and watching anime and Korean dramas. When she's not raising her panda army she's on Twitter and Instagram @CitlalinOssio.

Night Shift

PATSY PRATT-HERZOG

M elody Windywort, Magical Registered Nurse, fluttered her wings in agitation.

"Princess Ninnith," she said into her shell phone, "I realize there's a Cotillion tonight—I'd rather be dancing too—but you are the Princess-On-Call, and I have a frog that needs kissing."

"Yech," Ninnith complained. "Frogs? I don't do frogs, Melody."

"Well, you do tonight. Prince Roderick got himself cursed again, and this time he'll be a frog for a hundred years if a Princess doesn't kiss him by Midnight."

"That lecherous cad?" Ninnith asked. "Ha! He can stay a frog as far as I'm concerned."

Melody sighed. She shouldn't have told her which Prince it was. Roderick had once gone skinny dipping *au natural* with a bevy of buxom water nymphs at Princess Ninnith's garden party. It had taken her months to live down the scandal. "I know he's not your favorite Prince—"

"He's not anyone's favorite Prince," Ninnith interrupted. "He's a presumptuous, ill-mannered scoundrel."

"True, but he is also the Prince of Kingdom 1. His parents are the most powerful in all the 122 Kingdoms, so get down here and pucker up!" Melody dropped the shell phone back in its tank with a satisfying splash.

She had no patience for prima donnas tonight. The E.R. at the Recover-A-Spell Medical Center was hopping. Besides Roderick, she'd already healed the Prince of Kingdom 38's dragon burns, treated a satyr with pixie bites—served the degenerate peeping tom right in her opinion—*and* she'd cured the Princess of Kingdom 119 from a sleeping curse... again. She was a needy little thing, always putting herself to sleep in the hopes that a Prince would kiss her awake, but they weren't exactly banging down her door.

Roderick looked up at her from his bowl on the counter. "Ribbit."

She sighed. "I'm working on it, Your Highness. You really *must* stop courting sorceresses. They do not take well to your philandering ways."

"Ribbit," he replied, gazing up at her with his bulbous black eyes, a smirk on his froggy face.

The E.R. doors opened, a witch with frizzy red hair glided in and dismounted, leaning her broomstick against Melody's counter.

She was one of Melody's accident-prone "frequent flyers." Just last week, she'd singed her eyebrows off in a potion explosion.

"What can I do for you tonight, Esmeralda?" Melody asked, managing a smile.

Esmeralda hiccuped, and from above, a frog dropped onto the counter with a wet squelch. Melody's gaze went quickly to the Prince, but he was sitting placidly in his bowl.

She hiccuped again, and a second frog plopped down next to the first. Eyes wide, Esmeralda clapped both hands over her mouth.

"A case of the witchups?"

Esmeralda nodded.

Witchups could produce anything from spiders to full-grown dragons.

"Just frogs so far?" she asked warily, and Esmeralda nodded again.

"Have a seat, and I'll mix you up a tonic."

Melody bustled off to the potion room. She added a teaspoon of vinegar, a cube of sugar, and a pinch of cardamom to a pot of boiling water. She pulled her wand from her sleeve and mixed in a thimble of fairy magic and a dash of strawberry flavoring. Pouring the bubbling pink brew into a mug, she hurried back to the waiting room and nearly dropped the cup.

Croaking frogs covered nearly every surface in a sea of undulating green.

How? She'd only been gone a few minutes!

Esmeralda hiccupped, and seven frogs plopped onto the floor at her feet.

"Curses!"

Melody gestured Esmeralda forward, and the witch hitched up her skirts and tiptoed nimbly through the frogs.

Melody pressed the mug into her hands. "For pity's sake, drink it!"

Esmeralda took a cautious sip and grimaced.

"All of it! Straight down," Melody ordered.

A white coach and four horses drew up outside the E.R. and Princess Ninnith stepped out. In her frilly blue gown with her impeccably coifed hair, she looked none too pleased to be there. She came through the doors and froze, a look of abject horror on her face.

"I am not kissing all these frogs!"

"Don't be silly. I only want you to kiss *this* one," Melody said, pointing to the counter.

Ninnith stood on her toes, her brow furrowing. "Which one?"

Melody looked down. The Prince's bowl was empty.

"Curses!" She looked around at the teeming mass of amphibians and then back at the Princess in dismay.

Ninnith's eyes widened. "No!"

"Ninnith, you must! No matter how unpleasant, duty is duty. We have to find Prince Roderick before it's too late!"

"But Melody," Ninnith whined, "I hate slimy, disgusting frogs!"

Esmeralda hiccupped, and ten more frogs splotched onto the counter.

"For the love of Oberon, drink your medicine, Esmeralda!" Melody shouted.

Pinching her nose shut, Esmeralda obeyed, tipping the contents of the mug down her throat.

"Yuck!" she complained. "You know I hate strawberries!"

Melody caught movement out of the corner of her eye. She whipped out her wand and sent Esmeralda's broom to block Ninnith's attempted escape.

Ninnith turned to her with a panicked gaze. "Oh, Melody, I can't!"

"You must, and you will."

After they herded the frogs away from a chair by the window, Princess Ninnith was persuaded to sit.

Yellow skirts trailing behind her, Esmeralda scurried around the room, catching frogs and handing them to Melody, who held them out for a revolted Ninnith to kiss. As each failed to transmogrify into Prince Roderick, Melody dropped it out the window.

She looked at the clock, less than ten minutes until Midnight.

"Faster! We're running out of time!"

Frog after frog proved un-princely. Ninnith howled in woe as they were thrust at her faster-and-faster. The minutes ticked by, and the frogs thinned out as Esmeralda tipped them out of potted plants and pulled them from beneath chairs, but none of them proved to be the Prince.

"Where is he?" Melody cried, spinning frantically in circles.

Princess Ninnith let out a shriek and raised her feet. A frog, looking quite pleased with itself, hopped out from beneath her skirts.

Melody snatched it up and thrust it at Ninnith.

"Hurry, Princess! We have less than a minute!"

Looking as if she'd rather squash it flat, Ninnith planted a kiss on the frog's slimy lips. The creature started to twitch and glow, expanding before their eyes. Melody placed it on the ground, and soon, looking like he was sculpted by the gods, a very handsome, very naked Prince Roderick was kneeling at Ninnith's feet. She could certainly see why the dark-haired blue-eyed Royal had broken so many hearts around the 122 Kingdoms.

Esmeralda stared at him in open admiration, but cheeks flaming, Princess Ninnith averted her gaze.

Sighing, Melody pulled her wand from her sleeve and zapped some pants onto the errant Royal.

"Nice gams, Babe," Roderick said, shooting Ninnith a rakish grin.

"Really, Your Highness?" Melody admonished. "Can you not behave yourself for five minutes?"

Roderick waggled his eyebrows at her. "What fun would that be?"

He turned his attention back to Ninnith, placing his hands upon her knees. "I'm ready to get back under your skirts anytime you are, Babe."

"Oh!" she screeched. "I hope you get warts!" Nose in the air, she pushed him over and stormed out.

"Ninnith," he said, rolling to his feet and running after her. "Come on, Babe, you know you want me."

Shaking her head, Melody surveyed the chaos of frog slime and overturned furniture as she helped Esmeralda chase the last croaking amphibians out the door.

They watched with considerable amusement as Princess Ninnith gave up all pretense of lady-like behavior and dropped Roderick with a well-placed knee to his family jewels before she climbed into her waiting carriage.

"Well," Esmeralda said with a grin, "at least she didn't turn him back into a frog."

Meet Patsy Pratt-Herzog

Patsy Pratt-Herzog is an emerging freelance writer from Southwestern Ohio. Her favorite genres to write are Sci-Fi and Fantasy. When she's not writing, she enjoys painting and riding roller coasters with her teacher husband Tim. Her publishing credits include short stories in the following anthologies: Suspicious Activities, From A

Cat's Viewpoint II, Halloween Party 2019, Detective Mysteries Short Stories, Bodies in the Library Short Stories, and Accursed: a Horror Anthology. Check the featured publications page on my blog for more information.

https://patsyprattherzog.wordpress.com/featured-publications/

A Night to Remember

JEN BAIR

Tuning out parts of a group conversation was a fine art. I was no good at keeping comments to myself, and I had a lot of them. Selective listening helped. The prattle of teenage girls wasn't known for its intelligence, but my sister Veracity, most popular girl in school, would argue otherwise.

Sitting in the high school cafeteria, surrounded by her fellow admirers, Veracity was in her element. She'd been going on about how her new drink fit into her "beauty regimen."

"It sounds super yummy. Can I try it?" This from one of Veracity's vapid groupies.

"Eww, Britney," Veracity said, hugging the lidded brown cup to her chest as if she thought she might get tackled for it. "Like I want your slobber all over my triple venti, soy, half-caff, half sweet, non-fat, no foam, caramel macchiato with extra whip." She rattled the words off without stopping for breath.

"Get your own beauty regimen." She took a delicate sip. "Mine has just enough caffeine to keep me energized for the day, but not so much that it dries out my pores, plus the extra whip gives me that much-needed calorie boost. You know, because my metabolism is so high?"

I tried to focus on my book, but it was hard with the beverage brigade debating the benefits of soy versus non-fat dairy like they were in charge of deciding the official national drink. I would have finished the series already, but Veracity had spent the past two days insisting I look at dresses with her online.

"Let's ask Dahlia."

I looked up to see Veracity giving my book a pointed stare. Her groupies were staring at me, too, like a bunch of rejects from the set of *Children of the Corn*.

I hid my grimace. Veracity asked my opinion about everything, as if being born a year older gave me plus five wisdom. "Ask me what?" Were we still talking about organic almond milk or had we moved on? I tried to replay snippets of what I'd heard most recently, but came up with nothing.

"Is Brett going to like me more in the blue dress or the red gown?" Veracity spoke like she was talking to a particularly dim-witted child, enunciating the words.

I thought about it. I *could* just pick a color, but then she'd want reasons for it and I'd be sucked into a debate over a question I didn't care about. "Have you asked him?" I tried.

Her nose wrinkled in distaste. "I can't do that. He'd see what the dress looks like."

"And that's bad because...?" I prompted.

"Ugh," she said, exasperated, "because then he wouldn't be surprised when I walk down the stairs in all my glory on Prom night. Duh."

It was my turn to wrinkle my nose. "Our house doesn't have stairs."

"Not *literal* stairs," she said, as if that should have been obvious. "Metaphysical stairs, like you see in the movies."

Metaphorical, I corrected, though I didn't say it out loud. I didn't need another lecture on how hard she worked to "culture her image" and how it "depleted her confident energy" when I corrected her.

"You could just ask him what his favorite color is," I suggested.

She gave a short nod. "Brown. Because that's the color of my eyes. But can you *imagine* me wearing brown?" She scoffed. "It's *so* drab."

"Have you... talked to him?" I hedged. Brett was a Junior. Veracity was a Sophomore. She wouldn't admit it, but I knew she was nervous he hadn't asked her to Prom yet.

Veracity sat on the plastic cafeteria table staring at her nails. As she opened her mouth, Brett walked in next to a teammate, their navy-and-gold letterman jackets standing out from the crowd. His smile, always genuine, radiated kindness.

She spotted him and squealed, "Brett!" Waving her arm like she was in a Miss America pageant. He made his way to our table.

"Hey, Veracity," he said politely. "How's your morning going?"

She tapped her cheek and waited like she always did.

Blushing furiously at the demand with her groupies standing around, he gave her a quick peck. A collective sigh could be heard from all the girls.

"Wonderful," she said, running her arm down his jacket sleeve until her hand was in his, keeping him planted amid the gaggle of girls. I knew all the fawning made him uncomfortable.

Brett was captain of the football team. He was a people person and, unlike most jocks, he was very humble. I had seen him go out of his way to cheer people up after a fumbled ball or a lost game. He was a decent, all-around guy with a strong boy-next-door vibe.

His eyes connected with mine, and he gave me a sheepish grin. We hadn't said more than a handful of words to each other, mainly because I couldn't find my tongue when he was around, but I could tell he felt just as awkward around her groupies as I did.

The thing was, Veracity hadn't always had the hangers-on. Last year, she wasn't one of the preppy girls. She had acne, glasses, and braces and just wanted to survive her teen years. Her short, choppy hair looked like an evil lawnmower had given her a makeover, which didn't help.

Then she started hanging out with Britney, the new girl, who was obsessed with fashion magazines. Over the summer, Veracity had morphed into a clear-complected diva draped in false confidence, her insecurities masked by layers of makeup. Obsessed with finding the perfect boyfriend, she started plotting a way to get Brett into her clutches on the first day of her Sophomore year. The two of them had amassed a following with Veracity clearly in the lead.

"Now that I've had my good-luck kiss," she said, giving him a dazzling smile, "let's put it to the test."

He blinked. I held my breath. Veracity was supposed to do this out in the parking lot, not in the middle of the cafeteria.

"Prom is next month," she prompted, pulling him around to face her as she fussed over his jacket, dusting it off and tugging it straight as if she were already imagining him in a tux. "And we're going to want to arrive in style, of course."

Judging by the deer-in-the-headlights look he wore, he hadn't been expecting this conversation. A dozen heartbeats passed in silence. I caught Veracity's slow blink, something she did to keep herself from shifting nervously.

"I can probably get my parents to spring for a limo," she said slowly. "But I need to know what time they should have the driver ready." She smiled demurely up at him, waiting.

Brett's gaze panned around to the groupies, all leaned in, listening for his reply. His eyes landed on mine and I cringed in sympathy. His shoulders slumped. He wouldn't turn her down in front of her entire group of friends. That's why she had cornered him here. It was mean and I felt bad for Brett. Veracity made a habit of taking advantage of his kindness.

She hadn't always been so callous. We used to just watch television and eat pizza and laugh over stupid jokes. She would talk about starting programs where she'd collect used designer dresses from red-carpet events and give them to poor kids who wanted to look beautiful at school dances.

The bell rang, saving Brett from the spotlight. At the rustling of bodies, he leaned in and whispered something to Veracity before giving her another quick kiss and heading off to class.

She gave him a sour look that told me he hadn't given her a straight answer. I got stuck waiting for the gaggle of groupies to disperse. All but Britney, who seemed to be muttering under her breath while she tracked Veracity's progress through the room.

✧

"What are they fighting about now?" I asked, listening to our parents argue in whispers from their bedroom. Veracity had snuck into my room like she always did when the house became tense. She sat neatly tucked into the beige beanbag in the corner of my room while I lay on the bed staring at the ceiling.

It took her a long moment to answer. "The limo."

I wasn't sure how she had gotten Brett to invite her to Prom, but I knew for a fact that he didn't care about a limo. His mom was happy to drive them. Brett had told her after school he had no problem with that, but Veracity had objected. Hard.

"You can't show up to the Promenade in your mother's car," she'd told him. "What will people think?"

Listening to our parents argue, I wondered if it was worth it to her. "Who cares what you guys show up in?"

"Hi. I'm your sister. Have we met?"

She was my sister, but she wasn't the same sister I'd grown up with. She'd changed. I wanted to ask her why everyone else's opinion suddenly mattered so much. Instead, I just brooded until her light snoring lulled me to sleep.

I awoke to grunting and muttered curses. Rubbing my eyes, I sat up to see Veracity with the neck of her nightgown pulled down to her chest. She was scratching madly at her neck and shoulders.

"What are you doing?" I asked.

"I itch like *crazy*," she said. "I think I'm breaking out or something."

I turned on the light and took a knee in front of her. "Okay, stop scratching it for a minute." I checked her skin, which was spotted with flat, splotchy welts. "It looks like you've got hives," I said.

"What?" she screeched. "I can't have hives. I've never had hives. And Prom is in a *week*. I can*not* have hives." She started gasping for breath and I worried she would hyperventilate.

"It's not that bad. I don't think hives last that long."

"What do they look like?" she demanded. "Are they all pus-filled and gross?"

"No," I assured her. "They're like mosquito bites." Really big mosquito bites. Her neck looked like a topographical map.

She fluttered her hands in the air, fanning herself. "Okay, I need a mirror." She shoved me aside and ran to the bathroom.

I went to my closet and pulled out a black turtleneck before researching hives on the computer.

She came back, looking panicked. "I can't go to school this way. I look hideous."

Honestly, with her night gown properly in place, they were barely noticeable, though I knew that wasn't going to be good enough for her. I pointed to the turtleneck laid out on the bed and she lunged for it.

"You're the best. Kim Kardashian *wishes* she had a sister as good as you," she said, stripping off her nightgown.

"It looks like hives can be caused by allergies and a bunch of other things, including stress. I'm going with that one."

"You think," she muttered, her head stuck in the long tube of the neck, making her look like one of those air-filled dolls that wave outside car stores.

"It says they only last a few days. They should be gone before Prom."

"Oh, thank goodness."

I went to dig out my own set of clothes. "It says you can take allergy meds to reduce the itchiness."

"Oh, gross. I would never," she scoffed. "Do you know how badly allergy medication dries out your pores?"

I threw on my favorite jeans, a gray shirt, and a white button up that I left open. "Well, maybe tonight you can do a search for homeopathic remedies for hives that won't dry out your skin." I ran a brush through my hair and was ready to go. "Just don't scratch at them."

It took another half hour for Veracity to complete her morning ritual. She fidgeted with her collar all the way to school. We walked into the cafeteria and I raised my voice so she could hear me. "If stress is causing them, you're not helping anything by worrying about it. Try to relax. You'll be hive-free before the dance on Saturday, I'm sure of it."

A suspicious voice piped in from behind us. "Did you say hives?"

With a gasp, Veracity spun around, her hand at her throat,

looking for all the world like she had just been accused of murder. Eyes wide, she locked eyes with the same dim-witted groupie that had wanted a sip of her not-tea.

"Britney!" she said with false cheer. "What did you say? Something about wives?" She let out a forced laugh that sounded like it came from a hyena-donkey hybrid. "Brett and I are together, but there's no talk of *marriage*." She glanced down at her hand, as if considering the notion. "Yet."

Britney wasn't paying any attention to Veracity's hand. She was eyeing the black top. "That's a turtleneck," she said, her tone flat.

Veracity's hand went to her chest, self-conscious. "And?"

"It's Tuesday. You only wear turtlenecks on Friday. And only if it's below seventy degrees out." Her brows drew together in concern and she stepped closer to whisper, "Which it's not. You never break your own fashion rules."

I bit back a groan. *Now* the dim-wit wanted to have brains. And *of course* it revolved around Veracity's fashion choices.

Veracity looked ready to panic. She smoothed her top. "Do you think people will notice?" I hated how small and vulnerable she sounded. Yes, Britney was the one who got Veracity hooked on fashion trends, but it bugged me that, despite being an airhead, she had the power to hurt my sister.

Britney gave her an encouraging smile. "Not if I tell them I let you borrow my necklace, but *insisted* you wear it with a black top because I wanted it to really stand out." She reached up under her strawberry-blonde hair to unclasp the silver chain from around her neck. At the end of it dangled a deep green teardrop gemstone with silver filagree swirling around the edges.

Veracity took it, casting a furtive look around to see if there was anyone watching before she handed it to me, lifting her hair and turning her back so I could hook it around her neck.

"One more thing," Britney said, digging around in her purse. Her hand emerged with a dark brown bottle about two inches tall. "This is peppermint essential oil and it does *wonders* for relaxation. You just rub it on your temples or your neck or your wrists and it calms you right down."

"Really?" Veracity said. "That's so sweet." She let her hair down once I finished putting on her necklace. The dark brown locks had grown past her shoulders since her evil-lawnmower days. "I'm still not letting you drink any of my triple venti, soy, half-caff, half sweet, non-fat, no foam, caramel macchiato with extra whip, *but*," she paused for effect, "I might buy you one of your own."

They did a girl squeal of solidarity and walked to our usual table with their hands clasped. I was just happy Veracity had a game plan. I was in the middle of my latest fantasy book, a story about a young homeless girl that signs on with an assassin's guild, just to wind up running the Academy of Magical Intelligence. I sat at the far end of the table, just beyond the last of the groupies, and soon I was hunched over my book, lost in a world of incantations and murder.

A voice intruded on my thoughts. "Looks like a pretty interesting book."

I looked up to see Brett smiling down at me and my stomach fluttered. He took a seat across the table. I glanced at Veracity, who seemed to be in the middle of an animated tale that involved hair, if her gesturing was any indication.

"So, is it?" he asked.

It took me a minute to remember he had asked about my book. "Yes," I answered simply, the world of intrigue calling me back to the pages.

"What's it about?"

I flipped the book closed so he could see the cover.

"*Assassin of the Occult*," he read. "That's a good series. It's one of my top ten, for sure."

"You read fantasy?" I asked.

He nodded. "Every chance I get."

Our brief conversation was interrupted by Veracity. "Brett!" she called, doing her princess wave. Britney turned to see Brett and the smile she was wearing melted. Everyone wanted to bask in Veracity's attention. The problem was it never stayed in one place for long.

Brett smiled. "My queen beckons," he said, standing. "You should check out Marstaff's series, *Mark of the Dour*," he called back at me as he headed off to give Veracity her good-luck kiss.

I was surprised at his good taste in books, if not girlfriends. I had read Marstaff at least a half-dozen times. It was one of my favorites, as well.

✧

By Wednesday, Veracity's hives were gone. All that remained were faint, red splotches that could be covered with makeup. We were sure the discoloration would be gone by Saturday.

We were wrong.

By Thursday evening, the faint redness had become more noticeable.

By Friday, her face looked like a toddler had fed her berries and couldn't figure out where her mouth was. The splotches had turned into a rash that crept up her face. Mom had taken her to the doctor and had come home with a steroid cream. Mom let her skip school after Veracity convinced her there was nothing important happening in class since it was the day before Prom.

She was up at the crack of dawn Saturday, crying her eyes out, which didn't do her complexion any favors. Not that I could blame her. The rash had turned shiny and wrinkly and she reeked of candy canes.

"Good grief, Veracity. How much of that peppermint oil did you use?"

She just cried harder, blubbering about how no amount of makeup could save her now. "And this stupid cream can take over two weeks to work!" she wailed, throwing the tube of topical steroid at the wall.

I stroked her hair as I waited for her to recover. Veracity wasn't one to take unfortunate consequences laying down for long, though. Soon, she pulled herself together enough to blot her eyes.

"Where's your phone?" she asked, holding her hand out like I had it hidden somewhere in my pocket-less nightshirt.

I took it from the charging stand and handed it over. "Who are you calling?"

"Britney."

190

"It's a bit early, don't you think?" I asked, though *I* wouldn't have waited if *my* face made me look like it belonged in a burn unit.

She didn't bother responding, choosing to glower at my wall while she listened to the phone ring on Britney's end of the line. I heard a sleepy mumble come from the receiver, though I couldn't make out the words.

"Your peppermint oil turned me into a hag!" Veracity shrieked.

I cringed. Our parents were heavy sleepers, but they had their limits.

"How could you do this to me?"

I waited, sitting at my computer, looking up the side effects of overusing essential oils. The pictures I came across looked very much like Veracity's skin condition. Britney managed to calm Veracity down and she hung up the phone.

"She's coming over," Veracity said. "She has something she's sure will clear it up before the dance."

I watched her chew her lip nervously while she paced and I tried to gauge her mindset. Veracity was willing to listen to sense, but only if it didn't inconvenience her too much. Putting something new on her face in its current condition seemed like a bad idea. I didn't think she would listen to me if I told her that, though.

I decided to just wait and see what Britney brought over. Maybe it was her mom's hydrating cold cream mixed with baking soda or something. That probably wouldn't cause any detrimental reaction. "Okay, but let me do some research on whatever she brings before you put it on."

Veracity didn't reply.

As promised, Britney was over in no time. Her sister was a senior and, more importantly, had a driver's license. I ushered them both back to my room.

"Hey, Dahlia," Britney said in greeting. "You know my sister Abby, right—Oh my gosh!" she gasped, spotting Veracity. "You look terrible!" She rushed over to throw her arms around Veracity.

Abby strolled in wearing ripped jeans and a shirt with a heavy metal band logo written in jagged letters on it. The silver chain hanging from her belt clinked as she moved. I had seen Abby around school. She hung out with a group of pot heads. I never would have guessed she was Britney's sister. They were so different.

She eyed Veracity before saying, "Someone's out of the running for Prom Queen."

Britney turned to give her a venomous glare. Unbothered, Abby shrugged before turning to me. "Hey," she said in greeting.

"Hey." Something niggled at my brain, but it took some focus to figure out what. Standing there in her torn clothes, I couldn't help but feel like she was casing my room. She had a mystic, creepy quality to her. Reluctantly, I turned away as Veracity loudly demanded her miracle cure.

"Funny you should call it that," Britney said. "Because it really is a miracle."

I rolled my eyes. Every beauty product Veracity owned had the word miracle or magic or age-defying or some such promotional malarkey printed on it somewhere.

"It works great," Abby affirmed, holding up a little silver packet with words printed on it in black. "We've got connections."

"Shut up!" Britney said, suddenly venomous.

Everybody froze. Veracity and I stared at Britney like she'd grown a third head.

"What?" Abby asked, gesturing to Veracity. "Look what you did to her. You think she doesn't know?"

"Know what?" Veracity and I asked in unison.

"Shut up," Britney repeated, though calmer this time. She turned an apologetic look on Veracity. "She's delusional. She did some family history project for school, and now she keeps insisting we come from a line of witches. Just ignore her."

Abby held her hands up. "Hey, don't shoot the messenger." She held up a shiny little packet. "This stuff is foolproof. I guarantee it will give you an amazing complexion."

Veracity's eyes locked on the packet, almost feral in intensity. "I'll buy you both a latte if it works."

With the packet dangling in the air, Veracity rushed over, but I snatched it away from Abby before she could reach it. I held a hand up to ward her off while I read what it said.

"Georgina's Magic Balm," I said. "Beauty guaranteed by the Pretty Bayou Coven of Florida." I snorted, moving on to the ingredients list, which was printed so small I thought I might need a magnifying glass.

I got as far as formaldehyde before the packet was snatched out of my hands. Veracity ripped it open and squeezed silvery goo out onto her fingers, smearing it on her face in rushed movements.

"Veracity, slow down. That stuff's got formaldehyde in it. They use that to preserve dead bodies."

She paused, then resumed lathering. "Well, if it can make a corpse look decent, I'm sure it'll do wonders for me."

I groaned, already sure this was going to end badly.

I picked up the empty packet from Veracity's dresser and read the rest of the ingredients. She had torn it right across the finely printed list, so all I could make out was utque vitae and lingua bova. I sat at my computer and ran them through the search engine. They were Latin for "horn of life" and "ox tongue."

I would have shared my findings with Veracity, but she would most likely think spreading ox tongue on her face was some new fad from India or something.

"I think it's working," she said. "My face feels smoother."

"Oh, it totally does!" Britney said, clapping in glee and bouncing on her toes, excited not to have caused the downfall of her idol.

"Yay," Abby said, deadpan. "It's time to go, Britney. You still have my chores to do." She let out a big yawn. "And I'm going back to sleep."

"You're going to look totally fab tonight. Like, unreal," Britney said, giving Veracity a fake kiss on each cheek, making sure not to get any of the shimmery, translucent goo on her. "A unicorn among goats."

Veracity's eyes lit up at the phrase. Abby was already out the door and then Britney was gone, too. I went back to look at Veracity's face. The goo had soaked into the cracked creases of her skin, filling them in and drying to a powdery shine. It did seem to be reducing redness. Or maybe it just covered it up.

"That doesn't sting or anything?" I asked.

She shook her head, turning to hold up a handheld mirror and stare at her reflection. "It feels soft, like liquid satin. Maybe it will permanently close my pores so I'll never get blackheads or, like, sweat or anything."

I left the lecture on how sweat regulated your body temperature to her science teacher.

We watched television for the first half of the day, and I was shocked to see that the cracked skin seemed to improve at a miraculous rate. The redness and creasing had completely disappeared by noon. Veracity was ecstatic. I was still skeptical.

By lunch, her skin had improved beyond anything we could have hoped for. It still had the shimmery quality, but it had faded to a powder-soft finish that left her skin looking like it was made of porcelain.

"Look at this, Dahlia," she breathed. "I won't even need to wear makeup at this point." She bit her lip in excitement. "Well, maybe some color around my eyes," she amended.

I ended up reading a book while Veracity talked on the phone with Britney about where she could get more of the magic lotion in case she had another facial crisis. From what I could hear, it sounded like there wasn't any more.

I got to start the last book of my *Assassin of the Occult* series, which had such a gripping opening that it was an hour before I noticed Veracity was still on the phone. I glanced up to see that her face had continued to change.

She was still beautiful, but she was, maybe, *too* beautiful? Her face no longer had the powder finish to it, instead having an airbrushed quality, like she had been digitally altered and walked right off the page of a magazine.

When she got off the phone, she checked herself out again, saying, "Ah-mazing."

Her skin looked a bit fake to me, but she could get away with it. Nobody's face looked natural at Prom. Still, I figured it wouldn't hurt to take precautions. "You might want to wash your face in case there's still some residue on it," I suggested.

She looked aghast. "Are you kidding? This stuff is still working. I

194

look better every minute. Just my luck, I'll wash it off and turn into a hag again. No way. This face is staying just like it is until I'm sixty years old."

We watched Carrie with the lights off to kill time before getting her dolled up. As it turned out, she should have washed the goo off.

When we turned the lights back on I gaped at her like a fish out of water. She ran to the bathroom, excited to see what new level of beauty had unfolded while Carrie was getting soaked in blood.

I didn't even react when I heard her scream. I was grateful my mom and dad had gone to see a matinee and an early dinner.

"I don't look human!" she screeched.

She was right. Her face looked more like a Barbie doll than ever. At least in the sense that it looked like hard plastic. Her skin wasn't actually stiff, but whatever expression she wore, it looked like it was frozen on her face until it changed to a different expression. And it was weird watching her facial expressions change. Creepy.

I didn't bother to ask my computer what to do about it. I wasn't even sure how to ask the question.

"What am I going to do? I can't go to Prom looking like *this*," she cried from the bathroom.

I let out a strangled laugh. I knew she shouldn't have used Britney's hare-brained ideas, but she wouldn't listen. What were we going to do now?

"Help me, Dahlia!" Veracity said, rushing back into the room. She was holding a wet washcloth. "It won't come off. I don't even care about Prom anymore. Just don't let me turn into a plastic girl. I want to be a real girl!"

Her eyes filled with tears. As they spilled over, they rolled down her cheeks in perfect little spheres. They didn't spread out or soak into her skin at all, which was more disturbing than anything.

"Okay, I have a plan," I said. "We need to get Britney over here to fix this."

"I'll do anything she says."

Didn't I know it.

Britney, as if on standby, answered the phone on the first ring. I explained as best I could and heard her yelling for her sister before she hung up. When they arrived, Britney was in tears. "I'm so sorry," she wailed.

"What happened to fool-proof?" Veracity asked, exasperated.

Abby said, "I told you so," looking at her sister.

"I didn't mean to. I promise." Britney's teary eyes pleaded with Veracity, who glowered at her.

"You did this intentionally?"

"No, really, I didn't. I wasn't even sure it was me until just now," she said.

"You'd better explain," I told her. "Start from the beginning."

Britney swiped at her eyes. "It started Monday when you asked Brett to Prom."

"I didn't ask him to Prom, I simply discussed our options," Veracity said primly.

"Well, it just got me thinking. He doesn't get you at all. He's not interested in any of the same things you are." She bit her lip. "I guess I just don't know what you see in him."

"What does that have to do with anything?"

"Abby said my negative energy is what caused your hives. I thought she was being stupid. I mean, that's insane, right? Just because I didn't think you and Brett were good together didn't mean I had the power to destroy your complexion."

"You're right. That's dumb," I said.

"Only, I had the thought that if you got a zit or something, you'd probably stay at home and he wouldn't even understand why. Like, he doesn't get the social aspect of fashion and beauty, you know?"

I remembered her muttering to herself after the bell rang that morning. But, no. That was ridiculous.

"And then I felt bad when you got hives, but I didn't think that was me," she said, snorting in disbelief. "But I gave you that peppermint oil and totally expected it to help. Except you ended up talking with Brett all morning and making more plans for Prom and..." She sighed. "It just got to me, you know?"

Veracity didn't respond, though the icy look on her face spoke volumes.

"Anyway, when I saw what it did to your face, I really did feel responsible." Her pleading look turned timid. "Though, you probably shouldn't have used so much."

I turned to give Veracity a dry look. She ignored me, turning her nose up at both of us.

Britney hurried on. "Abby said that cream would for sure fix your face. Just in case she was right about my negative thoughts, I made sure to think good thoughts. I felt so bad that your big night was going to be ruined, so I pictured you radiant and flawless. Like... Barbie." She winced as she said it.

"And that's when you figured maybe your thoughts have magic?" I asked, floored at her logic. A person can't just think something and make it happen. That's like something out of a book. That stopped me. It actually was something out of a book. My book. In *Mark of the Dour*, magic relied wholly on the intent of the caster.

I had an idea. "Wait right here," I said.

I put some acetone on a cotton ball and handed it to Britney. "Make sure your thoughts are focused on her health, not her beauty this time," I advised.

Nodding meekly, she swiped gently along the side of Veracity's chin. The motion was gentle and caring and had an oddly intimate quality to it I wasn't expecting. Maybe there was more than one reason she was upset about Brett.

"Tell me if it burns or itches or anything," I instructed.

At first, nothing happened, but eventually the plastic residue came off in thin, gunky layers until only pink, irritated skin was left.

It took an entire bag of cotton balls and most of the acetone. Veracity's skin looked bright red and angry and faint cracks were still visible in patches, but overall, it looked better than it had in days. Well, minus the pre-plastic perfection. She sighed in relief.

The doorbell rang.

She glanced down at her watch. "Ack! That's Brett!" She turned to me, eyes wide. "Go answer the door for me. Stall him!"

I wasn't sure why she didn't want me to just tell him she wasn't feeling well. It wasn't like she was going to let him see her with her current sun-blasted face. I went to answer the door.

"Hey, Dahlia." Brett wore a tux that made him look so dashing I found it hard to breathe. "Is Veracity ready?"

My brain had glitched out, and I just stared at him until I realized my jaw was hanging open. I snapped it shut, feeling a flush crawl up my neck. "She's here," I said. "She's just...uh..."

Veracity came out of the back room. "I'm so sorry." Her hair was pulled into a ponytail and her face was covered in fluffy white cream.

My mouth dropped back open. "Veracity?"

She looked like she was in the middle of a spa treatment. She ignored me. "Hey, Brett. You look really nice." She sounded off, and it took me a moment to realize her voice didn't have the airhead quality she had adopted over the summer.

Brett's smile was good-natured, but he was obviously confused. "Yours isn't the look I was expecting, but with your confidence, I expect you could pull it off."

"I could if I was standing next to you," she said, smiling back. It was the most genuine smile I'd ever seen from her. "But I won't be."

She turned to me. "I'm going to bow out of tonight. Dahlia can wear my dress. She gets ready a lot faster than I do, so you guys won't be all that late."

I shook my head, suddenly panicked at the thought of going out with Brett, even if just for a night. "Veracity, no. What are you doing?"

She gave Brett a look of apology, raising a finger as she pulled me back down the hallway so we could talk a little more privately.

"I want you to go out with him," she insisted. "Really."

I gaped at her, wondering if she was running a fever.

She reached out to grasp my hand. "You told me to wait before using that stupid lotion earlier and I ignored you. I should have known better, because you always, *always* have my best interest at heart."

She was definitely acting weird. Maybe the lotion seeped into her brain and she was malfunctioning. Was that possible? Where was Britney? She better be thinking positive thoughts.

Veracity glanced at Brett, standing in the doorway, eyes casually running across my living room. "At first, I wanted to be with Brett because, you know," a leer spread across her face, "he's smoking hot."

Her eyes danced with laughter as she caught my blush. I couldn't argue with her on that count. "But as I got to know him, I wanted to be with him because he seemed to care about other people more than himself." She gave me a sheepish smile. "He reminds me of you." She waved one hand dismissively. "Except, like, in boy form."

I chuckled. "Yeah?"

"Yeah," she said. "You two are the same kind of people. And I've seen how you get all flustered around him. Besides, he's your age, not mine, and despite being older, you both like books about dragons, which is totally weird." She smiled again. "I know you'll be great together. I think I always knew that. But I was selfish. I didn't put you first. And I should have."

I wanted to tell her she was wrong. That I was selfish, too. I had been wanting to talk to Brett for a long time, and that desire had only increased since he asked me about my book. I didn't, though, because I was afraid. I was afraid that the spark I felt for him would turn into something more and that I'd end up hurting Veracity. She was family and you didn't do that to family. Really, I wouldn't do that to anyone, but I especially wouldn't do that to family.

She sensed my hesitation. "You have my full blessing on one condition."

"What's that?" I asked, narrowing my eyes.

"Don't blow it. At least not any worse than I did."

Could I do it? Could I just leave her here, recuperating from her traumatic day and run off with her boyfriend? Did having permission change anything?

My moral dilemma was solved when Britney appeared in the doorway of Veracity's bedroom. Veracity gave her a considering look. "I think we'll be needing some privacy to talk about a few things tonight, anyway."

I raised an eyebrow at her and she held her hands in front of her.

"I promise I won't put anything strange on my skin, okay?"

I chuckled. "Yeah, like I believe *that* for a second."

She acted all offended, shoving me off toward Brett. "You two have fun," she said, heading back to her room where Britney looked about as hopeful as I'd ever seen her.

I blushed, standing awkwardly near Brett, but he gave me that easygoing smile of his. He didn't look the least bit disappointed. I couldn't help my return grin. "So," I said. "What should we do?"

He held one arm up, gesturing at where a blue sedan sat on the curb. "I was thinking we should cancel that limo and take my mom's car to the bookstore. There's a new one over by the old drive-in theater."

He held his elbow out and I looped my arm through his. "I think that's a splendid idea."

Meet Jen Bair

Jen Bair is an Air Force brat, Army veteran, and military wife. She and her husband shamelessly drag their sons all over the world on one adventure after another. Jen has lived in 12 U.S. States, the Philippines, Guam, Korea, and Germany...so far. She fully believes in world exploration as a lifestyle. Much of her time is spent homeschooling her four children, training her energetic Malinois, or planning the next family vacation. She loves travelling to foreign places, real or imaginary. Her family is her life. Her writing is her passion. Check out her published works at www.JenBair.com or write to her at author@JenBair.com. She'd love to hear from you.

Casting Blame

REBEKAH AMAN

O ur family was perfect. Mom and Dad doted on me—sometimes more than I wanted—but they let me play outside often and gave me yummy treats regularly, so I didn't mind all that much. Everything would have continued in idyllic family bliss, but they just had to bring home a new bundle of joy.

"Look, princess! It's your new baby brother," Dad said excitedly as he presented the squirming thing for my inspection.

At first, I didn't know what to make of him. Maybe he'd be okay. We could play together, and I could easily blame my wrongdoings on him. However, the first time I heard that child wail, I knew this wasn't going to work out.

I watched Mom and Dad coddle the little creature, bouncing him, rubbing his back, cooing to him. They should be doing all that to *me*, but their entire focus had shifted. I was no longer the center of their universe. A usurper had entered my domain. They weren't even giving me meals at the proper times anymore. I was an afterthought, and that just wouldn't do.

In my defense, I did not initially plan to create chaos.

It all started rather innocently. I was sitting in the baby's room, watching him wave his arms at the spinning mobile. The thought even crossed my mind that he looked somewhat cute. Then Mom walked in, and I, of course, perked up and tried to look even cuter than the baby. But she didn't pay me even the slightest attention. She walked straight to the crib to talk to him in that ridiculous baby tone, at which point, I made a sound to inform her of my disgust.

"Oh, princess, I didn't know you were in here! Keeping your baby brother company?" she asked.

I turned away from her to look out the window. She had ignored me, so it was only fair that I return the favor. She chuckled.

"Don't be upset, princess. Babies require a lot of attention, but things will get back to normal soon. I promise," she said as she leaned over to give me a kiss.

I was almost ready to forgive her when the little creature in the crib started crying, and she instantly ran over to him. The audacity! How dare he pull my mom away from me when she finally showed me some attention! I would not stand for it.

"Oh, you need a fresh diaper," Mom muttered in the background as she rushed over to the changing table, "and of course we're out over here. Just a minute, little one, Mommy will be right back."

As I said before, there was no plan involved with what happened next. I didn't want him to be in the crib when Mom came back because then she would pick him up and love him, and I wanted her attention on me. As I watched my baby brother begin to float toward the ceiling, I realized my wish was granted. It wasn't a surprise, exactly. I knew I was magical because I'd done small things before—snuck some extra snacks or hidden the keys from Dad so he wouldn't be able to leave for work—but I also hadn't let my parents know because neither of them were magical. I didn't think they would handle it very well.

Hearing Mom's panicked scream when she returned to find my baby brother tangled up in the mobile solidified my decision to not let them know about my powers.

"Our baby has powers, Nick!" Mom yelled with wide eyes.

"How is that possible? Neither of our families are magical," he said in alarm.

Mom shook her head. "I don't know! But... I heard that sometimes it happens. In rare cases."

My eyes bounced back and forth between them as they stared at each other in shock, trying to digest the fact that their child was magical. It was definitely best that they blamed the baby for all this. And that's when a wicked little thought took root in my mind. Well, not really *wicked*, just mischievous. I would make my baby brother the outcast of the family. He would cause so much trouble for Mom and Dad with *his* magic that they would start doting on me again. I would be the good one, the one much more deserving of their love.

Thus began my campaign to sabotage the new creature in the house.

"Oh, honey, look! The baby's crawling!" Mom yelled excitedly one day.

I turned to look, and sure enough, the thing was half-crawling, half-dragging himself across the carpet... and then onto the chair... and then up the wall. A glance toward my once-pleased parents revealed the frightened horror on their faces.

"Get the ladder!" Dad called as he rushed over to the baby that was just out of reach. "How is he doing this?"

They spread blankets and pillows all over the house after that, which made lounging around comfortably much easier for me. Unfortunately, they started paying even more attention to my brother, so I changed tactics.

While eating in the kitchen one morning, baby brother tossed his food onto the floor. So I decided to make other things fall on the floor as well—the vase of flowers sitting in the middle of the dining table, the jug of orange juice on the counter, Mom's coffee—it was such a beautiful mess.

I was allowed to play outside for quite a while after that so they could clean up without me getting in the way. I had a wonderful time exploring the backyard in search of treasure. I even found some treasure that I brought inside with me, certain that I would receive Mom and Dad's praise. However, they were cooing over the baby again.

"Such a gifted boy, you are." Mom praised him. "We will teach you how to control your magic, and you will be so helpful around the house."

"It'll be a bit tough until he learns, though." Dad chuckled as he tickled my brother under the chin.

I stood in unhappy silence in the doorway watching them, pleased when they finally looked my way.

"Hi, princess! Did you have fun outside? Everything is cleaned up now, so it's safe for you to come back in," Dad said with a smile.

That earned him back some of my favor, so I decided to show him my treasure, but apparently a small snake was cause for a terrified uproar with loud screaming as opposed to praise. Stupid parents. It was just a harmless, little snake. That lost me my outside play privileges for like forever because it wasn't "safe." It didn't matter how much I demanded to go outside, they were stubborn. I did come to find, though, that they were happy to placate me with anything else I requested just after they so rudely refused me, so I guess it all worked out okay in the end.

The baby still hogged all their focus, though, so I knew I had to come up with something else. Harmless floating had become routine for Mom and Dad by now; the messes were apparently standard for a baby, just usually on a smaller scale; so now I needed something drastic. I focused on the things that Mom and Dad would get onto me about, even though they were completely unjustified in doing so.

I decided that destruction of their things would work. Mom had been angry for weeks after I accidentally knocked an expensive, crystal bowl off the side bar. My baby brother was going to take it a step further. I chose the time very strategically. It wouldn't do for them to think it was me, after all, but I also had to make sure they couldn't stop the mayhem or it would become another cute baby mishap to joke about.

Dinner prep seemed the ideal time. Mom would be distracted, and Dad was generally watching the news. They were around but not really *present*. Cue the floating collectibles: vintage cars, pristinely boxed action figures, comic books. It was an adult mobile of personally priceless junk circling just outside the range of the ceiling fan. Dad still hadn't noticed anything. But it wasn't good enough to just destroy Dad's keepsakes. Mom had to feel the pain and disappointment of loss as well.

That's where the wedding curio came into play. It took no time at all to open the door and whisk several items out to join Dad's more colorful baubles still hovering around the ceiling fan. Everything was in place, so now it was time to draw their attention.

I yelled loudly and began jumping up and down. Of course, they were slow to realize they weren't supposed to be looking at me but at the place I focused my eyes on. Oh, the horror that filled their faces. I actually did feel some guilt when I shifted the path of their toys and memories to allow the fan blades to smash into them and send bits and pieces hurtling into the walls. The baby's happy giggles were icing on the cake. This was fun for him.

By the time they turned the fan off, it was much too late. The damage had been done. Mom cried, while Dad looked like he wanted to as he patted her back. As the good child, I moved over to their little huddle on the floor to provide comfort. It was a wonderful night.

Unexpectedly, the next morning was back to normal. More baby doting. How? What did I have to do to make them stop showering the usurper with love and attention that was supposed to belong to me? They hadn't even gotten onto him for it! Stupid baby.

My last scheme had been drastic and had failed. This next strategy was going to move into dangerous territory. Just like my parents had refused my outside time because the snake was danger-ous, I could make the baby suffer similar treatment with a bit of dangerous magic. I thought about overturning the large bookcase, but that would mess up my favorite play area. If I was going to be inconvenienced, it wasn't worth the trouble. Making the crib fall over while baby brother was inside also seemed promising, but I didn't actually want him to get hurt. That was a bit too risky even for me.

Mom was the one that caused my ultimate epiphany. She was cutting up an apple and nicked her finger.

"Knives are dangerous, princess. Remember that," she warned me as she ran water over the wound. "We don't play with knives."

My eyes slid over to the block of wood filled with the deadly implements. Yep, knives were dangerous.

Peace and contentment filled the dining room as we all enjoyed our meal as a family. It felt good—the laughter and smiles. Everyone's guard was down. I made sure to studiously focus on my food as the knives encircled the table, but once they were all in place, I carefully stood and positioned myself in front of one gleamingly sharp end.

"Aurora!" Dad shouted and pointed. "Stay there!"

With mock surprise, I turned toward where he was pointing and made sure to jump and make a startled noise upon locating the danger. Mom rushed around the table to me, grabbed the knife, and hugged me to her chest. Dad carefully gathered the other knives, some of which bobbed just out of reach. Ultimately, he ended up shoving the knives he was able to collect into a drawer and shuffling us all into the safety of the living room.

"We have to do something about this, honey," he said shaking his head. "He's endangering himself, Aurora, the two of us. He doesn't even understand what he's doing."

I was certain at this point they were going to get rid of my former baby brother, but I was careful to hide my excitement.

"Some of my magical friends have recommended someone that is very skilled in handling this kind of thing," Mom replied softly. "I'll call in the morning."

I slept very well that night and was pleased to see the baby bundled up and leaving the house with Mom the next day. Bye-bye, usurper. You were tough, I grant you, but you were no match for me. Smugness rolled off me in waves for several hours after that. I had won, and it felt so good. When Mom's car pulled in, I rushed to the door. She had a lot of misplaced attention to make up for, and I expected her to start as soon as she walked into the house.

The lock clicked back, the door opened, her shout of "Honey, I'm back" echoed through the crack, and then I heard a giggle. My heart stopped. Surely, I misheard. Then the door swung open, and mom walked in with that creature in her arms. What was this? I had gotten rid of him. Why was he back?

"How did it go? What did the doctor say?" Dad asked as he poked his head out of his office.

Mom shook her head with a frown. "That's the thing. He said he didn't sense any magic from him."

"What?"

Mom shrugged. "He said that it happens sometimes. When kids are really little like this, magic kind of flickers, like a lightbulb."

"Huh. So... what do we do?"

"Well, the doctor has to see that he has magic before anything can be done, so I'm just supposed to call when strange things happen again."

So the scheming had to begin again. He was lucky the first time, but I'd make that doctor believe my little brother had magic, and then he'd be dealt with permanently.

I'll admit that despite my internal declaration of war, I was having trouble coming up with more effective strategies. Part of the problem was ensuring that I wouldn't get caught because now Mom and Dad watched the baby extremely closely, ready in a moment to call the doctor. I couldn't risk them finding out I was the actual culprit and getting shipped off in the usurper's place. It was a tricky conundrum.

Ultimately, though, I decided to do a simple but harmless floating trick while the baby was alone in the living room. I was, of course, looking down on him from the stairs, but Mom and Dad didn't know I was there so nothing would come back to me. The phone call was made, and then we waited. It was boring. I may have fallen asleep briefly.

The ringing doorbell startled me, and I looked down to see Mom moving to answer it.

"I hope he starts back up again, or we just wasted the doctor's time," my mom said worriedly.

This was it. This was my moment. I may have failed initially but not this time.

"Come in, Dr. Forman. He's in the living room," Mom greeted. "Thank you for coming out. His toys were floating everywhere, but it stopped a few minutes ago. I did take a video, if you want to see it."

The doctor shook his head. "I believe that magic is happening around the boy, but the source of it must be determined. I can do nothing with him until I know he is the source."

Perfect. You'll see, doctor. He's the source. Take him away so my mom and dad will focus on me again. I was very pleased with myself as I made the toys float. My nemesis watched gleefully, his little arms waving his excitement at the display.

"There, see!" Mom shouted unnecessarily.

"Hmmm," the doctor walked over, his head tilting this way and that. He muttered a few things I couldn't hear, then shook his head before straightening. "It's not him."

Silence. I blinked. How did he know? Fear coursed through me. If he knew it wasn't my brother, then would he blame me? I quietly snuck away and found a hiding place. He couldn't know it was me, right? I was a bundle of nerves. That doctor was a genius. I wasn't going to be able to fool him. I'm not sure how long I stayed hidden, but I did hear my parent's worriedly calling for me after about an hour. I was too scared to come out. What if the doctor had blamed me, and they were searching to have him drag me away from my home forever?

My growling tummy informed me when it was dinnertime, but I refused to leave my refuge. Mom and Dad renewed their efforts to locate me, and it wasn't long before Dad peeked into my hiding place.

"There you are, princess. Aren't you hungry? Why are you hiding?" he asked as he reached for me. "The doctor scared you, huh? Don't worry. He's nice. He's trying to help us. Let's get you some dinner."

I rested my head against Dad's shoulder as he rubbed my back. He wasn't angry with me, and he wasn't talking about giving me to the doctor. That meant he didn't know, right? My secret was safe. I saw my brother sitting in his highchair eating happily. My secret was safe, but I still had a problem. What was I supposed to do now?

My mopey disposition was not lost on my parents over the next several days. They commented about it and tried to pull me from my doldrums, but I just wasn't in the mood to deal with them. They were the reason I was in this mess in the first place. Didn't they realize how miserable they had made me?

I lounged grumpily on the couch, glaring at my baby brother as he toddled around. Mom and Dad were watching television, all snuggled up together. I wanted to snuggle with them, but they deserved punishment for their ill-treatment of me with this whole little brother thing. I needed another idea, one that wouldn't risk revealing my secret. What could I do?

I huffed.

"Aurora is pouting," Dad commented with a raised brow.

"What's the matter, princess?" Mom asked sweetly.

I turned to face the television, giving it my attention in obstinate response. What were they watching, anyway? It seemed boring. They always watched the boring shows without bright colors and happy chatter. This one was panning through an old house with a narrator explaining things in an incredibly dull tone.

I closed my eyes in disgust, then a little something caught my attention.

"...this haunted house. Many magical families have tested themselves inside, certain they would overcome the spirit residing within, but often, a family member disappears. Because of this..."

I tuned him back out again. A family member disappeared because of a haunted house? Well, wasn't that handy.

Instilled with renewed purpose, my focus shifted slightly away from my enemy and onto the house as a whole. I realized that if the entire house was to be haunted, I needed to create disturbances in rooms when the baby wasn't present. I was careful, of course, and made sure that I was only occasionally in those haunted rooms as well.

Pictures would fall off walls; candles would randomly light; books would be shifted around. I caused all sorts of mischief, and it was really fun. My parents were getting increasingly more irritated, especially when something they needed went missing. Just a bit more pushing and they would realize the house was haunted. Then my baby brother would disappear like the TV man said.

"She's here," my mom called one afternoon while looking out the window.

I pushed my way in front of her to see and found a beat-up car in our driveway. Who was this?

Mom had the door open before the ancient, round woman with heavy perfume and gaudy jewelry had a chance to knock. Why was Mom so excited to see this person? She was weird.

"Thank you so much for coming," my mom greeted.

The woman clapped once a hairsbreadth from her face. It startled both of us. I cut my eyes over to Mom in silent query, but she seemed disinclined to answer my wordless question. The perfume wafting from the woman was horribly overpowering, so I ran from the room. Whatever that smelly woman was, I planned to avoid her. Unfortunately, that was easier said than done. Mom was walking her throughout the house, and the woman held some smoking bundle of weeds and waved it around. They almost had me cornered in one room, but I managed to whisk out of the way just in time—well, almost. That nasty perfume still got up my nose.

I settled in the living room, despite my baby brother being there, because the smelly woman had already done an inspection of this room. It seemed the safest place. I was ready for her to leave. Why was she even here anyway?

"I sense nothing, my dear," her loud voice rang through the kitchen.

Great. She was getting closer.

"Nothing? But so many strange things have been happening around the house," Mom replied.

My ears perked. Maybe I should have been paying more attention to this woman after all.

"At first, we thought our son was magical because all the strange things happened around him, but his doctor said that he had absolutely no magic. After that, the whole house started to behave abnormally, whether he was in the room or not," Mom continued. "The house must be haunted."

Oh, so she was the lady that was supposed to announce the house was haunted and then make my brother disappear. This was terrible! I hadn't been doing anything to convince the weird lady. Was it too late now?

"You and your husband are not magical?" the lady inquired.

"No, no one in our family on either side has ever had magical abilities either."

"Hmmm..."

I crept over to the archway separating the living room from the kitchen. The woman was looking around with a frown.

"There is no history in this house to cause a haunting," the lady finally said. "I think, perhaps, you are mistaken."

No, no, no, no, no! This was my last chance. I made the refrigerator door swing open and shook the pot rack. Both women jumped.

"See?" Mom stressed, her hand still covering her heart.

That should do it. I didn't want to be implicated, though, so I decided to return to my seat on the floor of the living room where my baby brother and Dad were both present. A few minutes of extreme quiet had me growing a bit uncomfortable though. I glanced toward the kitchen. What were they doing? How long did it take to pronounce a house haunted? Maybe I should do one more thing for good measure.

The dining room was in range since it adjoined the kitchen, so Mom and the lady were sure to notice if I did something there. I started tugging on the end of the tablecloth. One gentle tug, two, three. I couldn't see Mom or the lady, so I didn't know if it had caught their attention yet. Tug. Tug. My mom gasped. Perfect. Just a bit more. I looked down at the floor and started pushing a block back and forth, but my mind was still focused on tugging the tablecloth. Tug. Tug.

"It cannot be!" the woman exclaimed.

One more tug would convince her. Just be nonchalant here in the living room, playing with a block. Tug.

"Impossible," the woman whispered, though it didn't sound like she was in the kitchen anymore.

"What? What is it?" my mom asked anxiously.

My dad stood and walked their way.

"Your house is not haunted," the woman said faintly.

What? My head shot up, my eyes locking onto the smelly woman's. She stared at me in awe and surprise, mouth agape.

"What do you mean, the house is not haunted?" my dad asked. "The baby isn't magical; the house isn't haunted; *something* is causing all of this!"

Slowly, the woman nodded, her arm drifting up to point at me. My eyes widened. No. Stop.

"Her."

My mom's brows drew together. "Aurora? That's crazy."

"That's not possible," my dad argued.

That's right, Mom and Dad. Tell her. Tell her it isn't me. She's wrong. There are rules in this world. Some things just can't be. I am your precious princess. You see that; you know that. Right? My heart was pounding as I looked from Mom to Dad to Mom to Dad. They were shocked; they wanted to argue, but I saw understanding on their faces. Everything began to click for them, and I wanted to disappear.

"The world is full of mystery," the smelly lady remarked with an almost ethereal cadence. "Because we have not yet seen something does not mean it fails to exist."

Stop talking, weird lady! You are messing up everything!

She smiled at me as she walked over and knelt.

"Aurora," her hand began to reach out like she was going to touch me, the horrible woman. She wasn't allowed to touch me, not after this betrayal.

Yet again, my wish became true without conscious thought on my part. I disappeared before she could touch me and slinked away from her. Mom and Dad both gasped, and my menace brother clapped.

The weird lady did not seem bothered by my attitude, though. Instead, she laughed before standing and facing my parents.

"Aurora is a treasure," she said. "I think the addition of your son has just soured her a bit. Let her know how much you value her as a member of the family, and your little magical problems should lessen."

Mom and Dad were clearly still in shock. They had no response.

"I'll see myself out," the weird lady said as she hobbled toward the front door.

I followed her to ensure she actually left our home, though I was still invisible. She paused on the stoop with the door cracked.

"Take good care of them, Aurora," she whispered, looking down toward me through the small opening.

I glanced at myself to ensure I wasn't visible. She shouldn't be able to see me. I looked back at her, and she winked. How did she know?

"Be proud. You are one in a million." She turned away to look at the sky. "In all my years, I never thought I would live to see a magical cat."

Meet Rebekah Aman

In addition to writing, Rebekah works full-time as an accountant in Tallahassee, Florida. She also enjoys singing and has performed in several musicals, which include The Sound of Music, Marvelous Wonderettes, Winter Wonderettes, and Beehive. Joining another collaborative work with the Legion of Dorks is an honor; the unique fun and challenge of each of their writing prompts truly allows for out-of-the-box, creative expression. Rebekah is the author of the young adult, fantasy series Keepers of the Essence, which currently has four books available. The fifth book is planned for release later this year. She and her mother, Carol Aman, also co-authored the related children's picture book series KotE Tales, illustrated by Jinsey Amber Smith, with one book available. For more information, visit her websites www.beks-books.com and www.keepersoftheessence.com. To view Jinsey's creations, you can visit her website at www.jinseysmith.com.

Vanished

JESSICA GUERNSEY

Are you really wearing that, Brandt?"

Cassie was one to talk. She wore a blue sequin leotard and fishnet stockings with too-high heels. Keeping upright as she strode across the old wood stage was one of the many talents she possessed.

I flourished the red satin-lined cloak, feeling like freakin' Dracula. "What? I look fantastic." I wanted to run my hand through my dark hair, but it was pretty firmly gelled in place. I'd spent so long getting it perfect I wasn't about to mess it up now.

"But doesn't that belong to...our boss?"

"Of course it does." I adjusted the ribbon on the huge-ass fake sapphire at my neck. "I can't go into this stream wearing Vans and a hoodie. I gotta look the part, Cass."

Not to mention that these clothes didn't smell like old dust and stale popcorn, like everything else in the theater. These had a sort of clove smell that was actually kind of nice.

She rolled her heavily-lined blue eyes and shook her head a little, her blonde curls so sprayed into place they barely moved. "Pretty sure you didn't ask Henry though."

"Well, not exactly," I said, checking the cufflinks on the sleeves. I wasn't sure I'd done them right. How did cufflinks work anyway? So useless. Good thing me and Henry were about the same height, though his shoes were a little loose. "But he'll never know. Besides, what could go wrong?"

I winked at her and earned a smile. Damn, she was hot in those fishnet stockings.

"Ready for this?" I strapped the streaming camera around my chest, checking that the fake sapphire wouldn't smack it and ruin the sound quality. A quick glance behind the prop table showed me the laptop was ready to go, with a second webcam catching a wider shot of the stage. At least I'd get some of my handsome mug on screen. The split screen showed the stage shot with my camera's half still black, waiting for it to go live and start the stream.

"You sure you want to do the vanishing cabinet? You haven't done that one on stage yet."

"True," I said, squeezing her hand. "I'm just here to wave my hands and use fake Latin-ish words. We both know that it's the lovely assistant that does all the magic for this one. "

Cass put on her stage-smile, the one that stretched her lips wide over her teeth and made her look a little crazy. But the audience loved her. And so did I. She was the reason the old magician took me on as his apprentice. While it was weird doing the finger stretches, I had to admit the man had shown me some pretty cool stuff, even if he still hadn't taught me how his levitation trick worked.

"Your pronunciation is too sloppy," Henry would say whenever I asked about levitation.

Well, of course it was sloppy. I took Latin for a semester as a freshman back in high school, because I had a crush on a girl who wanted to be a doctor. Not my fault Henry wasn't using real Latin, and I kept saying it the *correct* way. I didn't know what learning all these fake words had to do with sleight of hand and distraction. I mean, it wasn't like Cassie actually disappeared when she went in that cabinet. It was all smoke and mirrors. Or sliding panels and my super flexible girlfriend. But that didn't stop Henry from having me work on my "incantations" while I cleaned his apartment. Henry would call corrections from the other room as he read a book or newspaper or whatever. Seriously, who reads newspapers anymore? The ancient guy that was my master, that's who.

215

Henry was nice enough. He paid much better than I could make working in foodservice, which, after my borderline graduation, was about all I could expect. And he'd let me do the Sunday matinee show all by myself a couple of times now. He even let me keep the tips the old-timers in the audience left. Not that Henry had a big audience. Like ever. The ancient theater probably only sat about a hundred people, but I'd never seen the seats more than half full. And the regulars were primarily gray hairs.

I had plans to change all that. Tonight, in an effort to become the next viral channel, I was livestreaming the show. Or at least the parts that I knew, anyway. Once my show went viral, I'd bring in the crowds. Younger people. A cooler group. We'd turn this theater around, Cassie and me. Then maybe her grandpa, who owned the place, could retire. The old guy had done so much for Cassie and her mom that he deserved the rest.

"Ready for fame and fortune, my dear?" I said.

Cassie giggled.

I pressed the Stream button on the camera. The image in front of me appeared on the second half of the laptop screen. The red LIVE button lit up.

I cleared my throat, readying my stage voice Henry had coached me on. It was deeper than my natural voice, with the hint of an English accent, like Henry had, but not as stuffy. "Good evening, and welcome to the magic channel, Sleight of Brandt," I said.

"That's the name you're going with?" I heard Cassie whisper and hoped the mic didn't pick it up.

"Tonight, live from the Guiding Star Theater on Main Street, I'll be presenting a few of the wonders of magic." I waved my hands in front of the camera. I didn't wear gloves like Henry. I wanted to let the audience see that there was no place to hide, especially since the close-up shot would mostly show my hands.

I turned over my hands to reveal a deck of cards and splayed them out. I used a few flourishes—only the ones I was solid on—and then did a short card trick with a snap change to the "correct" card.

Next, coins pulled from Cassie's ear, hair, and even from her open, clearly empty hand. I nearly dropped the last coin before I set it on the table—rookie mistake. Hopefully, no one watching the stream noticed.

I turned to the velvet-covered table with more favorite tricks. The linked rings were an oldie but a goodie. I had to admit, a little bit of the child in me died when Henry showed me the secret to that one.

As with all of his tricks, I used the fake Latin terms. "*Nexus Noxus.*" I separated the rings.

Next came the never-ending handkerchiefs, usually ending in polka-dot boxers, but I'd switched out the underwear for a lacy red thong. Cassie pretended to be shocked, and her gasp was too adorable.

After releasing a pigeon from a hidden compartment in a top hat, I turned to Cassie.

"Next, my *lovely* assistant Cassie will vanish before your very eyes."

She preened and posed. I had to swallow a little and remind myself to focus on the trick and not on just how amazing she looked right now. The gross mothball smell of the cabinet helped me focus.

She stepped to the side and opened one door of the gaudily painted cabinet. I'd have to talk to Henry about making it a little cooler. I mean, who paints purple moons and gold stars all over these things anymore?

I opened the other door and brought the camera in close. I had no fears about spoiling anything. I'd been all over this thing, and even I couldn't tell where the false back was. Couldn't see if the sides tapered to allow extra space where Cassie had to be hiding. It was an excellent cabinet, even if the paint was stupid.

I guided Cassie inside, her sequins and curls sparkling under the stage lights. She blew the camera a kiss as I shut the doors with a thunk, stifling a sneeze through the huff of dust it shot into my face.

There were two locks on the cabinet, one oversized padlock on each door, to be locked as the cabinet was turned and the lame magic words chanted over it, copying how he said it as much as I could. "*Porta Porteri.*"

I did it precisely as Henry showed me—like I'd seen him do countless times. I couldn't even feel Cassie's weight shift as I spun the thing; she was that good. The cabinet was bulky but moved smoothly enough. I was wiry but I was also pretty strong. Or so I thought. Maybe I had overdone it on the cologne, because my head felt a little heavy and my stomach did a weird swishing thing. Or it could just be the nerves from doing this live on a stream.

I opened the locks, spun the cabinet again to undo each one, and opened the doors.

It was empty.

I made sure to get a good look inside with the camera, showing that she wasn't hiding in the ceiling either. Then I closed the doors, respun the cabinet, saying the same words as I locked it.

Was this taking too long? From the corner of my eye, I could see a steady stream of comments popping up on the laptop. Were they complaining? Oh no. What if they thought this was lame? A bead of cold sweat dribbled down the back of my neck as I unhooked the second lock. I chalked it up to wearing the cloak under the stage lights. Or maybe it was nerves.

This time when I opened the door, I reached my hand in for Cassie.

But it was empty.

I waited for a beat longer, not quite believing what I was or *wasn't* seeing.

I opened the other door.

No girlfriend. Just dumb stars.

"You spun it in the wrong direction."

I nearly jumped right out of those too-big dress shoes.

Henry stepped up beside me, bringing a faint smell of cloves, his brown eyes darker than mine and looking none too happy. "The second time. You spun it clockwise. You're supposed to do it counter-clockwise to bring her back."

"Huh?" was my brilliant response.

He gave me a dry look; arms crossed over his white button-down shirt. Even without the cloak, he looked far more like a real magician than I did.

"Is that my medallion?" he nodded toward the fake blue stone around my neck.

"How did you know—?"

"Son, I can taste magic from a hundred miles away, and you thought you could work these spells on *my* stage?"

"Sorry, I should have—"

He raised a hand. "We've got bigger problems than my stolen wardrobe." He lowered his eyebrows and looked down at me. "Cassie's been in there too long. And if I know one thing about my assistant, it's that she gets bored easily. She'll likely wander off."

"From inside the cabinet?" I asked, sounding every bit like the idiot I was. "Where would she go?"

He raised an eyebrow, motioned for the medallion. I slipped it off and handed it over.

"This won't take but a moment." He wrapped the medallion's ribbon around his hand and faced the cabinet.

In record time, he had the cabinet closed, locked, and spun. But then he walked around the outside, removing the locks, which wasn't how the trick usually went. When he opened the door, he motioned for me to join him. "We don't have a lot of time, and I'm not entirely sure I can explain sufficiently what's going on."

"What *is* going on?" I joined him at the cabinet.

Instead of those stupid stars, there was a narrow hallway, only the cabinet's width, stretching off into the dark.

Henry was already inside.

Questions flooded my mind as I stumbled to follow. *What? How? No, really...what?*

"Where are we?"

Henry paused a little way inside, opened his palm in front of him, and conjured a ball of light. I don't mean he popped open a flashlight. There was an actual ball of white light hovering above his palm. He casually flung it in the air, and as it rose to the ceiling, it grew brighter, lighting us several yards further down.

The walls were painted just like the inside of the cabinet, and the floor had the same give as if we were walking on plywood. And it smelled cold, though I didn't feel a temperature change.

"This is my little reality." Henry spread his arms out, easily touching both walls at his sides. "Well, a pocket reality. We haven't left the stage, exactly."

"A what?"

Henry gave me that look again. He gave me the same look when I told him the Latin he used wasn't right. "This is a conversation we will have to have on the run, so to speak." He turned and moved down the hall.

"See, the real reason I agreed to take you on as my apprentice was not because Cassie asked me to or that her grandfather told me I had to," he directed a pointed look at me, and I felt my neck get hot. So maybe he'd overheard those conversations with Cassie?

"I took you on, Brandt, because you have latent magical ability." He'd stopped, pressing his hand against the wall before moving on a little farther. "You might not believe it, and that's quite alright. But I thought it better to teach you to control those nascent notions before you self-combusted into a big mess later."

"Self-*combusted*?"

"Oh, it's rare, sure. But it has been known to happen." This time when he stopped, Henry spread his fingers over the wall's surface. "*Avem Arvancus*."

"Couldn't let that happen to Cassie's boyfriend, now could I?" Henry smiled at me before turning the knob on a door I hadn't noticed before and opened it into a room. He motioned me forward.

I poked my head inside just in time to get a face full of white feathers. I might have squawked louder than the dove that flapped through my hair and flew away. The room looked like an overfull aviary with dozens of birds—mostly the typical white doves Henry used on stage—perched on bar after bar strung between the walls. The noise was intense, but the smell? Not so much.

"Thought it'd be...stinkier in here."

Henry barked a laugh, pushed me back and shut the door. "Nah. Not the way a pocket dimension works. See, as long as I'm not actively manipulating it, things are pretty much in stasis. Well, at least they are inside the rooms. I never linked the cabinet to one single room as I required access to all of it. So Cassie won't be tucked away somewhere safe, like those birds. And since she wasn't waiting for us in the hallway, it means she's wandered off."

Henry lagged off, staring into the darkness.

"So where is she?"

"Hmm?" he startled, looking at me as if he'd forgotten I was there.

I mean, the guy was frequently spacey, especially right after a show. I just figured it was because he was getting up there in years.

"Where is Cassie?" I repeated.

"Ah, yes. Well." He turned and pressed the opposite wall. "The trick is to find which door she would have entered."

Henry spoke, but the blood pounding in my ears blocked out whatever he said. This time, I saw the door before he turned the knob. It hadn't been there the moment before. It really hadn't. I was watching this time.

Henry sighed. "No Cassie. Just cards."

"Cards?"

Henry gave a small smile, folded his arms, and leaned against the door frame, nodding his head inside.

I held my breath and leaned forward slightly.

Sure enough, there were stacks and crates of playing cards all over the space. Filing cabinets lined one wall, each drawer marked with a specific card, 53 drawers in all, including Jokers.

"Of course," he said, taking a slow look around the room. "How else am I supposed to pull the four of hearts from an entire deck?"

I could feel the wrinkles forming on my forehead. "Four of hearts?" I knew I sounded like a less-intelligent echo, but this was all so *weird*.

"You know the trick," he said, nudging a scattered stack back into the room, so it didn't spill into the hallway. "Pick a card, any card. You flourish the deck a bit and then bring their exact card back. Well, not the exact one. One from this room."

"But it's just some sleight of hand? It's a card trick, right?" I thought my voice got a little too high toward the end.

"Sure, sure," Henry said as he pulled the door closed. "For stage magicians. But I'm a wizard. Instead of all that shuffling nonsense, I just use my intuition to know what card they pulled and then pop a finger into this room here to grab the right one. Fairly straightforward."

My head started to throb a little, and my throat was dry from my mouth hanging open.

"That's what I've been trying to explain, Brandt." This time when Henry paused, he sort of stared at a blank wall for a moment. "Pocket reality overlaps the same space as the stage. I just reach in when I need something to appear or to make something disappear." Henry looked down the hallway. Maybe it was the ball of drifting light overhead as it followed us down the hall, but he looked a little paler.

"You okay?" I asked.

"Hmm?" He looked at me, blinked, and then looked back down the hallway. "Absolutely. Fine. I was simply thinking. It takes up quite a bit of headspace to keep the pocket reality open long enough for a hand to slip in. It's a bit more taxing for two whole people to be walking around."

"Is that bad?" I tried looking down the hall where he kept glancing but didn't see anything beyond the painted stars and moon. I needed to talk to him about making it cooler.

"Not bad," he said slowly. "Just difficult to focus. Yes. Focusing." He turned back to the wall. *"Nexus Noxus."*

I blinked and the door was there. Henry just sort of stared at the knob so I reached out and turned it. An unruly pile of linking rings in different sizes and colors was heaped in the middle of the tiny space.

"Rings," Henry's tone was dreamy. "But not Cassiopeia."

"She better not hear you call her that," I said and pulled the door closed. "She hates that name."

Henry nodded absently and shuffled off down the hall. He probably knew that, had probably gotten the near-screaming rant from her before about her "hippie" name and to never, ever call her that. I'd only made that mistake once. Once was enough. But honestly, I thought the name was awesome. I mean, the girl was named after a star constellation. How cool was that? My mom named me after some character on a TV show she liked as a teenager.

The old guy had stopped at yet another spot in the hallway and ran his hands over his pockets, as if searching for his cell phone.

"Lose something?" I asked.

Henry slowly removed the sapphire, which I wasn't so sure was fake after all. "I think you might have to take over, my apprentice." He held the ribbon out to me. He'd looked pale before, but now he had added a sheen of sweat to that pastiness.

I looped the ribbon over my hand, keeping the sapphire in my palm. "You feelin' okay?"

"No," he said, voice rough. "No, I am not."

"What do I do?" I moved a little closer to him.

"What's the next trick you do after the rings?"

"Uh," I stalled, running through the stage act in my head. "Hand-kerchiefs."

"Good, good," he said, his eyes closed now. "Do that here."

I moved in front of Henry and faced the wall, and said, "*Pannes Plures.*"

The door was there as soon as the words left my lips, the handle cool to the touch and smooth. Just like millions of other handles on normal doors. But this wasn't a normal door. My stomach constricted a little. Had I just done magic? Real magic?

I wrenched the door open.

Piles of attached fabric triangles (and underwear). No Cassie.

I pulled the door closed a little harder than I should. The room was real. The door was real. Magic was real. And Cassie had really vanished from the cabinet.

"This is a waste of time," I said. I turned to face the stretched-out hallway, fist clenching the stone in my hand. "Cassie?" I raised my voice "Cass-"

Henry's hand clamped over my mouth.

"Not a good idea to be yelling in here, Brandt." His whisper was fierce.

I didn't move, didn't breathe.

He removed his hand.

He glanced down the hall. "You, I, and Cassie aren't the *only* people in here. And I'm not entirely certain that we won't be heard by something less savory."

"What?" I squeaked.

"The rooms are in stasis when I'm not using them, true. But I'm fairly certain they are all active at the moment. You saw those birds. They weren't sitting still."

I swallowed, but my throat wanted to close. "Who...who else is in...here?" I managed to rasp.

Henry pressed his lips together. "Larry the Flint."

"Larry *Flynt*?"

"No, no." Henry had a hand to his eyes. "Larry *the* Flint. He probably thought he was original with that moniker. Though he does resemble a rather large pile of rocks."

"What's he doing in here? Does he help with your magic show?"

Henry ran his hand down his face. "He's here as a favor to Cassie's grandfather."

I stepped back, my face going all scrunched up as I tried to process this. "What, you gave him a place to live here? Was the guy homeless or something?"

"No." Henry coughed a laugh. "Definitely not homeless. Had a splendid place down in the valley. Lovely car, too."

I waited as Henry took in a few deep breaths.

"Cassie's grandfather. Mr. Reynolds. He's a good man. Wouldn't you agree, Brandt?" He turned to face me directly. "That if you saw a way to help him, you'd do it?"

"Well, yeah." I shrugged. "He took care of Cassie's mom and then Cassie, too. He got me this job, because he knew I needed it. He's a good guy."

Henry nodded, his forehead lined. "Exactly. When Larry the Flint took an interest in Mr. Reynolds's business, it wasn't to see the old man prosper or keep him safe from other characters. I had to find a place to keep Mr. Flint where he couldn't harm our mutual friend."

A hard knot formed in my gut. "Oh. So he was like, a gang member?"

"Mob enforcer, I believe."

"The mob? How long has he been in here?"

"Roughly..." Henry pulled out a fancy silver pocket watch, clicked it open, studied the face, then clicked it shut again. "Twenty-seven years."

I could feel my eyebrows crawling up my forehead. "How is he still alive?"

Now Henry shrugged. "Stasis. I'm not entirely certain he *is* alive. When I first put him in a room, I used to feel him *kick*, as it were, now and then, when I popped in and out during a show. I haven't felt that in years. No, I don't think he's dead. I think he simply got used to the place."

He squinted at the ball of light overhead, hands slipping into his pockets.

"The thing about magic," Henry's voice had a lower quality than before; slower, too. Like talking took concentration. "Is that if people know what you can do, they expect you to do it for them." He took a couple of deep breaths. "Mr. Reynolds is not like that. He knows what I can do, and he only ever sought to give me a safe place to be who I am. Of course, I would do what I could to protect him."

I swallowed hard. "So what do we do if we open his door?"

"We close it as quickly as possible and hope he doesn't notice."

That sounded like an awful plan. I'd only ever been in one fight in my life, and that was in the fifth grade. I wasn't ready for something like this.

A thought hit me harder than that jerk from the mall after I wouldn't let him cut in line. I stopped, reaching for Henry's arm at the same moment, turning him toward me.

"What if Cassie is in that room?"

Henry's forehead wrinkled even more. He didn't answer.

A couple more doors and a couple more rooms with no Cassie in them. Then I felt it. A sort of static in the air as we came to one section.

Henry had stopped, too.

"Is there a door here?" I asked.

Henry looked at me out of the corner of his eye, thin lips quirking into a small smile. "Now you're getting it."

I grinned back at him, feeling with my hands which side the door was on, then worked the next spell. Lots of black hats. No Cassie.

I shut the door, but a thought hit me hard enough to stop me in my tracks. "Wait."

Henry stopped, half-turned toward me.

"If we have to use magic to get inside, then how would Cassie get inside a room? She doesn't know that fake Latin stuff."

As he tucked his hands in the pockets of his slacks, Henry's smile was sad, and his eyes lost focus a little. "Do you honestly believe a girl named for the stars could not touch magic?"

"Cassie has latent abilities, too?"

"Most definitely *not* latent." Henry leaned against a wall. "Not since the day she was born. Her mother is very similar. It's why I originally came here, started working for Mr. Reynolds. Self-combustion, remember? But Cassie wasn't interested in learning the tricks or magic. When she was old enough, I asked her to be my assistant instead, teaching her what and when I could."

"So the vanishing cabinet?" I leaned hard into the wall across from him. "It's not because she's flexible?"

Henry barked that dry laugh again. "Dear me, no. She's been in here nearly as often as I have. Only I never leave her alone long enough for her to turn around." He started back down the hallway.

I stood a moment, staring at the door I'd used magic to open, imagining Cassie in the flashy magician's cloak, trying to keep a deck of cards palmed. I heard as much as felt a thud on the soft plywood floor.

Henry lay sprawled behind me.

I rushed to him, and he rolled to his side, batting away my hands.

"This is proving to be more difficult than I had anticipated." He ran the back of his hand along his forehead, then blinked at the collected moisture. "I'm afraid we shall have to test your senses far sooner than expected."

After a few deep breaths, he let me help him to his feet.

"Is it your heart or something?" I asked as he put his arm around my shoulders, taking some of his weight.

"My heart?"

"Well, yeah, because you're, you know, older?"

He scoffed. "I would very much like to see you hold a few dozen pocket realities while also messing about inside them. It's quite difficult."

I nodded and smiled.

Henry grimaced. "Focus, please. Seek out the feeling you had before when you found the door."

Keeping one arm around his back, I reached out with my other hand, and we started down the hall. I stopped a short distance as the static caught my fingertips. My face said it all as I turned to Henry.

"Vanishing..." Henry made vague motions toward the wall, breath gasping.

"But you said my incantation was sloppy," I said, beads of perspiration appearing on my forehead just to gang up on me.

"You did it before," Henry gasped.

I stared back at the wall that shimmered with the shape of a door, shaking my hand out to my side. "Right. Okay. This is for Cassie. Focus."

I closed my eyes and took a few deep breaths as I ran the words through my mind. *Porta Porteri. Porta Porteri.* I could do this.

I held out my hand. "*Porta Porteri.*"

Behind me, Henry snorted.

"It's not Spanish, son." He coughed, his breathing ragged. "Try it again. There's just the slightest hint of a 'th' sound in there. Keep it tiny."

I turned my head from side to side, listening to the vertebra pop, and held my hand back up to the wall. "*Porta Porteri.*" I even mimicked his dumb British accent.

With a pop, the door was right there, the handle smooth under my fingers. I did it. My stomach rolled in celebration. I had to admit I was also on the verge of jumping up and down and squeeing like a fangirl.

I grabbed the handle, slightly warm to the touch, and twisted it as I glanced back at Henry, giving him my most triumphant grin.

When I looked back at the new room, it wasn't the sparkling blue eyes of my wandering girlfriend that met me. These eyes were green. And bloodshot. And glaring.

Before I could get out the words "Larry the Flint," the massive shape barreled toward the door, ripping it from my grip. A huge hand

227

almost too big to fit slammed into my chest, knocking all breath and thought out of me as I flew back.

I hit the opposite wall as the doorway filled with a mountain of muscle. Give the man a black leather jacket and a Harley, and he'd be the ideal leader of the Hell's Angels. But this guy was dressed in a three-piece suit that had to be custom tailored. His full mustache was a little dated, but I had to say, it worked for him as a balance against his hairless scalp.

He growled as he eased his massive shoulders through the doorway, his eyes never stopped boring into mine. He moved closer, and I could smell some severe man stench with just a whiff of expensive cologne.

Through the pounding of my heart in my throat, I barely felt Henry's touch on my hand and then the words *"Avem Arvancus!"* sent a flock of white birds directly at the mobster.

Larry's hands flew to his face, but birds would only distract him for so long.

The effort of the magic put Henry on the floor again. I couldn't expect any more help from him.

Words Henry forced me to commit to memory blurred through my head. I plucked one out and held up my hands. *"Complur Charta!"*

A deck of cards appeared in my empty hands. While I wanted to bask in the moment, Larry growled and lunged toward me. I threw the cards at his face, watching as they scattered, while I shoved myself to the side, out of his path.

Larry's bald head smacked the wall, which had the effect of making him growl louder.

Cards and birds wouldn't work. There had to be something more solid. And painful.

Or *less* solid.

Words popped into my head from the endless times I'd watched Henry's show. I knew most of the terms Henry used were at least Latin-based, though usually altered, so they usually rhymed. The levitation spell Henry used was *"Erago Ego"* and only worked on him. But if I changed the "ego/me" to "eum/him"...

228

It was worth a shot because Larry shook off his concussion and took aim at me.

I held out my hands, ready for my stomach to do that weird clenching thing. "*Erago Eum!*"

Larry's eyes bulged, his fist just a few inches from my pretty, pretty face. He wasn't frozen since his mouth moved, spewing all kinds of things I typically only heard playing video games against preteens. But he was floating, his legs rising to lay him out flat, just like how Henry looked so Cassie could pass the hula hoop along him. Larry's arms thrashed, but he looked more like he was swimming than trying to punch me.

I stood still, just staring for a moment. My stomach was doing some sort of weird dubstep, and I thought that if I moved too much, I might leave my dinner behind.

"Well done," came Henry's breathless praise. "I'm rather...impressed."

I grinned like an idiot. This was possibly the coolest thing ever to happen to me. Magic was real. And I could use it. Even if it kinda made me want to puke.

Henry motioned at Larry the *Float* but couldn't seem to find the strength to make words. Right. This guy was flailing all over. I needed to restrain him.

I summoned the endless handkerchiefs. The underwear at the end never fails to get a laugh. And I had to admit I was chuckling by the time I wrapped the lengths as tight as I could a couple dozen times around his massive body, wadding up the boxers to stuff in Larry's mouth, narrowly missing getting chomped by his teeth.

Grabbing ahold of one of the loops, I dragged Larry, now weightless as well as speechless, back into his dark little room. The space was smaller than my room at home, though there was a bed. I made sure he hovered over the mattress.

There was no point in staying. Cassie wasn't in here. I closed the door firmly.

Henry had dragged himself up to sitting but looked at me with heavy eyelids, dark circles forming under his eyes. His breathing was labored; I wasn't sure how much longer he could do this. But he would as long as possible. For Cassie.

I heaved him up to standing, and we continued, me with one arm around him, and the other stretched in front of me, feeling for the tingly static that meant another door.

After far too many shuffling steps forward, I felt it.

"There's one here," I said, leaning Henry against the wall, where he slid down until he sat on the painted floor. "But I don't know any more words to open a door."

Henry took a shuddering breath and then spoke. "*Dolus...Lepus...*"

"Deceitful...*rabbit*?" I asked.

He nodded weakly, a small smile forming.

I shrugged, then turned to the wall, repeating the words as best I could. It took me a couple of tries, using different inflections, but finally, the door was there, the handle warm.

Inside were dozens of rabbits in just about every breed and color. The one that caught my eye was a particularly fluffy gray beast with flopped ears. It was also currently wrapped in the arms of my beautiful, wandering girlfriend.

"Cassie!" I rushed into the room, snatching her up, bunny and all. "We found you!"

"Brandt, careful." She pushed me back enough to give the fluffy guy space. "Don't smoosh him." She cooed to the bunny, planting a kiss on its head before setting it down.

"What took you so long?" she said, hands planted on hips. "I was so bored until I found the bunnies."

"What...took..." words failed me as the image of Larry the Flint charging at me filled my head. "We gotta get out of here, babe. Henry's not doing so great."

"Oh no," Cassie's eyes went wide. "Henry found out about your stream?"

I glanced down at my chest. The "stream" link still lit. I had forgotten about it.

"No, well, yes, but that's not the point." I grabbed her hand and pulled her toward the door, using the toe of my dress shoe to nudge back a white rabbit investigating the opening.

Cassie started to protest, wanting to say goodbye to her furry friends, but she was immediately at his side as soon as she saw Henry.

I closed the door and joined her in helping Henry stand.

Despite the hundreds of yards we must have walked while finding all the doors, the journey back to the open vanishing cabinet took only a minute, even with our master supported between us.

As we approached the bright lights of the stage, I saw shapes moving just outside the door.

I looked at Henry, and he returned my wary look as I eased his arm off my shoulders, letting him lean against the wall with Cassie.

I adjusted the sapphire in my hand and stepped through the door.

Henry had a specific way he liked to end his show. I thought it was just some cool lighting effects that resembled fireworks but knowing what I did now I had an idea.

The dark shapes immediately swarmed toward me. I may have to send them all levitating, even if it meant throwing up on the stage.

Holding the sapphire up, I bellowed, "*Lux Lumen!*"

I was not entirely prepared for the bursts of light that showered the stage, the first several rows of chairs, and all the people gathered. Many of whom I now recognized.

The closest one was Mr. Reynolds, both hands over his eyes but still trying to move closer to the cabinet from which Henry and Cassie emerged.

I was also not prepared for the applause that began. Neither was Mr. Reynolds because he dropped his hands and turned to look at the people around him, his gaping expression probably very similar to mine. I then closed my mouth and tried to look authoritative and intimidating while black dots still speckled my vision.

The group clustered around me, and out of the corner of my eye, I saw a blue-sequined leotard twinkle as Cassie spun the vanishing cabinet.

I blinked into the lights. "What're you people doing here?"

"Only witnessing the best livestream ever!" an overly enthusiastic blonde said, clapping her hands.

A girl I vaguely recognized from high school rushed forward, clinging to my arm. "Are you kidding? That was the best ARG I've ever seen! Like, I was totally fearing for your life! It's why I had to come down here immediately!"

"ARG?" said the guy that worked the concessions stand, still wearing his striped apron. "No way that was your 'augmented reality' crap. That was all real. Magic is *real*, right, bro?"

"Real or not," said another guy, "I came to see some more of that. Do another trick right now!"

And suddenly, a couple of dozen faces focused on me, smiles wide and expectant.

Here was my audience, waiting for me. Fame and fortune wouldn't be too far behind. I put on my stage face, smiling broadly, and opened my arms wide before giving a little bow.

I produced a deck of cards and went through a series of flourishes and cuts, keeping their attention while I had time to think. Did Henry say anything about protecting the secret of magic? Sure, I wasn't supposed to give away his stage tricks but this was different. What had he said? I couldn't remember, but it wasn't like he was buying up ad space, bragging that he was a wizard.

A fat hand knocked the cards from my hands. "No dumb card tricks," said the behemoth in front of me, and I briefly wondered if Larry the Flint had a son. "Show us the *good* stuff."

Several others voiced their agreement, and I may have swallowed a little hard.

A much more refined hand rested on my shoulder. I turned and saw Henry's brown eyes, still exhausted, but he also had on his game face. I could hear his words from before, echoing in more than my memory. *"If people know what you can do, they expect you to do it for them."*

So instead, I grinned at Henry, and he smiled back. Then we both started to laugh, though his side of it was a little more forced.

"Guys, guys," I said, wrapping an arm around Cassie's waist as she slipped in next to me, her stage smile glowing. "That wasn't real. I mean, I'm flattered that you liked the show, but it was just a show. For the stream. Showing you all those magician's tricks and then building up to real magic? We had a script and everything. Which reminds me." I turned my head to Henry. "You got a little too into the whole 'I may be dying' part of your role. Touch over-acted."

Henry's eyes narrowed, but he kept his grin. "I'll do better next time."

"So there *will* be a next time?" the blonde asked.

"Absolutely," I said. "We've got plans for a whole season of streams."

Half the crowd appeared to love this idea, while the other half didn't look too happy about being tricked. Eventually, the first half's enthusiasm won out, and by the time the crowd filed out the doors, everyone talked about the next show.

Before we could move to follow them, Mr. Reynolds stood in our path.

Arms folded, I think he was going for an angry posture, but his frantic glances toward Cassie sapped all the strength from it. "A whole season?" he said, eyes not stopping on any one of us for long.

Cassie and Henry both turned to look at me, one radiant excitement and the other weary wariness. Guess which one was which.

"Well," I said, deciding I liked looking at Cass a whole lot right then. "We'll have to work in some special effects and maybe another 'bad guy' to combat or something. But I'm pretty sure the livestreams will drive up interest in your theater, Mr. Reynolds."

Henry rolled his eyes and shook his head before running a hand over his face. "I'm not doing another show inside the vanishing cabinet. And you must learn to use cufflinks properly."

Cassie leaned forward to look at our boss. "But you *are* doing another show, right?"

Henry looked between her and me before throwing his hands up in the air. "What is it that they say in theater? The show must go on?"

I hugged Cassie, and we laughed. "Fame and fortune, Cassiopeia. Fame and fortune."

She punched me right in the gut.

Meet Jessica Guernsey

Jessica Guernsey writes Urban and Contemporary Fantasy novels and short stories. A BYU alumna with a degree in Journalism, her work is published in magazines and anthologies. By day, she crushes dreams as a slush pile reader for three publishers for a combined 12 years' experience. During November's NaNoWriMo, Jessica is a Municipal Liaison for the Utah::Elsewhere Region. Frequently, she can be found at writing conferences. She isn't difficult to spot; just look for the extrovert. While she spent her teenage angst in Texas, she now lives on a mountain in Utah. Discover more stories at https://jessicaguernsey.com.

Hidden Magic

SEAN MCKAY

The alarm goes off at 0500. It didn't matter how many years had passed since Merle was active duty, he couldn't shake military time. He didn't really have to be awake until 0600, but this early hour allowed him to get up and start his day before most of his neighbors had awoken. He started up the stack on his Magnavox stereo. "Things Ain't What They Used to Be" by ol' Duke started wafting through the old, dingy apartment he had called home for the past ten years. He'd discovered jazz music was the only thing that quieted the voices from the other apartments.

That first year after what happened, before that miraculous discovery, had almost driven him to insanity. So many voices, so many pleas, so many violent thoughts he couldn't control, only hear.

"The saxophone saved my life," Merle used to say to his buddies in the PTSD support group over at the VA. If they only knew what he really meant.

By the time the next wax disc hit the turntable—a little Buddy Guy action at this point—Merle was showered and dressed for work. He bustled about the kitchen, making his morning brew and cooking breakfast. The eggs and bacon managed themselves in the skillet, but Merle preferred to brew the coffee himself. He was too picky about his beloved coffee to give up control. As Merle sat down with his hot cup of joe, the eggs and bacon flipped onto the plate and slid across the counter to the breakfast bar where he was sitting.

"Perfect every time," he thought. "I've gotten pretty good at this over the years."

Merle Newman hadn't always had these magical abilities. He'd come from a patriotic family and joined the Army back in the 60s, just like his father and grandfather before him. But when the US entered the Vietnam Conflict, he knew he couldn't handle combat. So, when the opportunity came up in basic training to volunteer for a specialized program that would let him serve his country *and* avoid combat, Merle jumped at the chance. Within two weeks he was at CIA Headquarters to participate as a subject in something they were calling "MK Ultra." He was handed a badge that had "MKU" on one side, and his picture with "Merle N." underneath on the other. He quickly realized that MK Ultra was a secret CIA project using LSD and a variety of other less-than-legal substances in an attempt to unlock mind control powers in test subjects. The goal was to use operatives with telepathic powers for interrogation, espionage, and political assassination operations in the US fight against the growing Communist threat.

For the next two years, Merle lived a drug-fueled life of experiments, probes, tests, and recovery. He saw men die of drug overdoses, go insane, commit suicide. Those were the lucky ones. The worst cases, though, were the successes. Once in a blue moon, somebody would start to demonstrate actual powers, actual superhero stuff. Merle saw their power once, then he never saw them again. Rumor was they were sent off to another location for training and mission planning. Years later, no one knew where they were or even if they were alive.

Then one day it happened. To this day, Merle doesn't know what drug cocktail they hit him with. But as he was blacking out from the overdose, he heard other voices in his head, voices he recognized as in the room, but they weren't speaking. When he finally came out of the coma a month later, he realized he was awake not because his eyes were open, but because he could hear the voices of the nurses and doctor, though no one else was in the room with him.

"*Shit.*" It was the only word he could think of when he realized he could hear others' thoughts. Turns out he was telepathic *and* telekinetic. He couldn't control minds like MKU wanted him to, but he could hear and insert thoughts and move things by visualizing it in his head. Merle knew they would make him disappear too if he didn't keep his newfound abilities secret. So, he went through all their tests, allowed himself to be poked and prodded, lied his ass off, and acted like it was just a regular old OD, not the world-gone-crazy unlocking OD that it was.

"Screw this. If I have to disappear, it's going to be on my terms, not theirs." That's when Operation Hide in Plain Sight, as he liked to call it, started. He wandered about aimlessly–and homelessly–for a year struggling to maintain his sanity with the voices in his head. It was like never having privacy but at the same time being completely alone. It wasn't until he discovered that jazz music quieted the voices to the point he could function and work that he turned his life around. And here he was ten years later, a janitor at the Ford plant in Detroit. Same day, every day. Hiding in plain sight.

"Enough with the reminiscing," Merle thought to himself. Voices quietly developed in the back of his head as his neighbors started to wake. Through jazz and years of practice, though, he was able to keep them at a level low enough to feel normal. With a flick of his finger, the dirty dishes from breakfast slid back into the sink, washing themselves.

"Now that's what you call a cheap dishwasher," he laughed, as he headed out the door for work.

Merle had made a pact with himself all those years ago when he went into hiding: help somebody in some way every day of your life. Sure, he could dive headlong into the whole "superhero" thing, but he knew that was a risk. He *knew* there were others like him out there, but there were no "superheroes." That told him they were either still being used as tools of the government or had been killed off by that same government. He was not taking that kind of a risk. So instead, he became content with the little things.

Every day on his commute, he tried to find someone to help. Today was no different. It was Detroit, so there was no shortage of people in need. There was the homeless man in the alley outside his building, the little girl crying at the bus stop, the distracted woman almost wandering off into traffic.

But it was the old woman he saw sitting alone on the park bench that stole his attention. Something in the way she looked, eyes down and glazed, shoulders stooped over, aimlessly dropping crumbs for the pigeons just pulled his attention to her. As he stood there, he just closed his eyes and concentrated on her.

First came the pain. Not physical pain, but a grieving, yearning pain. His whole body became heavier as the weight of her pain pulled him down. Then he heard her thoughts and knew the source. Her husband of fifty-four years had just died from complications of Alzheimer's. She was lonely. She was lost. She was *alone* for the first time in as long as she could remember. Images flashed through her head of taking care of him, washing him, feeding him, being yelled at by him when he no longer remembered her. He felt her mix of emotions of her undying love and pain at watching her beloved deteriorate and forget who the love of his life was even though she was right in front of him.

All Merle could see and hear in her head was pain and sadness. *Surely there is more to their story than pain*, he thought.

So he dug. It was a weird thing digging deeper into someone's memories. It was almost like being caught under a parachute and trying to feel your way out, blindly pushing through memories and following connection to connection until you find your way. And out of the pain he did. He found memories of their first date back in 1924, their wedding, the birth of their children, and summers in the cabin in the Upper Peninsula. So many memories. So much love. She had just forgotten, buried under the pain of the last several years.

Merle helped her to remember. He pulled up one memory after another and gently pushed them in front of the pain. He opened his eyes to see the woman pause, then slowly, begin to smile. He watched her sit back, relax, and lose herself in thought, fighting through both tears and laughter. He could still feel the pain of her loss but could now also feel so strongly love and gratitude as she remembered the life they had experienced. And Merle felt hope.

He smiled at his efforts, then winced. Using his powers to help others was his way to change the world, but there was always a cost in doing so. Her memories, her pain, her sadness, didn't leave him when he stopped listening. They lingered like fingers digging through his brain. Though the sensation would eventually fade, a shadow of the experience always stuck with him. He shared an intimate moment with the woman, but she would never know. And he couldn't share his experience with anyone. He loved helping people in this way, but he hated the loneliness and isolation he confronted every time he did.

Merle wanted so badly to share these small acts of grace with others, but he couldn't risk his secret getting out. He couldn't share his *life* with others. Sure, he wanted to feel the comfort of a woman, someone he could love and trust. But he could not bear the thought of them learning his secret as he let his guard down, putting his life at risk *and* hers. God forbid, they ever had any kids.

So, every day became the same. Keep it hidden. Keep it safe. Small mercies. Merle had to be satisfied with being the anonymous benefactor of strangers and living a life of quiet solitude. It was the only way he could survive.

All this thought about relationships and loneliness made him think of Grace. Man, she was something. She was new at the factory, working in the little medical office for all the smashed fingers, bruises, and occasional broken bones. She was a little rough around the edges but had a quietness about her he liked.

They also had stuff in common. While he was off with MKU, she was a nurse serving in the war in Vietnam, helping all his brothers with lost body parts, lost lives. No wonder she was rough around the edges. She had definitely seen the worst humanity had to offer.

She knew he was a vet from Vietnam too, but neither really talked about it. No vets really talked about it. Vietnam vets were kind of *persona non grata* in the US, so it became easier to deny their trauma than talk about it. Grace didn't know he had not served in combat over there, just assumed he had. He was fine letting her believe that. It helped avoid any questions. Still, there were the quiet nods of recognition between them, shared trauma—different kinds, but still trauma.

"Morning, Grace." Merle always tried to be polite and friendly to her, but in his way of making minimal eye contact and keeping himself on his social island. Always protecting himself. Always protecting others. He desperately wanted to stare into those eyes of hers though.

"Well, good morning to you too, Merle," she said. "How was your weekend?"

"Same old, same old. The usual." Never giving details. "Yours?"

"Well, nothing special. Ran some errands, talked to my sister. I did go to one of those VA support groups for veterans. I don't know. Just not for me. All those angry and bitter guys. Angry at the country. The government. The enemy. Themselves. Too much for me to handle. I mean, yeah, I saw stuff too. In fact, I saw ALL the shit. But I can't be angry all the time. Drains me too much and makes me sad. Might be a good place for you to go, though. Seems like you shoulder a big burden walking around this place, Merle. I hate seeing that."

Amazing how she experienced the stuff she had and wasn't bitter. And care for him instead? How can she just open up and share so easily? It made Merle angry and jealous at the same time.

"Nah, I've been to those things. Just not for me. I don't like opening up too much about that stuff." He lied. He so desperately wanted to talk about his life but just knew he couldn't. "Nope. Just give me my Walkman and my jazz, and I'm good."

"Well, just think about it. If you'd like," Grace said, "I'd go with you if it would make it easier."

"OK. I'll think about it. Later, Grace. Better get down to the basement and get to work." Merle knew it was time to cut the conversation short or he'd want to stay longer. And the longer he stayed, the more he'd try to listen to her thoughts and risk revealing himself. Nope. Time to go. Keep it hidden. Keep it safe.

As he walked off, he smiled thinking about the fact that Grace was the only person he knew whose thoughts he could not hear. He had tried. It was the most pleasant and perplexing thing he had experienced in ten years of the voices. It scared him a little, but intrigued

240

him too. Apart from Grace's personality and compassion, it was the fact that she was a separate thing, a private entity that he couldn't just "know." That drew him to her.

He wanted to know her more, and it kind of excited him that he couldn't. The flip side of that coin, though, was it only heightened his sense of loneliness. He knew so much of people he didn't want to know, but he couldn't know anything about the one person he wanted to know.

The closer he got to the basement and janitorial department where he worked, though, the more the smile turned into a grim frown. It was a job, a good paying job with benefits, a job easy to hide in. But the people? They were another story. They were a hard lot: hardworking, hard playing, hard attitudes. Unfortunately, Merle's quiet demeanor just made him an easy target. On top of it all, he could hear The Kid in his head getting louder and louder.

"Hey, Newman! You're late, you asshole!"

"It's 0800. I am right on time."

"It's 0800 and 5 seconds! Drop and give me twenty or hit the kitchen for KP!" His supervisor—a long slick-backed haired weasel who must have been the kid of one of the higher ups—loved to make fun of the fact Merle was a military veteran. The Kid reeked of un-earned privilege, lack of motivation, and elitist attitude that likely meant he'd never be anything more than the Janitorial Services su-pervisor and, in his own head, lord it over his workers like some kind of fiefdom where they owed tribute.

"Ha. Funny one, sir. OK, grabbing my gear and heading out to the floor." Getting away from The Kid as quickly as possible was defi-nitely the right thing to do. But Merle couldn't resist a parting shot.

"Sonofabitch!"

Merle could hear The Kid yelling and screaming as his coffee inexplicably spilled all over his white, short-sleeved-with-tie-blue-collar-white-collar-wannabe shirt. Merle's smile came back just a little.

But as he approached the factory floor, Merle got sad again like he does after using his powers. All he had wanted to do was help people, defend people, and do the right thing. The powers should have given him so many opportunities to do just that. But with the way he got them, and *who* he got them from, he knew his only choice for survival and saving his soul was to stay in hiding and do the little things, hidden things, secret things. I mean, it was good and all, but how much was he really helping anyway? And at what cost? He had been fine with that for years. He had been content with his life, his jazz music, his small miracles.

But then there was Grace. Nina Simone's "Feeling Good" started playing in his head, instinctively.

Until Merle had met her, being solitary hadn't been lonely. Sure, he felt isolated after using his powers, but not lonely. He considered it his mission, so to speak, to protect the world—and what the government would have used him for—by staying hidden. It had been fine because there was no one worth missing. Grace had changed that for Merle.

"Stop it," he said. "Button that shit up, soldier. You ain't got time for this. You know your mission. Hold the line."

And with that, he shut it all off, put the headphones on from his Walkman, and headed off to the factory line to start the long, monotonous, and hiding-in-plain-sight task of keeping the place clean. That was the cool thing about being a janitor. Merle saw everything, came in contact with everyone, but he was invisible. Rarely was he looked at, and even more rarely was he spoken to. This gave him the chance to see people, see their lives, and almost live in them, unheeded and unnoticed. So, when "small miracles" happened, there was no way to connect it to him, because no one *was* connected to him.

He liked to have a competition with himself and see how many small miracles he could create in a day. He laughed when he thought about his record of thirty-two but shrugged it off because according to what he defined as "helping" he didn't really think it counted. It was that day the heat shut off at the factory, and he just slowly increased the vibration of the air around him to stay warm. Thirty-two people that day commented to him as he was cleaning that it felt like the heat was coming back on, only to complain about it being cold soon after he left. Yeah, thirty-two people felt it that day, but in his mind, it was just one miracle—keeping his own ass warm. Still, it was an important day because it taught him that there were ways to use his powers that he had never considered before.

Other than that day, though, it was pretty boring stuff: move buckets to keep people from tripping and falling, inserting a joke in someone's head who was having a bad day, stuff like that. Merle had always wanted to be able to use his gift for something bigger, but between trying to hide in plain sight and no real opportunities to use them for big things, he had settled into his life and realized this was what it would be. He had learned to be content.

He felt the screaming in his head before he heard it in his ears. Then came all the sounds at once, a cacophony of voices yelling and cursing and barking orders. Then the alarm sounded in the whole factory. All that noise slamming into his brain at once was disorienting, like being at the epicenter of a grenade explosion with shrapnel flying off in every direction. He stumbled and leaned his hand against the wall to balance himself.

"Merle, are you alright?"

Merle quickly wheeled around to see Grace standing right there, concerned look in her eyes. "I'm fine! Just lost my balance. That alarm caught me off guard! Wait, why are you here? The med office is on the other side of the plant!"

"I was taking some medical waste to the disposal, heard the alarm, and came running!"

Why was she carrying her med kit, then? How could she have planned for this?

They started running toward the sound. Merle wasn't thinking about what he would do, or how he could help, or that this was a chance to do something big. His instinctive nature to help went into overdrive. As he was running, Merle searched out the source of the screams, frantically searching through thoughts as he found them. Shock. Panic. Fear. Confusion. Then the pain.

Ahead of him in the middle of the assembly line, a line worker laid screaming on the floor under the weight of a car. Apparently, the assembly harnesses for the autos under construction had snapped, pinning this poor soul completely under its weight. Blood seeped out from under the car on either side of the man, almost like a full man-sized tick had popped. Merle tried to assess the situation before he got close enough to help.

What could Merle do? He couldn't simply lift the car off the guy. That was too obvious, but he had to help.

As other people panicked, Grace grabbed his arm and said, "You know what to do."

Well, of course, he knew they had to get the car off the guy. But did she expect him to lift the damn car by himself? Merle just dropped his head and backed away. To an observer, it appeared he was praying, but really, he was concentrating. Grace looked frustrated and turned to the scene in front of them.

Merle did what he knew to do. All he knew to do. First, he tried his best to send messages to the man, images of calm and peace, a voice to tell him it would be okay. Merle didn't know if it was shock or if what he was trying worked, but the man's screams quieted to a dull whimper and he stopped flailing his arms.

Second, Merle knew they had to get that car off this poor man before it was too late. He looked at Grace as she stood there trying her best to assess the situation. Then he saw her look directly at him. He couldn't figure out what her expression was, but there was an expectancy in her eyes. It made him feel even worse that he thought Grace was disappointed in him. Too many weird thoughts confused him right now. Grace's voice brought him back to the moment.

"Everybody move and give me some room!" she yelled.

He stood in amazement as he watched Grace quickly approach and assess the man pinned by the Mustang. It was like she was back in Vietnam taking care of injured soldiers. The, well, grace with which Grace assessed the man and administered a shot in one fluid motion was a sight to behold. Merle didn't know if it was what he did or what Grace gave him, but the poor guy almost seemed calm at this point.

"OK, he's sedated, but we have got to get this car off him." Grace barked to everybody. "Get in here and try to lift this thing."

Men circled the car and started grunting and yelling trying to lift it. It wasn't budging. Men, being men, just kept yelling and grunting.

Merle realized this was a waste of time with that bracket still attached to the crane. It almost pinned the man to the floor. He gathered an image of the bracket and crane and visualized the metal getting softer, bending. He pictured the molecules stretching apart, weakening, and becoming more brittle. He had never bent anything like this before and didn't know if he could, but he had to try. His head throbbed, blood rushed in his ears, and his heart pounded in his chest.

"Bend...break...snap damn it!"

Suddenly there was a loud metal clang and pop, and the men surrounding the car yelled in triumph as the bracket broke. They thought their might and their grunting was the magic power here, snapping the six-inch thick, metal bracket by brute force. Merle didn't have time to celebrate and didn't care what they thought. His head was hurting too much to care, and he still had work to do.

Merle knew there were enough men to lift the car straight up. However, he also knew there was no way they could lift it high enough or hold it long enough for Grace to get under the car and provide initial triage and critical care. So, he moved on to the next job. He remembered changing the air temperature before, but had not considered it as a way to change air pressure. He hoped his idea would work, but he had never really tried to actually change the density of air to create a force field of sorts. He wasn't trying to create some kind of impenetrable thing, he just wanted to create a little extra resistance to fight gravity just enough to help the guys keep the car up.

Change the temperature, change the density. Slow the molecules. Pull them closer together. Make it cold.

Again, because all this stuff was invisible to everybody—hell, even to Merle—he wasn't sure if it was helping or not. However, he could feel the air beneath the car was noticeably colder than the rest of the air in the factory. He could only hope the men were straining so much they wouldn't notice. But what about Grace? He instinctively looked in her direction only to find her staring directly, intensely, back at him. Was that a smile on her face? It was almost imperceptible, but Merle could swear it was there. That smile scared him.

As he was thinking all this, he realized the car was up. The guys were doing it.

Shit! Bleeding!

This one was easy for Merle. It was simply a matter of focusing on the broken blood vessels and closing off the arteries. Merle knew he couldn't completely make them leak-proof, but at least he could slow it down enough to give Grace another minute or two to do her thing. He didn't have time to think about it. He had to do it if the guy was going to make it. The car was no sooner off the floor than Grace was sliding underneath the car. She gasped.

"What the hell?" Grace said. "Blood's everywhere but he's not bleeding."

As she looked at the man's crushed legs, her expression changed. First, shock, then... recognition? Her gaze moved from the man's legs directly to Merle. As Merle saw this happening, he watched Grace's face. Was that knowing acknowledgement on her face? Did she know? How could she know it was him? But somehow, he knew. She knew. He was done. His secret was out. But then he was overcome with something: suddenly he could feel her thoughts, "see" what she was seeing. He saw individual blood vessels from her point of view and closed them off as he saw them. Was Grace guiding him? The mixture of thoughts and emotions was making it difficult for Merle to concentrate.

It was just a split moment in time, and then Grace's focus was back on the man. She grabbed a tourniquet out of her med kit and in one quick motion slung it around one leg, cinching it up tight to prevent any further bleeding. There was the other leg though. Looking at Merle, she yelled at him to pull his attention to *her*. "Merle! Hey soldier! What the hell are you doing?! Give me your belt!"

Hearing that word "Soldier!" snapped him out of it. He didn't know if it was snapping him into the military mentality or triggering a trauma response that kicked in his fight-or-flight, but it didn't matter. Without a thought, he ripped off the belt and threw it to her. She grabbed it, slapped it on, and made sure no more bleeding would happen.

246

As she was climbing out from under the car, EMT's arrived and took over treatment and extraction. She walked directly over to Merle, covered in blood, full of adrenaline. Merle, on the other hand, was feeling weak and shaky. He had stretched his abilities more than he ever had and was exhausted. All the thoughts rushing through his head left him bewildered and scared, too. Merle could feel his knees start to buckle so he just leaned against the wall and just slid to the floor.

"You OK? You look pretty pale, Merle," Grace said.

"Yeah, just haven't seen stuff like that since 'Nam." *Keep up the lie. Hope she doesn't know.* "You were pretty amazing, there, Grace," he said weakly.

"No, Merle. *You* were amazing. I've never seen anything like that," Grace whispered.

"What are you talking about? I froze and just stood here. You had to yell at me to get me to throw you my belt! Most I did was just stand here and pray." Merle was desperately trying to hold on to the lie. But he knew he was discovered. He knew his life was about to change. He knew what he had to do.

"Whatever, Merle," Grace said. "You keep telling yourself that, but I think you and I have more things to talk about. I think there's more to you than people know."

At that moment, all the men who had been standing around started crowding around Grace, congratulating her for what she did to save the man's life. They ignored Merle. Perfect timing for him. As Grace was distracted by the crowd, Merle snuck away.

Merle didn't waste any time. He went straight to his locker, changed out of his work clothes and left them there with his ID, put his Walkman back on, and headed straight out the front door of the factory. He was going to miss this place. He really did like his job and most of the people. But most of all, he was going to miss Grace. He knew he had to leave though. He was discovered so wasn't safe anymore. He normally rode the bus home, but he just needed to decompress from everything that happened. "Walkin'" by John Coltrane started playing in his ears from the Walkman. Perfect.

It wasn't a long walk home and it was generally a pleasant day, but he wasn't feeling pleasant at all. In fact, he was panicked, and his adrenaline was rushing. He didn't think he had much time to disappear. He could figure out how to restart his life later, but for now he just had to go. He knew he should have been more worried about what was going to happen to the man, but he couldn't help but be more concerned about himself and Grace for knowing. As sad as it made him that he would have to leave, those few seconds of acknowledgement from Grace was a kind of intimacy he had always wanted and never had. It just made him experience the pain of his loneliness even more. But no time to think about that now. He just knew that no more secret meant no more safety. He couldn't risk that for himself. Or for Grace.

Merle hit the door to his apartment and wasted no time. He grabbed two canvas duffle bags from his closet and started packing. Filled them both with clothes but made sure to leave room for any items that would identify him. And his music. The thought of leaving his Magnavox and record collection was tough, but he had all of that on his Walkman cassettes which were much more portable.

All packed. Everything checked. Nothing left to link him to this place. He could disappear now. He had to disappear now. He grabbed up the bags, slung them over his shoulders and turned to leave.

"Where are you running off to, soldier?" *They finally found me*, he thought and panicked. Simultaneous was the realization that he recognized the voice. As he spun around, the recognition hit him like a mortar blast.

Grace was standing in front of him. Merle's heart both soared and sunk at the same time.

"What the hell, Grace? You scared the shit out of me! How did you get in here?"

"I just walked through the door. I figured we had unfinished business from today."

"What are you talking about, 'unfinished business'?"

"Merle, I know. I've known for a long time."

How could she know? He had been so careful! Kept it hidden. Kept it safe! "What in the world are you talking about, Grace?! Breaking into my apartment is not cool! Who does that?"

"Merle. MK Ultra. The drugs. The experiments. The powers. People disappearing. I know about all of it."

How could she know? How the HELL could she know?

"I honestly have no clue what you are talking about or what is going on here!" As he said this, he walked to his door. It was locked.

He turned to Grace, face beginning to show fear. "Grace, how did you get in here?"

"Like I said, I just walked through the door." She smiled. "Merle. I know about MK Ultra, about the drugs, about everything. Because I was there."

Realization started to set in. "You worked there, Grace? I mean I knew you said you were a nurse in the war, but you did *this* to people? You, Grace? Do you have any idea how MKU tore my life apart? How it tore apart the lives of all those men?! How could you do that to innocent men? Treat us like guinea pigs?!"

"Merle, I said I knew. I didn't say I worked there. What? You think only men were used as guinea pigs? What do you think they wanted to use WOMEN for?" She visibly shuddered.

"You were in the program?" Merle said weakly.

"I know things, Merle. I don't know how I know things; I just *know* things. It was how I *knew* about you and your history the first time you walked in the clinic at the factory. Of course, I learned more about you and what you thought about me over time. I didn't need special abilities to see that." She grinned.

Merle pressed, still suspicious. "So, wait, how did you get out? Why did you not disappear like the others?"

"Well, when I woke up, I just *knew* what the plans were for any of us that showed 'promise.' Luckily, I also *knew* the patterns of all the staff in the program, so it became easy to work around their patterns to escape. Being a nurse, it became easy to find a way to assume the identity of some poor soul who had died and live under an assumed name. Like you, I have been hiding since."

"Well, what about today?"

"Like I said, I *know* things. I knew the second the car fell. I grabbed my kit and came running."

"Ok, well now it makes sense that you showed up with the med kit in hand. But how could you have "known" ahead of time? My reaction and you arriving couldn't have been more than seconds apart! What? You can tell the future too?"

Grace laughed out loud. "Oh, hell no!"

"Then how?"

"Um, I call it blinking. I only realized I could do it a couple of years ago. I think it is kind of like teleportation, sort of, but just short distances. How do you think I walked *through* your door?"

Merle's shocked face morphed in one fluid motion. He grinned. That grin turned into a smile. That smile turned into tears. He buried his face in his hands and sobbed.

For the first time in years, he didn't feel alone.

Grace gave Merle a couple of minutes. I mean, she was feeling it too. It was almost too much to bear thinking of being able to share her secret – share *anything* – with someone. Then she smiled and said sheepishly:

"Now about that unfinished business between us."

Meet Sean McKay

Sean is a clinical psychologist with over 20 years' experience who currently works with the US military. His love of nerd culture brought him to the Legion of Dorks a few years ago, and his life of service to others led him to write his story to contribute to a happy holiday season for children. When not busy with work and family, you can find him knee-deep in his hobbies which include sports, gaming, and podcasting. Sean currently co-hosts The Gene Pool

Variety Hour, a nerd culture podcast with his son Connor, where they have weekly geek debates and review movies chosen at random. They broadcast the podcast live Friday evenings on Twitch (twitch.tv/genepoolvarietyhour). They'd love to have you stop by and say hi!

Acknowledgments

I must thank the Legion of Dorks for being so supportive. This is the third installment of *Legion of Dorks presents* and each one has been a pleasure to edit. The community is incredibly creative. When I add in the other contributors who were willing to take a token payment since the anthology is for charity, I'm filled with gratitude of the writing community.

Without the enthusiastic support of the fans of this anthology series, we wouldn't make any money for charity at all. So for you I am most grateful. Thank you for purchasing copies every year for everyone you know. After all, what better winter holiday gift than stories along with the knowledge that the purchase helps children who need us.

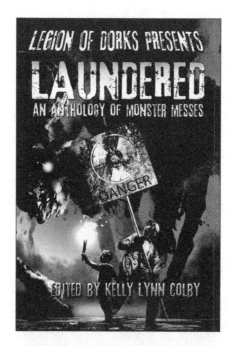

The hero defeats the monster, but who cleans up the ensuing mess? Meet the intrepid people who really save the day.

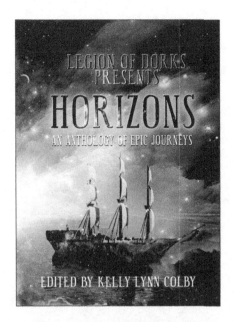

Only through travel can you discover who you really are.

Made in the USA
Monee, IL
10 November 2023

46216624R00156